LOVE *on the* RANGE

Books by Mary Connealy

From Bethany House Publishers

THE KINCAID BRIDES

Out of Control

In Too Deep

Over the Edge

TROUBLE IN TEXAS

Swept Away

Fired Up

Stuck Together

WILD AT HEART

Tried and True

Now and Forever

Fire and Ice

THE CIMARRON LEGACY

No Way Up

Long Time Gone

Too Far Down

HIGH SIERRA SWEETHEARTS

The Accidental Guardian

The Reluctant Warrior

The Unexpected Champion

BRIDES OF HOPE MOUNTAIN

Aiming for Love

Woman of Sunlight

Her Secret Song

BROTHERS IN ARMS

Braced for Love

A Man with a Past

Love on the Range

The Boden Birthright: A CIMARRON LEGACY *Novella*

Meeting Her Match: A Match Made in Texas *Novella*

Runaway Bride: A KINCAID BRIDES *and* TROUBLE IN TEXAS *Novella (*With This Ring? *Collection)*

The Tangled Ties That Bind: A KINCAID BRIDES *Novella (*Hearts Entwined *Collection)*

BROTHERS
IN ARMS

BOOK THREE

LOVE
on the
RANGE

MARY CONNEALY

BETHANYHOUSE

a division of Baker Publishing Group
Minneapolis, Minnesota

© 2021 by Mary Connealy

Published by Bethany House Publishers
11400 Hampshire Avenue South
Bloomington, Minnesota 55438
www.bethanyhouse.com

Bethany House Publishers is a division of
Baker Publishing Group, Grand Rapids, Michigan

Printed in the United States of America

Library of Congress Cataloging-in-Publication Data
Names: Connealy, Mary, author.
Title: Love on the range / Mary Connealy.
Description: Minneapolis, Minnesota : Bethany House Publishers, [2021] | Series:
    Brothers in arms ; 3
Identifiers: LCCN 2021011910 | ISBN 9780764237744 (trade paper) | ISBN
    9780764239359 (casebound) | ISBN 9781493433797 (ebook)
Subjects: GSAFD: Western stories. | Love stories.
Classification: LCC PS3603.O544 L68 2021 | DDC 813/.6—dc23
LC record available at https://lccn.loc.gov/2021011910

Scripture quotations are from the King James Version of the Bible.

This is a work of fiction. Names, characters, incidents, and dialogues are products of the author's imagination and are not to be construed as real. Any resemblance to actual events or persons, living or dead, is entirely coincidental.

Cover design by LOOK Design Studio
Cover photography by Aimee Christenson

Author is represented by the Natasha Kern Literary Agency.

21 22 23 24 25 26 27   7 6 5 4 3 2 1

ONE

olly Garner bent over Wyatt Hunt, bathing his fevered brow. How many gunshots did a woman have to tend in one lifetime?

This was her third in the last month. It might happen more if you were a doctor or fighting a war, but she thought she'd done more than her share, and she'd had several pointed conversations with God about why this kept happening to her.

Of course, she wasn't the one who had been shot. So she admitted, as much as she'd been called on to doctor people, she was better off than the wounded. And they weren't yet sure they'd caught whoever had shot Wyatt, so that danger remained until they got a confession out of one of the outlaws.

Yes, in calmer moments she admitted that tending gunshots

wasn't as bad as being shot. So she wasn't the only one who'd had it hard.

God's answer was to make Wyatt's fever come back up, so Molly tried to quit feeling sorry for herself and just pray for her patient, tend him, worry, and pray some more. His fever had been up and down several times.

The work didn't occupy her mind. It occupied endless hours with no sleep and precious little help, but soothing his fevered brow with ice-cold water and pouring willow bark tea and a few other concoctions she'd contrived didn't take much thinking. While she cared for Wyatt, she considered how much her life had changed in just a month's time.

One big change: Kansas.

She most certainly wasn't in Kansas anymore.

She had been born and raised there. Now she was long gone, living at a ranch in Wyoming. It was only two states away from Kansas, but they were *big* states. She thought of what she'd left behind in Kansas and fervently hoped they were big enough.

Another change: Kevin, her brother, got married. His bride, Winona Hawkins Hunt, seemed decent enough. She worked in the kitchen to keep the broth and tea brewing for Wyatt. She'd started talking to Molly a few times, as had Kevin, but it seemed they both had a talent for wanting to talk right when Wyatt started burning with fever.

A second wedding was joining Wyatt's big sister, Cheyenne, and his big brother Falcon. Molly would have enjoyed watching them explain that to the parson.

Andy, her little brother, was turning into some kind of cowboy.

And of course, Molly—her own life had changed.

Somehow she'd become the cook, housekeeper, and doctor for a crowd of strangers. What did they call it? She remembered something . . . oh yes, chief cook and bottle washer. Or maybe jack-of-all-trades, master of none.

Or just the dupe who'd found it her lot in life to care for a herd of thankless strangers who kept getting themselves shot.

She caught herself. Breathed in and out. Bathed Wyatt's fevered brow and calmed down, counting her blessings. Then she thought of Kevin getting shot and forgot about calm. He was no stranger. And he was mostly well by the time he got home, so he required no doctoring. And neither Kevin nor Andy was thankless, but they weren't around all that much.

And maybe worst of all, Kevin, her big brother, her closest confidant, the man she trusted most in the world, a man who had once saved her—he'd betrayed her.

And she couldn't wait to get shut of all of them.

She'd do it as soon as Wyatt got over this most recent gunshot.

She'd thought Kansas—before, during, and after the Civil War—had been dangerous. They'd called it Bleeding Kansas, after all. A state acting out the Civil War before the real one got started, with people deciding elections by shooting the opposition to stop them from voting. There was a half-witted way to run a state.

But Wyoming was no Sunday picnic party, either.

"Chey!" Wyatt tossed his head. His fever had come back up. He was calling for his sister, Cheyenne, whom he called Chey. It sounded like *shy*, and no woman Molly had ever met was less likely to be called shy.

But tough, dangerous, not-shy Cheyenne wasn't here to help with her brother. Her real brother—not the connected-but-not-by-blood brother she was marrying. And her absence upset Molly's patient. And that made Molly want to punch Cheyenne right in the face.

Of course, if she did, Cheyenne would probably beat her to a lump on the ground and shoot her, so Molly would just daydream about swinging a fist while doing *all the work and taking care of everyone.*

Something that, in all honesty, she felt like she'd been doing all her life.

She caught herself again. Breathed in and out. Bathed Wyatt's fevered brow and calmed down, counting her blessings.

"Chey. Chey." Wyatt tried to throw the covers back. He couldn't. Molly had a firm hold of his right hand, and his left arm was strapped tight to his body because, in Molly's doctorly opinion, he'd broken his collarbone. It wouldn't heal if it wasn't kept still.

Cheyenne should be here helping with this.

Yes, they'd gotten home late last night. Yes, they'd captured four gun-slinging outlaws. Yes, they'd found and rescued Amelia Bishop, who'd been kidnapped, and yes, they needed to go with the Pinkerton agent, Rachel Hobart, to talk to the sheriff today about the crimes committed by people far and wide. The wedding was going to be in there somewhere, so yes, they had a lot to do.

Yes.

Yes.

Yes.

Fine!

With a moment of desperate recklessness, Molly sat down beside Wyatt, cradled his rough, calloused hand as she'd seen Cheyenne do, dropped her voice to a hoarse whisper, the best she could do to imitate Cheyenne, and said, "I'm here, Wyatt. I'm here. This is Cheyenne."

She held tight. Her right hand to his. A bullet wound in his upper left shoulder. She rested more weight on him, trying to keep him still, and set the cool cloth on his forehead.

"I'm here. Stay still, please. Lie still."

For a moment, his eyes fluttered open. They were dazed and cloudy with the fever. The bullet wound didn't appear to be suppurating. It gave her hope that he just needed to beat this fever, and he'd be fine.

But that didn't help her get through this moment, right now.

"You're not Cheyenne." He'd quit thrashing at least.

"I'm taking care of you until Cheyenne gets back. She'll be here right away."

Let him think she just went to get supper or tidy her hair. Molly wasn't about to remind him that his sister was off marrying Falcon Hunt. That news had almost shot him out of bed before. Cheyenne had at least told him though. More than Kevin had managed when he'd sneaked off to his wedding.

"Why is it so h-hot?" Wyatt's throat worked as if he was parched. "Oh. Summer."

Molly gingerly released his hand, got a few sips of water down him, more willow bark tea. Then she dipped the cloth in the basin again to cool it, then wrung it out and folded it, keeping an eye on him in case he started rolling around.

Trying not to say anything that got past his dazed confusion. Once he started remembering things, like the bullet wound, who knew what all he might recall.

"You'll be fine. You need to rest." She had a doctor's voice, and she used it as best she could. She lifted the cloth away so he could see her, and he shook off the hold she had on his right hand, grabbed at her left with the cloth, and pressed it back to his brow.

"Feels good. Stay, stay with me." He held her hand with the cloth beneath it. "Burning. Hot. Hot."

His eyes locked with hers as he refused to let her go. Of course, she wasn't exactly fighting to escape. The poor man needed someone to care about him. His cheeks were flushed. His gazing eyes were that same brown shot through with gold that Kevin and Falcon both had. There was a dimple in his chin that was barely noticeable with his three-day scruff of beard. All three brothers had those eyes and that chin dimple in common, features they shared with their worthless father, Clovis Hunt.

Beyond that they didn't look much alike. Wyatt was a handsome man, though he could use a haircut. Falcon was a rough-looking mountain man dressed in homespun clothes with little interest in haircuts and shaves. She had her suspicions about his interest in baths, but Falcon had recently been swept a long way down a stream, and they'd cleaned him up when he got back, so that was two baths in a short stretch of days.

Kevin was . . . well, Kevin was her brother. It was hard to think of his looks because he just looked like himself.

Since Wyatt gave her no choice, she kept the cloth in place.

Slowly his grip relaxed. The willow bark tea mixed with yarrow was bringing the fever down. Before this most recent feverish stretch, she'd gotten a fair drink of water down him and some broth with bits of bread soaking in it. It combined to give him the strength to . . . sleep.

And he was one of the strongest men she knew, so that was a sad commentary on his condition.

He sank down into real sleep. She stayed with him, hoping the cool cloths fought his fever. Finally, she was satisfied the fever was coming down again.

This time she promised God no whining. No self-pity. Before her mind could start churning again, being awake for twenty-eight straight hours caught up with her.

TWO

Wyatt woke up to a woman in his bed. Very few things in his life had ever been stranger.

She had her hand resting flat on his chest, right over his heart. Her head lay on his uninjured shoulder. His arm was around her.

She was on top of the covers, and he was under, but it was still the strangest and most wonderful thing that'd ever happened to him.

And he'd once watched a cow sniff a little cloud that rolled into a mountain valley, leading a horde of clouds that settled into fog.

That fog rolling in like little balls of fluff and that sniffing cow had been the strangest and most wonderful thing . . . up until now.

Molly. And boy, oh boy, this was now number one. The sniffing cow wasn't even a close second.

Molly what? What was her last name? He'd hardly ever

talked to her. Well, a few times. And she'd served him deli-cious food. She was a way better cook than Cheyenne and a fair sight better than Win. She'd patched some of his clothes, washed them, hung them on the line. He'd seen her doing it. She'd cleaned up after all of them. She'd kept this house running through a time of madness.

And now she was sleeping in his bed, in his arms, and it felt . . . right.

Most everyone around here was named Hunt. His mind rabbited around to Win marrying Kevin, and then like a jolt of lightning, he remembered Cheyenne marrying Falcon. He leapt out of bed . . . except he didn't.

He tried. Realized he was all but tied up. Remembered why—his broken bone—and figured he was too late to stop the wedding anyway.

So he just stayed where he was and watched Molly sleep. He'd done some wiggling when he'd tried to sit up, and she'd slept through it, so she must be exhausted. Poor thing.

He realized that her name could be Hunt, too, if he mar-ried up with her. And shouldn't a man marry a woman he shared a bed with?

Especially when he was so uncommonly pleased to wake up next to her.

There were dark shadows under her eyes. His head was clear enough to remember being in and out of conscious-ness, fighting a blazing fever. A lot of it was blurred, but he knew whatever else was going on, whoever else was around, Molly had always been there.

Marrying a woman he really didn't know at all just be-cause he liked waking up next to her struck him as a lunatic notion. But his life was one lunatic moment after another lately.

Anyway, she didn't like him much. So he set the idea aside.

Garner. Molly Garner.

There, somehow knowing her name released him from any plans to change her name to Hunt by marrying up with her. He could remain single.

Relief swept through him, and that relief told him he'd made the right decision.

Still, she was a pretty little thing.

Her eyes fluttered open. Lashes long and dark around eyes blue as the Wyoming sky. Her fine, flyaway blond hair was a real mess. He wanted to smooth it down, but one arm was tied up, and the other was busy holding her.

She had on a dress in the same pale blue as her eyes. The dress was sprinkled with little white flowers. The whole thing was a mass of wrinkles. That's what came of sleeping in your clothes, and in fairness, it also came from working day and night, probably not taking the time to change, and for certain not taking the time to iron her dress.

His last clear memory was of morning, and now, judging by how the sun came in his window, it was near suppertime.

"How long have we been sleeping . . . together?" Some impish impulse made him add that last word.

She gasped, sitting up like she'd been bounced by a spring. Her fair skin flushed until he was afraid her head would light up like a torch and set her hair afire.

He smiled, couldn't stop himself. Then he laughed.

He hadn't laughed much for a long time.

"I-I—that is—we—"

Since words seemed to be beyond her, and he remembered how she'd cared for him, he figured asking for some kind of help would bump her off her stuttering.

"Can I have a drink of water?"

She grabbed that request like it was a lifeline thrown to her in a rampaging river.

Picking up the tin cup, still with water in it, she slid an arm behind his shoulders. Getting close to him just like she'd been, but now it was work.

He took a sip. "That tastes like a bit of heaven." He drained the whole cup. Then saw a slice of bread on the bedside table. "Can I have that bread, too? I think my stomach is waking up along with me."

The flush was fading as she found work to do. She picked up the bread, then frowned and tapped it, dry as the Mojave, against the plate it lay on.

"You just stay still." She had a pert little voice. Bossy, but in a way so cute, he didn't mind taking orders, much.

"I'll be right back with fresh bread and warm broth."

"I would greatly appreciate that."

She patted him on his good shoulder and ran out of the room. Whether to escape the embarrassing situation of waking up in his arms or because she was hustling to give him whatever he needed, it didn't matter. Both left him oddly cheerful, and there wasn't much cheerful that'd gone on around here lately.

And he had no intention of staying still.

Wyatt sat up slowly. He found he wasn't really tied down, just bound tightly to his own body. He was careful not to move his strapped-down arm. He found his thoughts turning

. . . buzzy. Like a swarm of bees filled his head. His vision did something weird, something that was darker and darker. Using his good arm, he leaned back a bit and braced himself. If he passed out, he wanted to fall backward onto the bed, not forward onto the floor. That couldn't be good for what ailed him.

His vision went so far down that road to darkness he thought he was going to fall over, then it stopped getting worse and began to clear. The room came slowly back to its normal sunlit self. The buzzing eased, then faded.

All he wanted was a good, hearty drink of water, and he wanted to slip into the closet, where they kept a chamber pot.

Gripping the head of his bed tightly, he stood, testing his strength with every move. He wasn't being careless or reckless. But a few things a man needed to tend to for himself if at all possible.

When he was sure his legs would hold him, he walked, leaning when he could, into the closet. He was out quick, not wanting Molly to catch him.

He stopped by the water pitcher. His hand trembled as he poured a full cup of water and gulped it down. It stuffed his belly full to bursting. He tottered back to the bed and sat down, then lay down, feeling smug that he'd gotten away with something before his eagle-eyed doctor got back.

He heard Molly on the stairs, and she appeared, still a bit pink cheeked, with a tray holding a bowl and some bread. He smelled the soup before he saw it.

"I have a chicken soup for you. Mostly broth but a bit of chicken and vegetables so you can, I hope, regain your strength." She pulled a chair close and laid a napkin on his chest, then held out the bowl and handed him the spoon. He felt an odd twinge of pride that she was going to let him feed himself instead of trying to spoon the soup in herself, like a mother would a child.

He sat up straight and ate half the bowl before he had to stop. "I want the rest, but I need to let this settle."

"You'd have had room for more if you hadn't gotten up and had all that water." She arched her brows at him.

For just one second, he felt like a naughty schoolboy, and he remembered she'd been a schoolteacher. No doubt able to see through floors and walls and read minds, as well.

"Yes, I did. And used the . . . ahem . . . that is, I needed a necessary bit of privacy. I was cautious, made sure my head was clear before I stood."

She smiled. "And you're a strong man, an adult, fully capable of making such a decision for yourself. No need to sneak, and I appreciate it that you didn't try and lie to me."

"You've got a scolding tone that you use very well. It reminds me of the teacher I had."

"Oh, you had a pretty young teacher who cared for you and watched over you? A woman you liked and respected?" Molly sounded doubtful.

"I had an old bat who never had a kind word to say and could tear the bark off a tree when she was correcting you."

Molly looked a little hurt.

Which only made it more fun to go on. "I'm lucky I got through a single day without a whack or two with a ruler."

"No doubt you deserved it." She squared her shoulders. "Well, there'll be no ruler whacking in this house, nor in my school."

She leaned closer to him. "No matter how badly you deserve it."

Wyatt lay back as Molly set the soup aside. "Can you tell me what's been going on around here? Is Cheyenne really married?"

"They aren't back from town yet, but they rode off with that intention. So I imagine by now they are."

Wyatt's hazel eyes met hers. "When did that happen? I know I've been busy with branding, but you'd think I'd've noticed my sister and a man becoming . . . attached to each other." He shook his head.

"I never saw it coming with Kevin and Win." Molly told him about the betrayal of RHR hired hand Jeff Wells. He didn't remember that.

"He didn't have good cowhand skills. But I gave him a chance. I thought I was doing a good thing."

She talked about the Pinkerton agent and the search for Amelia Bishop.

"I missed all of that," Wyatt said. "Who is Amelia Bishop, and what is a Pinkerton agent?"

Molly explained to the extent she knew. "I've spent a lot of time tending you. I've missed plenty of what's going on, too. They've found more stolen cattle. Another whole pasture of them besides the ones that'd been stolen from the RHR and the Hawkins Ranch."

"I'm starting to remember some of this."

"Do you remember that a man from each of the area ranches was among the outlaw band?"

Wyatt thought hard but shook his head.

"It seems there were conspiratorial plans to kill the owners of each ranch and take possession of them. They had a decent chance with Oliver Hawkins, a man alone and no gunman. And possibly with Roger Hanson."

Wyatt interrupted, "Hanson's as tough as they come."

"But one man alone, Cheyenne said. It would only work if his hired hands didn't back him, and it sounds like his gunman was in on the plot."

"And Judd Black Wolf? He's as mean as a rabid badger and a knowing man. He wouldn't have men on his ranch that would betray him."

"It sounds like they were just conspiring to rustle cattle at first. But when all this turmoil happened on the RHR, they got ambitious. They thought if they struck hard and fast, they might pull it off. But they are fools, and now two of them are dead fools. Cheyenne and Falcon followed Percy Ralston, and he led them to his band of outlaws. The men had given up on taking the ranches and were making a break for it with their stolen cattle. Cheyenne and Falcon stopped them. They're straightening this all up with the sheriff right now."

"Before the wedding."

Molly nodded.

Wyatt had plenty of questions, and Molly answered what she could. When Wyatt thought he was hearing things he already knew, he paused. "What else has happened around here?"

Molly shrugged. "I can't think of anything more, but a lot of this has been going on with me too busy to pay it much mind."

Wyatt reached his working right hand up and gently

touched his left shoulder. "So then, who shot me? That's about the end of what I remember. I think we were believing it to be Hobart before Cheyenne took off and captured all those outlaws."

"Did you miss the part where Falcon caught Hobart sneaking into our house in the dark of night? It looked like she was coming to finish the killing she'd started."

"I might've slept through that."

"I came up and distracted you to keep you from noticing. Hobart convinced Cheyenne she hadn't been the one to take the shot. She was spying on Hawkins because she'd been hired to find Amelia Bishop—who'd been missing for a long time. Hobart expected she was dead, but her father is a powerful man and wanted answers. And Ralston was tied up, so he's not who shot you."

"One of Ralston's outlaw band must've done it."

"Must have. But two of them are dead, Ralston one of them, and they haven't got a confession out of anyone yet. Maybe Cheyenne will pound one out of someone before her wedding."

Wyatt had to be satisfied with that. For now.

Molly helped him eat the rest of the soup, and he ate a slice of bread and drank more water.

"I feel like I've got some energy from the food. My arm hurts like mad, and it's useless, but the rest of me is feeling decent. In fact, I'm feeling mighty good."

"Your fever has come up and gone down a few times. But you've never been this clearheaded nor shown any interest in eating." With a pleased nod, she said, "You're on the mend, Wyatt."

"Can I come downstairs?" He cringed a little because it sounded like he was asking permission. This was his ranch. He ran it. No one told him what he could and could not do. Except maybe his doctor.

"Are you willing to wait until one of the men comes back? I think you *should* come down. You're up to it, and it might do you some good to get out of bed for a while. But a fall down the stairs might be very serious, and you've only one arm to steady you."

She smiled and batted her eyelashes at him as if, instead of giving orders, she was trying to sweet-talk him into it. He had the sense that she was mocking him, or at least being some odd kind of flirting girl, only sarcastic under it. But it didn't stop him from doing what she wanted.

Truth was, with those pretty blue eyes batting at him, there weren't many orders he wouldn't take from this bossy woman.

And he didn't want to fall down the stairs, either.

"I'll wait."

Molly stood and reached for the tray and the empty dishes.

Without really thinking, Wyatt reached out and caught hold of her wrist. She stopped and looked at him.

"What is it? Do you need something more? You've only to ask."

"Thank you," he said. "You saved me, Molly."

A pink blush rose on her cheeks. "You're a strong man, Wyatt. You were always going to make it."

His grip tightened. "Don't dismiss what you've done for me. I appreciate it. I know you . . . you . . . well, you fell asleep beside me. . . ." He hadn't meant to bring that up. Clearing his throat, he forged on. "You fell asleep out of pure exhaustion. Yes, maybe I'd've healed up all on my own if they'd've just tossed me on a bed and gone on about their business, chasing outlaws and getting married, but . . ."

Her hand came and rested over his where he held on. "Doctoring you needed doing, and I knew what to do. If I lessened your suffering—"

"Or did things that'll help my arm heal straight."

She nodded. "Then it was my pleasure to do it, Wyatt. I'm glad you're feeling better."

For one second, one lunatic second, his hand drew her forward. She didn't seem averse to being drawn.

Then he realized his focus was on her lips. His memory was of her in his arms. That wasn't what he should be thinking of. That was no way for a man to truly thank a woman for her care.

He let her go, and she straightened, her hand rubbing her wrist where he'd held her. The color in her cheeks going from pink to rose.

"I'll send someone up for you as soon as they get home. Maybe you could get in a bit more sleep." She snatched up the tray and left so quickly it could almost be described as running away.

He smiled as he watched her leave. Then his smile faded. With a full belly and his head clear for the first time in a long while, he settled in to figuring out who'd tried to kill him.

THREE

*F*alcon Hunt stepped into Sheriff Corly's office with three women in tow.

Every single one of them more bloodthirsty than he was.

Strange feeling.

Amelia Bishop, who'd shot one of the dead men, Norm Mathers. She hadn't killed him, but she'd opened the ball, taking the first shot. And she'd winged him a couple of times, which sent him to shooting wild. And it looked like in his aimless shooting, Mathers had killed Percival Ralston.

Cheyenne, who'd taken the killing shot at Mathers, though not for lack of trying on Amelia's part. But Amelia was shooting with more rage than aim.

And the Pinkerton agent, Rachel Hobart, a cool, ruthless character if ever Falcon saw one. Hobart wanted out. She wanted to take her found-alive missing person back to Minnesota, wherever that was. Hobart probably had cash money to collect for the job.

Most everyone involved in the search—Amelia's pa, the state senator; her brother, the army general; and Hobart herself—had figured Amelia for dead, so taking her home alive and well, even if killin' mad, would make Hobart a hero.

Falcon led the three women in, hoping to make this quick because the woman who'd actually killed a man had agreed to marry up with him as soon as they were done.

And then it got complicated.

Oliver Hawkins showed up.

Falcon knew Hawkins had asked Cheyenne to marry him. She'd been sorely tempted when she lost her ranch.

Amelia, then later Hobart, had been his housekeepers, though Hobart had been what she called undercover. It sounded like the woman was a liar for a living, but she seemed to have no problem with that. Falcon decided to let that be between her and God and didn't bother fretting.

Hawkins strode into the jailhouse like a proud banty rooster. His eyes went straight to Amelia Bishop. "Amelia, where have you been? What is going on?"

With a quick look between the sheriff, Hobart, Falcon, and Cheyenne—looking for safety, Falcon reckoned—Amelia moved to hide behind Cheyenne. Good choice.

But the woman looked plumb scared. There was no sign of the bloodthirsty woman she'd been in the canyon.

"Don't you come near me, you foul, lecherous beast." Her voice was high-strung, a woman near terror.

Cheyenne's eyes narrowed at that. Amelia had said she'd run away from Hawkins with Percy Ralston because she didn't like her boss, but she'd never said just why.

Falcon wasn't sure what a lecherous beast was, but it sounded mighty bad.

He shifted so he stood shoulder to shoulder with Cheyenne. He was inclined to hate Hawkins just 'cuz he'd proposed to Cheyenne. If Amelia hated him, then Falcon would stand between Hawkins and her.

Cheyenne edged right next to Falcon, which was mighty nice. She whispered, "What's a lecherous beast?"

He glanced sideways at her and shrugged.

"It sounds mighty bad."

Falcon thought he and his feisty little Cheyenne were going to be about the happiest married folks who'd ever lived.

Cheyenne went back to standing straight, scowling at Hawkins. "We found Amelia. She'd run off with Ralston and married him. Now she's going home to her father."

"But, Amelia," Hawkins pleaded. "You were the best housekeeper I've ever had. I want you to stay with me."

"No, absolutely not. Cheyenne, don't let him touch me," Amelia whimpered.

Hobart came over and stood beside Cheyenne. "He will touch you only over my dead body, Amelia. You don't have to be afraid anymore."

While the women handled Hawkins, Falcon wondered if the two men left of the gang would be hanged. The outlaws had done a lot of trying and failing when it came to murder, and it was hard to say just who'd pulled the trigger on Wyatt.

But cattle rustling was a hanging offense, wasn't it? And they were all guilty of that. And which of them *had* shot Wyatt? He looked hard in the cell. Trying to judge. If they were smart, and there was no sign they were, as being a thieving rustler was, at its very root, stupid, they'd blame it on one of the dead guys.

"Amelia doesn't want to be a housekeeper anymore, Hawkins." Hobart spoke loud and clear. More sensible than any of them, it seemed. Being ruthless was helping her keep her head. "She wants to return to her father and stay with him."

"But Amelia—"

"Enough, Hawkins," Sheriff Corly interrupted. "Your housekeepers have both quit. You need to stop intruding when we've got prisoners to hang."

"Hey, I didn't hurt anyone. I didn't even belong to this gang when they were stealing cattle." Jeff Wells from the RHR was a weakling.

Falcon considered him for a bit. Weaklings were often willing to do plenty of talking when a noose was mentioned. Maybe he knew who'd shot Wyatt.

Cheyenne quit protecting Amelia, which wasn't a real big job. It was unlikely Hawkins was going to hurt her or drag her out of here with—Falcon counted quick—six witnesses, including the sheriff. He probably shouldn't count the outlaws locked up, but anyhow, there were plenty of folks who'd step in if Hawkins so much as touched her amiss.

Falcon sure wondered what it was that Hawkins had done to set Amelia so hard against him. He'd noticed Win didn't like her pa, either. Falcon intended to find out what was going on.

Cheyenne said, "Drag Wells out of there, Sheriff. I want to talk to him away from Bender."

Corly moved fast. Maybe he thought it was a good idea, or maybe he just knew he had a dangerous woman on his hands.

Sonny Bender, the other survivor of yesterday's shootout, shouted, "Wells, you'll keep your mouth shut, or you'll be sorry."

"I've got two cells. I'll put you in one of your own." Sheriff Corly had a firm grip on Wells, who showed no sign of resisting. Everyone but Bender went outside.

They were far enough from Corly's door not to hear the yelling anymore when a man galloped in with five riders. The leader looked like every other cowboy except his short hair, which only showed around his ears, was midnight black, his eyes black as coal. His skin a shade that didn't come from any suntan.

He swung down off his horse with a move Falcon swore to himself he'd learn. As graceful and powerful as a big, dangerous wildcat.

~

"Judd? Judd Black Wolf?" Cheyenne had thought she might see Judd before this was over. She was surprised how nice it was to see the kid—though he definitely wasn't a kid anymore.

The fierce look on the man's face faded and turned into a smile. "Yep, and you're Cheyenne Brewster from the RHR? I haven't seen you in years."

Cheyenne strode forward and stuck out her hand. Judd grabbed it and just held it. They'd had enough in common back in the day, with Indian blood flowing in their veins in a world being conquered by the white man, that she'd always felt a strong connection to him.

"You found cattle stolen from my place?"

"I was in on finding it." She quickly ran through enough of what had been going on, then she jerked her head at Falcon, who'd come up beside her. "He helped. We've got Sonny Bender locked up inside."

"Bender? One of my cowpokes is in on this?"

"Yep, he was in on it. They're forming a jury, and he'll hang. We listened in on a plot to kill you, Hanson, Hawkins, and those of us on the RHR. We think there are more traitors on every ranch, because they couldn't have hoped loyal cowhands would stand by while their boss was killed and someone else took over. So ride careful."

That's when she realized Judd was still holding her hand, and she quickly pulled it free. Judd looked between her and Falcon, then flashed a blinding white smile.

Then his smile faded as he really looked at Falcon. "You're the image of Clovis Hunt. I was unlucky enough to meet him a couple of times." He turned back to Cheyenne. "We've heard how he stole your father's land from you, Cheyenne. And now here you stand with the son of the man who stole from you?"

Cheyenne felt a wave of exhaustion sweep over her. She just wasn't up to a long explanation. "Falcon and Kevin are the brothers who were cut in. They're both decent men and are doing their best not to profit off of the legal thievery in Clovis's will. Falcon's a fine man and a better tracker than I am."

Judd arched both brows and looked longer at Falcon. "Is that so?"

"We're getting married, and I believe that gets me a goodly chunk of my ranch back. Now, do you want a thousand more details, or do you want to find your stolen cattle?"

"Your father was of my people, as you are, Cheyenne. I'd come to your aid if you needed it. That's true today and for all time."

"Clovis's will led to Falcon coming out west. That led to the outlaws being exposed. Falcon had no part in Clovis's thieving."

Sheriff Corly had taken the time to shackle Wells's hands.

Judd noticed. "And this is one of the cow thieves?" Judd glared at him in a way that would make a stronger man than Wells confess to any crime he'd ever thought of committing.

"Hey, not me." Wells raised his bound hands as if to protect his face.

"Yes, him," Cheyenne said. "But he just joined them, probably after they'd done all their rustling. Though he was willing to throw in with them, so he's guilty. But if he helps us, we might let him off with only a few years in prison instead of hanging him."

"Hanging?" Wells's hands dropped, his shoulders slumped, and his head bent down until his chin rested on his chest. Yes, he'd tell them everything he knew.

"Did my message make sense?" Cheyenne asked Judd. "Do you know where to go for your cattle?"

"I know the place you described, and I sent men on ahead of me. I'll go join them."

Cheyenne snaked out a hand and grabbed him. "Remember what I said about traitors. We think we've got the leaders, but watch for dry-gulchers, Judd. Watch real close."

Her hand tightened on his wrist until he flinched. Her eyes drilled into him. "My brother is lying in bed with a bullet wound. These men are ruthless coyotes, so be on guard. Wells here is the second turncoat we've found among our men, and we thought we could trust them all."

31

Judd nodded, his mouth a grim line.

She released him. He turned, leapt on his horse in a way so graceful Cheyenne felt like she was watching a cougar leap from the ground to a tree branch. The horse raced away, and Judd's men went with him.

Behind him.

Cheyenne said a prayer for his safety. For the safety of everyone trying to straighten this out.

Falcon's arm came firmly around her shoulders and turned her to face him. "Old friend?"

She looked into those hazel eyes and smiled. "He is an old friend, and a married man with, I think, three children. And I only know that because I've heard it around town. I haven't seen him in years." She leaned into that arm of his and said quietly, "I'm so glad I'm going to marry you."

She saw the jealous flare in Falcon's eyes calm, and he relaxed his grip.

She turned back to Wells. "If I need to beat a confession out of you"—Wells flinched and didn't seem to have the force of will to break eye contact with her—"I'll just think of my brother, wounded, feverish, only alive through the pure grace of God, and everyone here will need to get in line behind me. Now, tell us how long you've been mixed up with this crew and the name of every man on every ranch around here that's part of it."

~

"What did my father do to make Amelia Bishop, who is by all accounts a well-to-do, adventurous young woman with a powerful father, marry a poor choice like Percy Ralston and live in hiding for months?" Winona curled up in Kevin's arms.

He couldn't believe how nice it was to have such a fine woman as his wife. "I don't like your pa, what little I know of him. Add in the things you've told me of him and how fiercely you refused to live with him, and I can believe he did something so terrible Amelia thought she had to run and stay hidden."

Kevin felt bad that he and his beautiful new wife believed her father was capable of doing something awful. Kevin's father, Clovis Hunt, had done something awful, so he knew just how she felt.

"Cheyenne said Ralston lied to Amelia," Win said. "Convinced her she was still in danger. And seeing as he was a rustler, and he was stealing from my father, his motives were very personal."

"She picked a poor choice, for a fact. Why didn't she just have Ralston take her to town? She could have told the sheriff she was afraid of your pa and stayed near him until the train left for the east."

They sat together in the ramrod's house. Kevin could hardly bear to let her out of his sight. She seemed just as devoted to him. After they'd been married awhile and the danger had passed, they would probably loosen up, but for now, he was hanging on tight to her, enjoying every moment.

"I should find time to talk with Molly," Kevin said. "I tried to talk to her, but Wyatt's fever spiked, and I didn't really clear things up. The two of us were always partners running the farm, raising Andy. I feel like I've abandoned her."

"I started talking to her a couple of times, but it's hard

when we're taking care of Wyatt. We need to get over there and let her rest."

"He's past the worst of the danger. We'll start taking turns caring for Wyatt, and once Molly is rested, we can both spend more time with her. I want her to know this new family I've started with you . . ." He paused to kiss Win long and deep. God was truly taking care of him. God would take care of them both. "Well, she's part of that family. Marrying you doesn't mean she's not still my sister, partner, and friend."

Things had changed though. And they would stay changed. But he wanted Molly to be a part of that change.

And he'd tell her that, just as soon as he could find a minute when she wasn't busy, and he was able to pull himself away from his precious little wife.

Four

October 1870

"I'm going to unwrap your arm today." Molly remembered all her high-minded talk of being on her own, taking over the school, living independently.

Six weeks later, here she still was with the Hunt clan. On the RHR.

Everyone else spent time working the ranch; even Kevin was showing some skill at being a cowboy. And Cheyenne in particular was having trouble trusting her cowhands. The whole group of them seemed to be working hard and settling in.

Except her.

It'd taken some talking, but Falcon had agreed to live in the house. He couldn't stay forever, and no one believed he would. He talked of a small cabin in the woods, and Cheyenne talked of the house her parents had lived in before her pa had died.

But with Wyatt laid up, Kevin and Win in the ramrod's

house, and Cheyenne needing all the help she could get to take up all the work left by Wyatt and their betraying cowhands, there'd been no time to move out.

They'd had a cattle drive, and Falcon had gone along with Cheyenne. Andy too. Kevin and Win had stayed around. Because it was improper for Molly to stay in the house alone with Wyatt, Kevin and Win had moved in while everyone else was gone.

Molly and Kevin had a chance to talk. Enough to make Molly worry about intruding on his new marriage. She and Win had formed a friendliness that Molly had trouble turning into a friendship. It was a small distinction, but Molly knew the difference. What's more, it was her fault, and she knew it was rooted in the loss of Kevin as her best friend.

The cattle drive was over and done. The rustler business was behind them. They'd never gotten a satisfactory answer to who shot Wyatt, but they hoped, because there'd been no more trouble, that it had been one of the rustlers who was dead.

Falcon wanted to get moved before snowfall, which Molly understood came early in the highlands of Wyoming, early and deep.

Wyatt interrupted Molly's thoughts. "The wrap is coming off? You're not just saying that so you can laugh at me later when I get my hopes up?"

Molly smiled. "No, the pain seems to be gone, and six weeks is long enough for the bone to knit by my reckoning."

Wyatt, sitting up to the kitchen table, sighed. "I can't believe I missed the cattle drive. I haven't done that since I was old enough to sit on a horse. Might've been before that. I remember Ma telling a story of carting me along on her lap when I was about five months old. Nope, I've never missed one until now."

He glared at her.

"Don't look at me. I didn't shoot you."

"You're the one who poisoned the others against letting me go."

Shaking her head silently for a moment, Molly finally said, "You're welcome."

She untied the waist-level knot under his left arm while she talked. "The bullet wound is healed up. All you're left with is an interesting scar."

"Interesting?" He turned, and she realized, bent over as she was, their faces were very close.

"But the collarbone needed time to heal. Riding a horse wasn't possible." She resolutely ignored his handsome face. Her hands trembled slightly against the warmth of his side. The knot was stubborn, but it finally gave.

"I'm afraid it will be sore for a while," Molly said. "Your shoulder and elbow haven't moved in a long time. The muscles in your arm and chest may have gotten weak. But you'll get your strength back. You'll be fine."

She hoped.

"How is it you, a young schoolmarm, know so many healing skills?"

"I'm sure I've told you." She worked quickly to unwrap him, not unlike a Christmas present, wanting to get it done and step away from him. She'd become too aware of him while he'd been healing.

"Tell me again."

With an exasperated huff, she said, "The Civil War, remember? There was plenty of harm done on both sides during that trouble. My pa caused his share and was dealt his share. My ma got hurt a few times. Kevin and Andy, well, they were never hurt because Kevin got mighty good at keeping us hidden when the night was full of riders. But there was always someone getting knocked around by a cow or cut working a plow on a farm. Someone had to know where the salve was." The truth was so much worse.

The bandage fell away.

"Move your arm gently," Molly instructed. "Let me feel if your collarbone is solid when you move." She took a firm grip on his shoulder. The doctor back in Wheatfield had come out for Pa's broken arm. Molly had no idea what was wrong then. But later, when Ma had a broken collarbone, Molly remembered and knew what to do. Ma refused any doctor's help when she was hurt, so it was left for Molly to do the best she could.

Wyatt flinched as he raised his arm, rotated his shoulder, and straightened his elbow, but a smile bloomed on his face. "It feels good. Like you said, the joints hurt, but it's healed."

"You're right. Nothing shifted." Molly pressed along the line of his shoulder. "I feel a thickened place here, and that's normal for a broken bone."

She patted him on the back, then quit touching him and stepped away. "You'll need to treat the arm carefully for a bit."

Wyatt was out of his chair and striding for the back door, not being careful at all, when Cheyenne came thundering down the stairs. "Look at this, Wyatt."

"Why do you want my family Bible?" Falcon was on her heels. He looked mighty confused.

"The date Falcon was born is written in here." She bent her head over the book, open in her hand.

"It is?" Falcon tried to look over her shoulder.

"I thought you didn't know how old you were?" Wyatt came to Cheyenne's side.

"I don't." Falcon scratched his head. "Not exactly."

"You were twenty-nine last January."

"And I was three or four when Pa ran off. Ma died when I was ten."

"Are you sure about that? About your age?" Cheyenne asked.

Falcon nodded, but there was no great certainty in it.

"We have to track it down. Make sure." Cheyenne looked up from the old Bible in her hands and locked eyes with Wyatt.

"I can't read nor write," Falcon shrugged. "I couldn't write down the date she died in our Bible."

"If Falcon's right about his age when his ma died," Wyatt said, "Clovis's marriage to my ma isn't legal, and that means the will isn't legal and the land is Cheyenne's and mine."

"We have to make sure, but if we're right, this fixes everything." Cheyenne shoved the Bible into Wyatt's hands and rushed out of the room.

Falcon watched her go, then said sheepishly, "It's strange to have my wife all excited about me losing an inheritance. I don't care. I'm not a rancher. Honest, I'm happy for her. But it don't seem quite right."

Wyatt came to his side and slapped him on the shoulder. "You're married to her. I know from good old Pa that whatever she owns is yours. So instead of owning a third of the ranch, you now own half."

"And Kevin owns none." Falcon gave Molly a worried look.

"He stands to inherit all of Hawkins Ranch, even if he'll never get Win to go near it while her pa's alive," Wyatt said.

"You were alone in a cabin in the mountains from the age of ten?" Molly's heart twisted. "I was nine when my parents died. But I had Kevin."

"Yep, I was a mighty scared boy." Falcon got a faraway look in his eyes and was somber when he said, "Ma was ailin' awhile, so I knew it might happen. She talked herself blue trying to teach me to get by without her. I could hunt, and I'd worked the place with Ma since I was no bigger'n a sprout. I could plant and hoe the garden. I could find berries and nuts, there were roots growing wild. I could fetch 'round a possum or a brace of rabbits, snare a quail, and I sure enough knew how to go fishin'. Whatever I caught, I could skin, cook, and eat. I could make leather out of a hide. I knew how to load my gun and hit what I aimed at. I could use a bullet mold. I got by. But I was so alone my ears echoed like someone shoutin' down the holler."

Molly came to his other side and patted him a lot more gently than Wyatt.

Falcon looked to Wyatt on his left, then Molly on his right. "It's a whole lot better having family about."

Molly nodded, though some days she had her doubts.

"You got yourself untied." Falcon turned to look at Wyatt's arm. "You're well, then?"

"Seems like it. I'm crazy to get outside. Saddle up a horse and ride. Want to come?"

"Sure. If we're right, my wife owns half this ranch."

The two of them grinned at each other and charged outside.

Molly smiled after them. When the back door slammed, her smile faded. She felt . . . Well, Falcon had said it about right. She felt so alone her ears echoed.

She made plans to get on with her life. Find a job.

Then, plotting her escape, she turned to setting the kitchen to rights. All Wyatt's bandages were scattered about. And there was a noon meal to get. She'd ride to Bear Claw Pass right after she'd cleaned up. She hadn't heard who replaced Win for the teacher's job, but she'd make sure to see if they'd found someone. If not there, she'd find a diner that needed a cook. Or a hotel that needed a housekeeper.

Teaching was what she wanted though.

Before she headed for town, she'd see how the noon meal went.

It wasn't something she was proud of, it made her feel some shame in fact, but she wanted to be thanked for the food. Helped with the food. Appreciated for the clean house, the made-up beds. The scrubbed pots and pans. The laundry and mending. She wasn't sure quite how she'd ended up running this house alone.

All she knew was it hurt her.

Especially Kevin marrying Win, which was an absolutely normal thing for an adult man to do. But he hadn't talked to her before the wedding. They'd always been such partners, and now he had a new one.

He'd moved into the life of a completely reasonable adult.

She had to do it, too. Not just hang around here feeling pitiful.

And furious.

Both feelings, she was sure, were sins. And sins she was committing with great regularity. It had to end, and she'd end it by getting on with living.

She turned to her cooking. She'd make the noon meal the best they'd ever had. She was a better cook than Win and a far better cook than Cheyenne. Kevin was probably the second-best cook around here, Andy third. The rest of them were nothing to boast about. Although she had to admit that Falcon might do wonders with a possum.

An unworthy part of herself wanted them to miss her.

She'd fry chicken because she had a knack for that, and she knew just the chickens she'd use. A few young roosters were still about from the spring hatching.

Her chicken gravy was delicious, and her mashed potatoes smooth and fluffy.

Gleefully, she decided to make up a delicious custard with an unusual crunchy caramel topping that always left Andy and Kevin groaning with full bellies and pure bliss.

She hadn't made it since she'd come here.

Surely, they'd say thank you. Maybe they'd even show some kind of true appreciation for her. Maybe they'd even be so kind she'd settle down and decide to stay.

She thought of the way Wyatt had run off once he was free of the sling. Not even a backward glance.

When they all abandoned her again, she'd take her satchel and all her worldly goods and ride to town to find work. Maybe, if she was in a good mood, she'd leave them a note.

FIVE

"Where's supper?" Wyatt came in dragging after his first day back in the saddle. He'd taken it easy. He sure hadn't busted any broncs or thrown any cattle. But he'd ridden long hours and thrown in with his cowhands to herd cattle from one stretch of pasture to another.

He'd handed his horse's reins to Jesse, one of their younger cowhands, and come straight in from the chilly night. The sun was setting early, and the wind had a mean bite to it. His shoulder ached like a wolf had sunk fangs into it.

And he was starving.

"Molly's gone." Kevin slapped the note hard against Wyatt's chest. "I'm riding to town to find her and bring her back. Falcon's out saddling the horses. I stayed behind when I saw you coming. What did you do to her?"

Wyatt noticed Kevin's fist balled up tight and braced himself to take a punch to the jaw. "I didn't do anything to her. What did you do to her?"

"I didn't do anything." But Kevin's fist relaxed and worry

clouded his eyes. Almost like he thought maybe he *had* done something to her. Now Wyatt's fist clenched.

"Both of you shut up." Cheyenne shoved them apart.

Wyatt noticed Win stood behind Kevin with her hands clutched to her throat. A much more biddable kind of woman than Cheyenne. Wyatt would have said Molly was the biddable type, too, but then why'd she take off?

Wyatt's eyes went to Kevin's. "Did she say I did something to her?" He thought of waking up beside her. But that had been weeks ago. Nothing like that had ever happened again.

He'd thought of it though. Mercy, he'd thought of it a lot.

"Not in the note." Kevin looked at the sheet of paper in his hand.

"I never had any kind of trouble with her. No harsh words." Wyatt pulled the note away from Kevin and read it. "This says she's going to find work. Ranch life doesn't suit her. How could ranch life not suit someone?" Wyatt had trouble even imagining such a thing. There was no better way to live.

"It's not like we made her help with branding." Cheyenne stepped away, either figuring they'd passed on the fistfight or not caring if they went to slugging each other.

Win came up and caught Kevin's arm. "It's me. She's gone because she doesn't like that you got married. Or she just doesn't like me and doesn't want to have me in your family."

Kevin looked down at her, his color high from his earlier temper with Wyatt, but suddenly he looked uncertain, sad. "I felt like things were better between us. She was upset I didn't tell her I was getting married, but we've talked plenty since then."

He swallowed hard. "But maybe we didn't talk about important things. Maybe we just talked about day-to-day life. I thought things were good. I've never had any notion that she didn't like you, Win. But I guess when something is important, I've talked to you instead of her. Molly and I always talked about everything. It's not you who sent her off, it's me."

"No, she worked too hard doctoring me." Wyatt looked at the terse note again. "I was impatient and cranky all the time. It was me."

"We talked of being teachers." Win looked at the note, her brow furrowed with worry. "I thought we had that in common. She even mentioned getting my old teacher's job. But I told her they would've hired someone else by now. I thought all consideration of that was over and done. I should have known she wanted to leave here. It *was* me, Kevin."

"Well, it wasn't me. None of this is my fault." Cheyenne gave the kitchen stove a mean look, like it was her enemy and she was in no mood to fight a war tonight.

Kevin took the note back and crushed it in his hand. "She should have told us. Talked to us about it. She shouldn't have just run off like she did."

He looked at Win again, frowning. "I should have talked to her about plans, about the future. I should have made sure she knew I wanted her to live with us when we get a house built. But we haven't really talked about the future since . . . since . . ."

"Since you got married?" Win asked.

"Since I ran off and got married without talking to her, then mostly cut her out of my life since I got back." He bent

45

and kissed Win. "I love being married to you. My life seems so full, but to me that always included my sister and brother. Maybe she didn't understand that."

"She might have gone just 'cuz she thinks you've got a new family, Kevin," Wyatt said, "and she wants to let you get on with your life. Andy's working hard on the ranch. He doesn't even eat with us in the house anymore. It might not be about liking or not liking anyone, she might just think it's time she got on with her own life, and she doesn't see that being here at the ranch." Wyatt gave Cheyenne a nervous look.

"What?" she snapped. "You've thought of a way to blame this on me?"

"No, but it was this morning that you confirmed Pa probably wasn't legally married to Ma. If it's true, the will doesn't stand. Which means Kevin doesn't own any of it."

"I told you I don't want any part of a stolen ranch," Kevin fumed.

"Yes, and Falcon said it, too, and I believe you. That's real decent of you." Wyatt tried to trace down all Cheyenne had told him. "You're still my brothers, and you are welcome to have a home here on the RHR. But maybe Molly didn't see herself as part of that. She has no blood relation to me and Cheyenne. This ranch isn't in any way hers."

"Yes, but she's *my* family even if she's not yours. Leaving has to be—"

"Maybe," Cheyenne cut him off, "she just doesn't like cooking and cleaning all day every day. I know I wouldn't." Cheyenne's shoulders slumped as she trudged over to the stove. "She was a schoolmarm back in Kansas. Maybe she just quit a job that didn't suit her to get one that did."

Wyatt's exhaustion slid away as worry and regret gave him new energy, pushing him to find Molly. "I'll go with you to look for her, Kevin. If you and Molly haven't talked about how she fits into your future, it's a big part my fault because she's been fetching and carrying for me all day long. I've been so useless with my arm bound."

He circled his shoulder and winced. "She's done so much to care for me, and I don't know if she realizes how much I appreciated it." Had he said thank you? Or had he complained about being more or less tied up for six weeks?

And blamed it on Molly and her doctoring, as if *she'd* shot him and broken his collarbone.

Kevin turned to Win. "You stay here. It's cold."

Wyatt turned to Cheyenne. "We can't all go haring off and leave Win alone at home. It's not safe. And you're right. You've done nothing to be sorry for. It's me that needs to go. Kevin may be part of it, but I reckon she mostly just got tired of me." He thought of her warm and soft against him. "And she was too decent to leave until I was up and around."

"She made the most delicious thing I've ever had for dessert today." Cheyenne patted her stomach.

Wyatt thought of that custard. He guessed that'd be what they served for dessert in heaven. He could eat that for three meals a day, every day, for the rest of his life, though her fried chicken was the best he'd ever had, too. "We've got to get her back just so she can make more of that."

"We told her thank you, real nice, when she served that." Cheyenne looked at the tidy counter. "I wonder if there's any of it left?"

"I think I remember licking out the pan," Wyatt said with

a shrug. The pain from that motion made him immediately regret the movement. "You and Win can get some supper on. We can eat fried eggs and biscuits. I hope to be back in an hour, even if we have to throw Molly over a saddle and cart her home like a felled elk."

Bear Claw Pass was a half-hour ride if they goaded their horses. So they'd really have to just grab her and run.

"Hey, get out here," Falcon called from outside. He must have the horses ready.

Win grabbed Kevin's wrist. "Maybe you should ride beside her on the way home and have a good long talk."

Kevin nodded and kissed her.

Wyatt headed out, dreading Cheyenne's cooking. Especially when she was in a bad mood. He should have told her they'd just eat bread and butter. Molly was ahead with the baking. Cheyenne seemed to cook at a full gallop with little care for charred edges and rare innards. Sometimes, after her more rushed meals, he felt like *he* had charred edges and rare innards.

Win was a decent cook. She wasn't a patch on Molly, but she was decent. He hoped Win could manage Cheyenne and hog-tie a meal.

SIX

Molly had a job.

They had hired a new schoolmarm after Win, but she'd worked through a six-week stretch of school and was already quitting to get married. It was hard keeping a teacher in a town with five men to every one woman. Or was it fifty to one?

Molly had gotten hired on the spot, and the school board had walked her over to Parson Brownley's home.

Parson and Mrs. Brownley had acted delighted to have a new person to live with them. They seemed like lovely people.

She'd unpacked her satchel and washed thoroughly, and was out in time to help Ida Brownley with supper. She oughta make these two a custard. They'd be glad they'd had her come to stay.

The evening meal was a fine experience. Casual and friendly, not a gunshot victim to be seen anywhere.

The Brownleys were good company. Older but not elderly by any means. By the time they were done eating Ida's tasty ham steaks with mashed turnips, Molly had learned all about their three grown children. Two sons and a daughter, all married with children of their own and moved away.

The two seemed interested in adding someone younger back into their household. Why, they looked willing to adopt her.

Molly was just preparing to insist on clearing the table and washing the dishes when someone knocked on the front door. All right, it was pounding. Someone was slamming the side of their fist into the wood.

"Mercy." The parson rose quickly. "Someone must be badly in need of a parson."

He rushed to the door and swung it open.

Wyatt stood there, glowering.

Molly's stomach twisted. "I think they're here for me, Parson." Her voice rose so the Hunt brothers—all three of them—could hear her. "They must have doubts about allowing a self-supporting, intelligent, adult woman to make her own decisions and live her own life."

Mrs. Brownley arched one brow at her. Molly had no doubt her tone wasn't lost on Ida Brownley.

She saw Kevin looking worried. Probably because he had to leave his wife behind for more than ten minutes.

Falcon didn't look overly upset.

Wyatt charged in, followed by the other Hunt brothers . . . but only one of them actually her real brother.

Molly slapped her napkin on the table. She hadn't done anything wrong. "Are you three taking up brotherly outings now?"

Wyatt glowered like he had been since they opened the door. Kevin's brow furrowed with worry. Falcon grinned at her.

She knew, even if they didn't, that their protest was all out of guilt. They didn't really want her underfoot. They were all just bound up by their sense of responsibility.

"Come and join us at the table." Mrs. Brownley gestured. "Would you like some ham? I made quite a bit thinking of leftovers, but I'd be delighted to share it with you."

The parson pulled two extra chairs up. It was crowded, but there was enough room. Kevin rounded the table and shoved a chair in beside Molly, while Falcon and Wyatt sat across from them, Wyatt straight across from Molly.

"We haven't had supper, Mrs. Brownley." Wyatt seemed to be very friendly with the couple. "I'd be mighty glad to have some of your fried ham. On Sunday, I'll bring you in a couple of our older roosters for your stewpot."

"That sounds wonderful. We'd appreciate that."

Wyatt took a piece of tender, sliced ham from the serving platter. "I've had your fried ham at a church social, ma'am. It's a wonder what you can do with a slice of pork."

Mrs. Brownley pinked up nicely and passed a bowl still half full of turnips. The men started serving themselves as if . . . Molly scowled. As if she wasn't there with a hot meal when they came in at night. As if she wasn't there to wait on them hand and foot, and now they were starving and letting some other poor woman do it.

"It's a wonder, really, Wyatt, that you didn't starve to death before I arrived in Wyoming."

"Now, Molly." Kevin poured gravy over his turnips and ham. He near to drowned the whole plate. "We're here to fetch you home. We—that is—*I* don't want you to live away from us."

"Neither do I," Falcon said around a mouthful of cured pig.

"You're coming home, and that's that." Wyatt went back to chewing. Maybe he'd come in scowling because he blamed her that he was hungry.

"We want you out at the RHR, and we feel like . . . like . . ." Kevin gave Wyatt a desperate glance.

Molly knew it might be best to have this talk strictly between Kevin and her. No one else needed to hear their business.

Parson Brownley said, "Sometimes when there is strife in a family, it can help to talk about it with another person present. A parson."

"And his wife." Ida Brownley gave Molly a pointed look. Neither one of them was budging. Almost like they knew she wanted them to leave.

"I have a job. I'm sure you were going to ask soon."

"We heard the last schoolmarm got hitched." Falcon kept chomping away. "But we can't spare you. You're keeping us alive, and you're the best cook I ever heard tell of, and that's sayin' something because my first wife, Patsy, was a wonder with possum stew."

Molly had never eaten possum, nor did she want to. But she tried to keep the disgust off her face. "I'm sure you'll be fine. Win is a good cook, and Cheyenne, well, she works so hard outside it stands to reason she wouldn't have developed cooking skills, but you won't starve."

"No," Falcon said, grinning. "But we might want to."

Ida Brownley snatched up her pretty white cloth napkin and used it to cover her face. She tried to make it sound like she was coughing, but Molly was sure the woman was laughing.

"She's your wife." The parson was rubbing his mouth rather vigorously. "You might want to be more positive in your—your—comments about her cooking."

"She's the best wife a man ever had." For the first time that evening, Falcon seemed upset. "Whether she's a cook or not ain't nuthin' that I'd ever judge her on."

The parson nodded, and Kevin went on. "We know you got hired, because we asked around town while we were looking for you, and we also learned that school doesn't start until next Monday."

"Looked high and low. Figured you'd been taken away by some outlaw." Wyatt sounded grim.

"So please, Molly, please . . ." Kevin drew the word out for several seconds, "come home with us. We'd like your company until you start school."

"We honestly want you back to stay," Falcon said. "Can you make that custard again tomorrow?"

Molly balled up her napkin but refrained from throwing it at him. Falcon smirked, almost like he knew exactly what she was thinking.

Wyatt added, "Your brother is asking nicely, but you *are* going home tonight."

"I don't like seeing you all pressuring her." Mrs. Brownley lost all trace of humor.

Wyatt looked at Mrs. Brownley. "We all feel mighty bad that we weren't kind enough to her so that now she wants to leave us. It's me especially. I've been ailin', and all the work doctoring me fell to her."

He looked across the table at Molly. "Did I ever thank you?"

Molly heard the guilt in his voice. Saw the sincerity in his eyes. She felt herself weakening, blast it all.

"I've been so impatient to be well. I'm sure I snapped and snarled like a cur dog by way of letting you know you saved my life."

Kevin rested one of his strong hands on her back.

Wyatt went on. "Your knowledge and care are a miracle straight from God. I feel like the worst kind of sinner to have done something to drive you away."

To say he hadn't driven her away would make Kevin blame himself. To say he had driven her away would make Wyatt feel awful. Falcon just kept chewing, eating fast as if he knew they'd have to leave soon and wanted to fill his belly.

He swallowed and said, "Don't blame me. I didn't do nothing wrong."

Molly narrowed her eyes and uncharitably wished he'd choke on a turnip.

Instead of choking, he said, "Come back home with us, Miss Molly. Monday is near a full week away. Come home and spend the days before your job starts with your family. We may try and get you to want to stay, but in the end, it's your life, and as a self-supporting, intelligent, adult woman, it's a decision you get to make. But we're sure enough gonna miss you at the RHR and no denyin' it."

Molly was beat. She could feel her will crumbling. Not from Kevin's worry or Wyatt's anger. Those only made her more determined to stay away. But Falcon, blast him. And his guiltless invitation. He was making it impossible to stay here.

It was going to take a lot of doing to escape her family. But she was up to the job of escaping more than she was up to the job of taking care of this thankless pack of almost-kin.

"I've got five days until school starts." Molly slammed her napkin on the table and stood. Disgusted with herself. "During that time, I'm going to teach *someone* in that family to cook. If I do, none of you will ever notice I'm gone."

Wyatt's eyes flashed. Kevin's brow furrowed.

Falcon grinned. "It ain't gonna be me. Though, I could cook a possum over an open fire for us once a week."

Molly flinched. She turned to Mrs. Brownley. "I'll leave my things here, if it's all right with you. I'll be back next Sunday. I believe I'll stay after church."

"We'll look forward to it."

Molly got her coat and stuffed a satchel with her nightgown and a few things she'd need for a stay at the ranch. She wasn't going to think of it as home ever again.

SEVEN

*M*olly wasn't quite sure how she found herself cooking breakfast alone the next morning. It was odd really. Like yesterday, her escape, her job, her new future, had never happened.

Kevin had talked to her on the way home. It was a friendly talk, and she appreciated it. But it didn't close the divide between them. In some ways it widened it because he was so clear about how much he loved her. And yet he'd started a new life without her. As was right and proper.

The talk had helped her accept the new way of things and see that nothing would or should change that.

The thumping around upstairs told her Wyatt was up. There were other sets of footfalls, so Cheyenne and Falcon were stirring, too.

It was a chilly day. There'd been snow in the night. She saw it scudding along the ground. Not deep, and it wasn't the first snow by any means, but it was a reminder that once she got settled in town and the weather closed down the trails, she might not see her family for months. Not for Thanksgiving nor Christmas.

Squaring her shoulders, she accepted that. Parson and Mrs. Brownley would be good companions, and she'd see her family in the summer—but she refused to live out here as Win had done when school wasn't in session. When she made her break, though they'd always be family, she wasn't going to ever live with them again. It hurt too much for it to begin and end repeatedly. She'd learned that from being dragged home last night.

Turning her thoughts away from being separated from Kevin and Andy—as if she weren't already—she stirred a skillet full of scrambled eggs just as footsteps sounded on the stairs. She scraped the eggs onto a platter with the sharp sound of her metal spatula on the cast-iron frypan.

She set the eggs on the table as Wyatt came in. He went straight to his chair and sat.

The bacon was done and keeping warm on the back of the stove. She set that beside him. Then she pulled her drop biscuits from the oven. She'd grated some cheese into them and seasoned them with garlic, which she'd brought along from Kansas. She'd learned to grow it and loved what it added to a meal.

She slid the perfectly browned biscuits into a small cloth-lined basket and set it on the table. Wyatt grabbed the first one before she let go of the basket.

She added a ball of butter to the table, along with sparkling purple jelly that she'd found in the cellar. It must have been made from wild grapes. She'd have to find where they grew next summer and make more.

Then she caught herself. She didn't intend to ever live here again. Fine, she'd make jelly for Mrs. Brownley.

Cheyenne and Falcon came in next, and they all ate, singing her praises. They were acting like they wanted to make up for whatever had made her leave.

Molly cleared the table with so much help they were in each other's way.

Then Cheyenne said, "We don't know how long we'll be gone."

Molly turned from the sink and saw Falcon's back as he followed Cheyenne outside and swung the door shut.

Blinking at the sudden departure, she turned to Wyatt, who was standing there looking like a man who was afraid he'd say the wrong thing and make Molly move out again. He held a towel and a dripping plate, but he wasn't wiping. He was staring wide-eyed at her.

"Where are they off to? More cattle to move?" Molly asked. "And what did she mean by not knowing how long they'd be gone? I always make plenty for meals, so it doesn't matter if they turn up at mealtimes."

Wyatt seemed to come out of whatever strange mood of fear he'd been in. With a somewhat desperate grab at something to talk about, he said, "The house Cheyenne was born in sits on the border of Ma's land and Grandpa's. We've used it as a line shack."

"What's a line shack?" Ranching was eyeball deep in odd phrases.

"We have such a far-flung holding we send a man or two out to cabins we've built on the far edges of our property line. They live out there and can check the cattle nearby."

"And Cheyenne and Falcon might be moving to that cabin to live?" Molly went back to washing dishes, only to find out the cast-iron skillet in her hands was the last. Wyatt made her nervous for some reason. She'd prefer to keep busy.

"They are thinking of it. It's a nice cabin. Not nearly as big as this, but Cheyenne's pa was a good builder, and we've kept it in good repair. Not sure why they can't just stay here with me." Wyatt frowned. It was his little-brother frown, and Molly had felt a little-sister version of it before on her own face. She suspected it'd been on there near full time since Kevin got married.

She rinsed the skillet and handed it to Wyatt, then poured the basins of water down the handy drain hole in the kitchen sink. This really was a nice house.

Thinking desperately of what to do, she filled a pot with water from the hand pump that came right in the kitchen. Then she used that to refill the wells on the stove while Wyatt dried the skillet.

She forced herself to think of the noon meal. She had a nice elk roast Falcon had brought in.

While she poured the water carefully into the wells, Wyatt reached past her to hang the skillet from the nail on the wall behind the stove. She felt him too close to her as she poured and stepped aside, splattering water on the hot stove. It sent a hissing blast of hot steam straight up toward Wyatt's reaching arm.

He yelped, dropped the skillet with a loud bang, and jumped back.

"Oh, Wyatt, are you burned?"

He pumped the handle for water a couple of times and

cool water flowed out onto his wrist. He let the water soak his shirtsleeve, then sighed in relief. "No, it's not bad. Sorry to fuss like that."

Molly took over the pump handle and kept the water flowing.

Wyatt kept his arm there, so she knew it must hurt.

After a few more seconds, Wyatt said, "That's probably enough."

Molly quit pumping. He pulled his shirtsleeve up, then the sleeve to his longhandles.

"It's red." Molly leaned close. "But no blisters. They sometimes raise later."

She thought of the time her pa, in a temper, had thrown a full coffeepot of boiling water on her ma. Molly had doctored those burns and knew the different levels of seriousness.

"You need to keep something cool on it for a while though, until all the heat goes out of it. It will make the burn less serious." She grabbed a towel off a nail and soaked it quickly, wrung it out, then wrapped it around Wyatt's arm.

He allowed it, which surprised her. He'd often snapped at her when he was hurt and wanting to get out of his bandages so he could get to work.

"Does it hurt bad? I'm sorry I was so careless." Her right hand rested under his left arm, holding it still, while her left hand held the cool, wet towel pressed gently on the burn.

"It's not bad. I shouldn't have crowded you like that."

He shifted, so her back was to the sink, to keep her from leaning against the hot stove, probably.

Then he shifted a bit more and darned if he wasn't crowding her again.

She looked up, and their gazes held. She had his arm, and that was all the space between them.

"M-Molly, I've wanted to—to say . . . thank you. No, that's not what I wanted to say. Of course, I am thankful, but what I wanted to say is . . ." His voice dropped to a whisper. "W-waking up with you beside me, well, I have to admit I think about it now and then."

He looked so deeply into her eyes she felt like he could see her mind, her heart, her soul. And she could see his.

Slowly, an inch at a time, plenty of time for her to realize he was too close and realize his intention, he leaned down.

His lips met hers, and he kissed her.

And she most certainly kissed him back.

Just as slowly, just as surely, his arms came around her back. Hers slid up his strong chest and wrapped around his neck.

She vaguely wondered where the wet towel went. But it was gone for a fact. There was no space between them anymore.

One of his hands came up to cradle her face, then slid deeply into her hair. He tilted his head and deepened the kiss, and she clung to him as if fearing she'd collapse. Her knees were shaky enough she had to wonder.

Like a warning bell, the kitchen door handle rattled.

Wyatt was gone. She blinked her eyes open to see him striding toward the door, yanking it open. Kevin stood outside with Win a pace behind.

"Good. You're here. You and Win help Molly. I've got work." He squeezed past Kevin and got out before Win got in, and that was the last Molly saw because she whirled away

61

from Kevin, wondering what she looked like. Her cheeks felt flushed. Her lips felt swollen. Was her hair in disarray? Her thoughts certainly were.

She got very busy picking the wet towel up off the floor, then the skillet. She hung both up neatly, giving her face a chance to cool. That wasn't quite long enough, so she went back to filling the water wells. The stove would keep the water hot, and they'd have a ready supply of it all day.

How long had she been standing here, working in silence when *hello* or *good morning* was absolutely called for?

"What do—" Her voice was husky, all wrong. She cleared her throat and forged on. "What do you two have planned for today?"

The wells full, she pulled the large roasting pan out from a cupboard below the sink. Straightening, she glanced behind her all casual-like, trying to think of what she would normally do if Kevin and Win came in, and she wasn't all woolly-headed from the kiss she'd just shared with Wyatt.

A kiss.

Her first kiss.

Kevin and Win only had eyes for each other, as always, so Molly calmed down—leastways she calmed down about being caught. She'd be a while calming down about being kissed.

"Would you like a cup of coffee? I'll join you as soon as I get this roast on to cook."

"I'll pour it for us, Molly. Your coffee is so much better than mine. I wish I knew how you do it."

"If we all three have a cup, that'll drain the pot. I'll show you how I make it."

Win smiled. "Thank you, Molly." And somehow things were normal. Win was bustling around pouring coffee. Molly was focused on her meal, which didn't take long.

Then they sat at the table and talked like one of them hadn't just done the stupidest thing she'd ever heard tell of any woman doing in the history of the world.

EIGHT

*H*is first kiss. He'd really never thought much about kissing.

Well, some.

But honestly, there were no women around. Well, Cheyenne, but she didn't count.

And Win had lived here off and on for the last few years, but she didn't count, either.

Neither did Molly. What in tarnation was he thinking?

Kissing Molly, who'd shown clear as glass that she wanted to leave him, had even moved out until they'd near dragged her back. Kissing her had to be the stupidest thing a man had ever done.

And Wyatt wanted to do it again, bad.

The cowhands were so used to running the place without him while he'd been healing up from being shot that they'd spread out to do whatever needed doing without even talking to him.

And he'd have to track them down if he wanted something to do besides go charging back into the house and kissing Molly again. Right in front of her brother this time.

Oh, there was an idea fit to get a man shot.

He'd noticed Kevin, a usually easygoing farmer from Kansas, had a mean streak. Tough man. Protective. Kevin would feel bad if he shot his own brother. It might only be later, long after the gun smoke had cleared, but then he'd feel bad.

Wyatt reckoned he'd feel bad, too. And having just healed up from being shot, he had no wish to repeat the experience.

He still almost turned back. Fear of getting shot wasn't enough to stop him, so he near ran to the barn in the brisk wind and the blowing snow. None was coming down now, but what was already on the ground danced as if it were thrilled to be here on earth.

He saddled up a pretty sorrel gelding and rode hard for Cheyenne and Falcon's cabin. It wasn't far, which was the thing Wyatt liked most about it, but still too far—because they should've just stayed put. Stayed right there in the house instead of leaving Wyatt all alone with beautiful, yellow-haired Molly.

But Cheyenne was gone with her husband, reminding Wyatt he'd lost his place in his sister's life.

Just as Molly had lost her place in her brother's.

It made sense that he and Molly could find what they'd lost by turning to each other.

But he didn't know how to make her see sense.

He had two brothers. One of them had talked the prickliest woman in the whole territory of Wyoming into marrying him. The other one might shoot him just for bringing up his worries.

It was easy to choose Falcon to talk to.

Kevin would probably be cheerful enough about Molly marrying Wyatt and staying at the ranch, but he might not like all that went into bringing her around.

Wyatt was well and truly chilled by the time he got to the line shack. He hadn't been over this way for a while. Looking at the cabin as he rode up, he was struck by it being really small. Cheyenne was used to a fine house. This cabin had a main room that Nate Brewster had built in his bachelor days, then he'd added on a single bedroom when Ma had married him. Grandpa had lived in a house of similar size. After Nate died, Grandpa built the big house and welcomed Ma and little Cheyenne home.

There was a little entry room. That room slowed down the wind and kept the cabin warmer. The cabin was tightly built. There were sturdy shutters on the few small windows, a good wooden floor. Cupboards and a dry sink inside.

A windmill spun like mad in the late fall wind, and a small barn stood behind the cabin with room enough for a couple of horses and leather. A corral was tacked onto the barn.

That was it.

Wyatt heard chopping in the nearby woods that grew on a slope heading up the hill behind the cabin. Falcon must be fetching kindling for the fire. Instead of seeing if Cheyenne was in the house, he circled the house wide enough so that Cheyenne wouldn't notice him and rode toward the sound of the chopping.

"Falcon?" Wyatt stopped while he was still well back. He was a cautious man and had no desire for a felled tree to land smack on his head.

The chopping stopped. Falcon came rushing out of the forest, ax raised. "What happened?"

Falcon was always ready for trouble.

"Nothing happened." Wyatt swung off his horse. "I . . . well, I thought, maybe, uh, you could . . . could use some help over here." This wasn't quite true, but maybe chopping wood next to Falcon would help Wyatt get his thoughts in order. Of course, his arm was still a little tender.

"You can't chop wood the second day you have your sling off. We talked about it last night, and you agreed. So what's the matter?"

Wyatt met Falcon's eyes. They were a match in very few ways. They both had Clovis's eyes and the dimple in their chins. That was all that was the same between them.

"H-how . . ." Wyatt's throat went a little dry. He hitched his horse to a sapling and walked over to face Falcon, putting off the moment he had to speak. He wasn't much for talking about his troubles. Truth was, until Clovis's will, he'd've told you he didn't have any troubles. Well, except for stampeding cattle and unbroken mustangs and gunslinging rustlers, and the occasional rattlesnake, wolf, avalanche, blizzard, that kind of thing. But no *real* trouble.

He swallowed hard. "How did . . . did . . . did you, um, uh . . . talk Ch-Cheyenne into m-marrying you?"

The tension went out of Falcon's shoulders. The furrows on his brow smoothed out. Then he grinned. "Trouble with Molly, huh?"

Wyatt felt his face heat up. Being embarrassed was stupid, so instead he got mad. He wanted to slug Falcon in the face and stomp off. But then who'd he ask?

Falcon watched him mighty close—still grinning. And Wyatt had a feeling Falcon was reading what went on inside Wyatt mighty clear.

Including the punch. And he wasn't one speck afraid.

"Cheyenne's gonna notice I quit chopping. We really oughta go in and talk about this with her."

"No!" Wyatt was horrified. Cheyenne would never let him—

"What's the matter, Wyatt?"

He spun around to look his sister in the eye. She probably saw almost as much as Falcon. She knew him mighty well.

"Having trouble with Molly again?" she asked.

"How do you both know this?"

Cheyenne didn't smile, not like that half-wit Falcon. Instead, she came up and slung an arm around his shoulders. He wondered if Kevin and Win knew, too. He might've saved himself a long ride if he'd just dragged Kevin out of the house and talked to him.

"I think Molly is falling in love with you," Cheyenne said.

Wyatt's hopes soared.

"Nope, that ain't right." Falcon came up beside Wyatt but didn't touch him.

Good thing because his words made Wyatt sick and nervous. He didn't want to hear this.

"Molly *is* in love with you. No thinkin', no fallin'. She's all the way in."

Maybe he did want to hear it.

"How can either of you know such a thing?"

"I'm not sure what's going on with Molly leaving the way she did the other night." Cheyenne's arm tightened halfway to a hug. "We all decided different things. She wasn't appreci-ated. She was working hard at a thankless job."

"You were a growlin' old grizzly to her all the time." Falcon had to remind Wyatt of that.

He glared at Falcon. "I came over here thinking a brother might have some good advice. Now I wish you'd go back to chopping, and I could just talk to Cheyenne."

"Sparkin' a girl's the easiest thing in the world." Falcon grinned at Cheyenne.

Who grinned back.

Falcon had gotten lost in the woods, well, not lost ex-actly. He'd been shot, he'd fallen into a vicious, fast-moving stream, half-drowned and believed dead, and left to wander in the forest for a week with a head wound that wiped out his memory. Cheyenne hadn't met him yet, since it happened the first day he'd come to the ranch, and she'd left the ranch in a rage over having lost her inheritance to Wyatt and his surprise half brothers.

While wandering the woods, she'd seen tracks and won-dered who was skulking around her property. She traipsed around after him in the mountains and forests for nearly a week and never so much as caught sight of him.

"Falcon impressed me so much when I was trying to trail him. I was halfway in love with him before we met. He's right. It was easy."

"You two are no help." Wyatt grabbed his Stetson and dragged it off his head, then with his gloved hand, he shoved his hair back so it didn't hang in his eyes. He needed a hair-cut. He clapped his hat back on and decided to ride to Bear Claw Pass to the barber. Anything to get shut of these two.

And no, he wasn't gonna ask the barber what to do about Molly.

He took one long step.

Cheyenne grabbed hold of him. "Wait. Don't leave. You're right. We're a bad example of how to spark a woman."

"I sparked Patsy back home. My first wife."

Nodding, Cheyenne asked, "How'd you do that?"

"I met her in the woods skinnin' a possum. You should've seen that woman skin a possum." Falcon shook his head and seemed to be seeing into the past. "It was a wonder. I asked her if she was married, and she said no. So I asked her if she'd marry me, and she said yes."

Cheyenne leaned forward to look across Wyatt at Falcon. "Just like that?"

"She was a fine woman."

Cheyenne looked sideways at Wyatt.

He scowled at her. "I've never seen Molly skin anything. She expects the food to come to the house already skinned."

"Still, she's a fine cook." Falcon patted his stomach.

Wyatt expected Falcon and Cheyenne to show up for most meals back home . . . unless Molly moved away. Then they'd all starve.

"Just go back and ask her to marry you. That oughta fix things up, but I can go trap a possum for you if y'all want to test her first." Falcon's Southern drawl was a perfect echo of Clovis Hunt, their worthless father. Of the three brothers, Falcon resembled Clovis most. It was the thing Wyatt liked least about him.

Wyatt shoved Falcon, and he only moved because Wyatt

70

took him by surprise, and maybe because he was getting out of fist range and laughing at the same time.

Having brothers was turning out to be a chore.

"Molly isn't interested in marrying anyone," Wyatt said, feeling low. "Remember when we were talking about honoring our fathers, and all of us were wondering how to honor Clovis? Molly said, 'Mine was no great pillar of decency, either. I think honoring him is going to have to be one of those sins I just have to ask forgiveness for.'"

"You remember her exact words?" Falcon asked. "You were interested in her even back then?"

Cheyenne crossed her arms and frowned. "After Molly did so much doctoring on Win the night she got shot, I said something about Molly getting married someday. She said she'd never marry. And, cranky as I was then, I wasn't paying her much mind, but even at that, I was struck by her sounding solemn as the grave. She said her ma did a poor job of picking husbands, and she'd likely do just as poorly."

"Picking me wouldn't be doing poorly."

"That's sure enough true, but she might not see it that way, especially since you've been so growly."

He hadn't been growling when he'd kissed her. His head was a little fuzzy from it, but he was pretty sure she'd kissed him back. Before he'd heard the door, shoved her away, and ran. He winced at the memory. He doubted that had impressed her much.

"Kevin said his stepfather and his ma died a long time ago." Falcon tried to remember. "I think his pa was a . . . a night rider? Was that what he said? Threw in with men riding wild at night, thieving and burning, fighting for slavery before there was even a war. Molly's pa sounds like he was no prize. And we know Clovis was a dumb choice. So I can see why Molly's a little on edge when it comes to husbands."

Wyatt listened and wondered.

"You should ask her about it." Cheyenne shook her head while she gave advice.

Wyatt didn't think she noticed her head shaking, but he figured her head was being more honest than her mouth. "You never want to talk about anything that upsets you. Molly won't either."

It was hard being the youngest. As the man, he should've been the leader of his home, but Ma and Cheyenne were both stronger and smarter and faster at everything than him.

And now here he was asking his big sister personal questions. He said, "I know she's too skilled at healing."

"Did she learn that during the war?" Falcon asked.

"I don't know. Around the farm, I think. Were her parents hurt because of the war? How did they die? Was it in the war, or were they killed by men taking revenge on her pa's night riding?"

"Maybe Kevin would talk about it," Falcon said.

"I'm not talking to Kevin." Wyatt didn't know a thing about sparkin'. But he knew sure as shooting that talking to Kevin would be stupid.

"Maybe Win knows," Cheyenne said. "I could ask her."

That sounded like a good idea. Wyatt wouldn't have to do any more talking. He was worn clean out from all this talking.

"If she's determined not to marry, I doubt you can change

her mind. Prob'ly best to give up and go looking elsewhere for a woman." Falcon shoved his hands in his pockets.

"Big brother, you're not a lot of help. Between possum skinning and giving up, I should've just gone out looking for stray cows to herd in." Wyatt decided to do that right now.

"Now, Wyatt, let me talk to Win. I can at least ask. And you know what? You oughta take Molly somewhere. Take her riding."

"Too cold."

"Take her to town for a meal at the diner. You could do that today."

"She's a better cook than Hogback." The man who owned the diner called himself that and nothing else. No one knew his name.

Everyone knew he was a terrible cook.

"Um . . . I don't know where a man takes a woman here to court her." Cheyenne scratched her head. "I'll talk to Win and give some thought to how to woo Molly. In the meantime, it's cold, either come and help me sweep out the cabin or go home."

Falcon turned to the woods, his ax slung over his shoulder. Cheyenne gave Wyatt a kiss on the cheek. Something she'd hardly ever done before. Well, maybe when he was little, and maybe when he'd been shot, but he'd been mostly out of his head with fever so he wasn't sure.

"You're going soft, Cheyenne." He kissed her back.

He heard her chuckling softly as he swung up on his horse. She was halfway back to the cabin by the time he rode out of the yard. Back to the home he'd just run away from.

Molly's parents.

Her pa was no great pillar of decency. What did that even mean?

Then he thought, if he asked her about her parents, she could ask him about Clovis. And Clovis Hunt was a sidewinder if ever there was one. He'd also broken Wyatt's heart regularly when he was little, until Wyatt learned not to care. Or at least not to show he cared.

Did he have the nerve to ask her?

And if she asked back, did he have the nerve to answer?

NINE

*M*olly enjoyed cooking with a well-stocked pantry, and the RHR had a fine stove. But she'd just run off to town, and her excuse had been that she wanted to do some other job. Now here she stood, sliding a baked chicken out of the oven and sliding a pan of cinnamon rolls in.

An oversized rooster had fallen into her hands this afternoon, one who'd taken to sleeping in the rafters of the barn and had thereby escaped plucking. She'd made him up like a Thanksgiving turkey with stuffing.

Lifting the lid off the roasting pan, she saw the bird was done and browned perfectly. It would be ready to serve at the same time the cinnamon rolls came out of the oven. She had potatoes boiling, soon to be mashed. There were carrots, baked and glazed. It was a fine meal, and she enjoyed thinking of the nice fuss they'd make of it.

Win and Kevin would come, she'd asked them specially. She doubted Cheyenne and Falcon would be back, but there was plenty if they made the long ride. It wasn't impossibly long, but long enough if they were in the middle of repairing the cabin.

Andy, he liked it too much with the working men.

And Wyatt. She paused. Instead of lifting the chicken from the pan, she touched her lips. She could still feel the kiss. The heat of it. The intrigue. The sweetness.

Shaking her head, she said out loud, "No. I'm not getting married."

Not that Wyatt had asked. No, he'd run like a scared rabbit.

But if he had, the answer was no. She had no wish for marriage. No interest in binding herself to a man. Her own pa was reason enough. Her ma marrying badly twice made it worse. And knowing how a man could steal a woman's property was the final blow. She had plans to work, teach school. Starting next Monday, she'd be earning money, and it would be hers to keep. Maybe in a couple of years, when she was twenty-one, she could homestead, build a small cabin. Kevin and Andy would help her. If there was a place near Bear Claw Pass left to claim, she could work as the schoolmarm and set up a decent kitchen at her own home and cook for herself.

She wondered if she could eat a whole chicken before she tired of it. A whole pan of cinnamon rolls.

It didn't matter. Her life was all planned and in order.

And then Wyatt Hunt had kissed her.

And she really wanted him to do it again.

She put the chicken on a platter, then set plates and utensils on the table. She made gravy, scraping crunchy bits of chicken drippings from the bottom of the pan. She pulled out a pan of glazed carrots from the oven and turned them into a bowl. The cinnamon rolls smelled luscious and were minutes away from perfection.

The sun was well set as she mashed the potatoes. She heard the back door open and close quietly. Probably Wyatt, that kiss-stealing skunk.

"Molly."

Startled by the unfamiliar woman's voice, Molly spun around and flung a spoonful of potatoes through the air.

Rachel Hobart was out of range. "Where is everyone?"

"What are you doing back here?" Molly remembered her, but they'd only met briefly. After Wyatt had been shot. After Falcon had dragged the Pinkerton agent into the kitchen when he'd caught her slipping through the shadows on her way to the house.

At the time, Falcon figured her for the one who'd shot Wyatt. Molly had gone running upstairs because they heard Wyatt moving around and someone had to keep him from coming down because he was too unsteady for the stairs.

They'd met one other time while Molly was fighting for Wyatt's life. So Wyatt hadn't spent any time with her, either. The bullet had knocked him mighty low.

Molly knew the rest of the family had been persuaded to trust her, but now she was back, looking like a desperate woman with bad intentions.

Molly braced herself to fight her off with the potato masher.

Wyatt came in behind Rachel, likely having seen her arrive. "What are you doing back here?"

Molly took grim satisfaction in knowing Wyatt thought

like her. She was also glad she didn't have to get the knife out of her boot. She liked to keep it a secret. She and Win had both taken to carrying one. Cheyenne, of course, already did.

"You're Wyatt, right?" Rachel Hobart stuck out a hand, very manly.

Wyatt blinked. He hesitated but shook. Molly didn't like it.

"Answer my question," he said.

"That's exactly what I'm planning to do." Rachel looked from Wyatt to Molly. "Where is Falcon? And Cheyenne?"

"They aren't here," Wyatt said.

Rachel's jaw firmed, and her eyes flared with annoyance. "I got Amelia Bishop returned home to Minnesota. We had a long train ride to talk, and we compared our experiences with Oliver Hawkins. He bothered both of us."

"He bothers everyone." Wyatt shrugged.

"He bothered us in a way that was *improper*. He was overly familiar. As a single woman employed in his house, I can promise you he said and did things in an increasingly disturbing way. Amelia's experiences very closely matched mine. You weren't in town when Hawkins saw Amelia had been found. But it was clear she was frightened of him, and it was clear he wanted her back.

"On our trip home she said a big part of the reason she ran off and got married and lived in hiding was because she was afraid Hawkins meant her harm."

"Harm?" Wyatt's brow furrowed. "You mean he put his hands on her? Against her wishes?"

"I mean, Amelia's experience and mine aroused her father's suspicions to the point he asked me to continue investigating."

"But how can you investigate the way he treated you and Amelia when neither of you is still in his household?" Molly asked.

Rachel's eyes narrowed. Her mouth a straight, grim line, she said, "I've learned of two other housekeepers that worked for Hawkins. They disappeared without a trace. They had no influential, wealthy family, so no one sent an investigator. It's sad for the families left behind, but there was nothing done to find those housekeepers. After all, the West tends to swallow people up."

Molly knew it had swallowed her parents. In one big, ugly gulp.

"Checking up on Hawkins led me to checking on those missing housekeepers, and that led me to his wife."

"She died birthing a child," Wyatt said. "Everyone knows that."

"What everyone *knows* doesn't line up with the truth. In fact, I suspect he's a killer."

The door swung open.

Win came in. Kevin was a pace behind her.

Win's eyes went straight to Rachel. All the color drained from her face, and Molly wondered if she was going to faint.

"You collapsed before when we spoke." Rachel had a shrewd look in her eyes that Molly found cruel. And that look was aimed right at Win.

Molly didn't like that Win had stolen her brother. That made Molly feel unfair, unreasonable, and petty—and Molly didn't like feeling that way.

But what Molly really didn't like was that right this moment, she realized Win was her sister. And no one was going to upset her sister.

"Wh-what are you doing here?" Win reached for Kevin, missed him because her eyes were locked on Rachel. Kevin stepped up quickly and grabbed her hand to steady her.

"I'm here to ask you some questions you're not going to want to answer, Mrs. Hunt."

"What kind of questions?" But the tremor in Win's voice made her sound like she knew.

"Questions about your father and his unpleasant history with women."

Win nodded. The tiniest nod, the most reluctant show of agreement Molly had ever seen. Still holding tight to Kevin's hand, Win walked to the table and sat rather heavily in a chair.

"Supper's ready." Molly thought eating might as well go on. "There's plenty for you, Rachel, please join us."

Honestly, Molly would have preferred to boot her out of the house. But Rachel had a stubborn look about her.

Molly figured the woman was here to stay.

Another plate was added to the table, and Molly swiftly set out platters and bowls. Then they all sat down, said a prayer, and Molly braced herself for talk of murder.

TEN

I need to ask you questions about your father, Winona." Hobart picked up the platter of sliced chicken, served herself, and passed it to Wyatt, who sat at the head of the table.

He felt like he needed to guard his family from her. Protect Win, protect everyone.

Taking the chicken, he added it to his plate with some stuffing. Just the smell made his mouth water. He was sure Molly had again prepared an unusually delicious meal.

"I suspect your father of being a murderer." Hobart picked up the bowl of glazed carrots. "I think he killed your mother."

Molly's quiet gasp drew Wyatt's eyes. He handed her the chicken platter. And he had to hold it for too long. She wasn't paying attention to anyone but Win.

Kevin's arm came around Win. He said fiercely, "You don't have to talk to her, Win."

The way Kevin said it sharpened Wyatt's attention. From his earliest memory, Win had always stayed here. A little, motherless girl, then she'd vanished off to boarding school for years and never once came home, even for summers. When she had finally come home, she spent her free time here, not at her pa's house. Wyatt had never considered why. He didn't care much for Hawkins, and he just accepted that Win preferred the company of Cheyenne, her childhood friend, to her loud, lazy father.

Now he asked himself if there was more to it than that.

He wondered at Molly's reaction, too. It was a shocking statement by Hobart, but Molly seemed to be struck hard.

"I am blunt, Winona. I don't apologize for it. Yes, your husband is right, you don't have to talk to me. But I traveled to Chicago to find background on Hawkins. I couldn't find much before he married your mother. He was untraceable, and I'm good at tracing. I suspect he isn't using the name he was born with and most everything your mother knew about him was an invention. There were people willing to share suspicions with me—old friends of your mother and your grandparents. Their suspicions, combined with his treatment of me and Amelia Bishop, made me wonder. I looked closer and found two former housekeepers that disappeared. Can you remember when your mother died?"

Win closed her bright blue eyes and drew in a long, slow breath, as if gathering herself. Kevin pulled her closer.

Win's hand went to where his rested on her shoulder. She said to him, though not so quietly the whole table couldn't hear, "I need to tell her."

Kevin slowly, reluctantly, nodded.

"I-I sh-share your suspicions, Mrs. Hobart."

"Please, it's Rachel. No missus. I told your father I was a widow when I took the job."

Nodding, Win said, "I don't remember anything that will help you. I was told Ma died birthing a child. I remember no one had said that there was a baby on the way to me. It was a complete shock. The news of a child lost. The news of my ma dying. I got sent over here. Katherine, Wyatt and Cheyenne's mother, had come over and offered to take care of me."

"What about your father? He does no work that I could see. It's not like he was out laboring on the range every day."

Win shook her head, such a tiny motion . . . Wyatt could barely tell she heard and reacted.

"I guess he felt he wasn't up to caring for a child."

No one mentioned that she wasn't an infant. She didn't need care so much as love. Wyatt was glad she'd come over here where she had a chance to find it.

"I stayed here for a few years until I was old enough for boarding school."

"In St. Louis, not Chicago. That struck me as strange," Hobart said between bites of stuffing. "Why not send you back to the town where you were born, where your parents were from? Hawkins could have much more easily contacted someone there to ask about schools."

"I have few memories of my grandparents, but I met an elderly lady in St. Louis who'd known them. I found out they were wealthy, influential people in Chicago. They were completely against my parents' marriage. My ma, my grand-parents' only child, had been a bright, socially active woman who loved people and dancing and pretty gowns. After she married, she all but vanished from society. She had a child, and people didn't think it was so strange that she'd stay at home for that. But then there were rumors that she'd become frail. Melancholy. After my grandparents died, my parents moved out here. This woman in St. Louis was a good friend of my grandmother. She still carried all the worries Grand-mother had shared with her around like weights."

"I should have looked into the circumstances of their deaths," Hobart muttered to herself.

Win gasped. She swallowed hard and went on. "My pa wanted to be a land baron."

Wyatt made a particularly rude noise before he could stop himself.

No one looked away from Win. "Then Ma died. Since I talked with that woman in St. Louis, I've begun to remember things. Ma crying. Loud shouting. Bruises. It's all dim and muddled by the years and my youth."

Win's eyes came up and locked on Hobart. "I can hardly bear to be around Pa now. I've wondered if I'm being fair to him. But there's something there, something in his eyes. Maybe I'm imagining it, but he—he scares me."

Hobart's jaw tightened. "I know that look. I've seen it directed at me. Amelia knows that look, too."

Molly asked, "C-can a person still be arrested or hanged for something that happened so long ago?"

Hobart studied Molly's face for so long Wyatt wanted to grab Molly and drag her away from the woman.

Finally, Hobart said, "Have you heard the term *statute of limitations*?"

Wyatt looked around the table.

"*Statute* means law, I think," Win said.

"Yes, there are laws that limit how long a person can be arrested for crimes," Hobart explained. "Different crimes have different lengths of time, and most states and territo-ries have their own limits. If you rob a bank and they don't catch you for seven years, you got away with it. If someone realizes you did it up until that time—if that's the statute of limitations in your area—they can still arrest you."

"S-so what number of years is it for killing someone?" Molly had taken food onto her plate, but Wyatt noticed she hadn't touched it.

Hobart looked at Molly, then Win, then back to Molly. She said quietly, "There is no statute of limitations on murder."

Molly asked no further questions. And she didn't eat a bite.

～

"I thought I was going to be sick." Win rested her head on Kevin's shoulder. She shook, deep inside, her soul trembling. To have said out loud the deepest secret of her life. "I still don't feel steady. B-but it was right to talk to her, wasn't it?"

She and Kevin had returned to the ramrod's house where they'd taken up residence. Now they lay together, Kevin holding her close. A very present help in times of trouble. There was a psalm that spoke of God being a present help in times of trouble. Win thought it described her husband right now, too.

She prayed to God and clung to her husband and trembled.

"I think . . ." Kevin was silent for far too long. "I think one of the reasons you've never spoken of it is because you saw no way to prove what you suspected. It would just be a young woman who'd listened to gossip back in St. Louis. Your pa is a wealthy man. It would put you in a terrible position to have spoken of your worries under those circumstances. But now, with Hobart here investigating, it was right and good that you spoke up."

Win snuggled closer. Kevin had such strength, and she leaned into every bit of it.

She whispered, "Did you see how Molly reacted when Hobart talked about there not being a statute of limitations on murder?"

"I saw." Kevin spoke as if his jaw was clenched tight. "Molly and I have never spoken of how our parents died. But I could see her fear. I came in and found them dead and Molly bleeding. I hid the bodies, and we never spoke of them again. Ma was a near recluse due to Pa's hard fists and her shame over the bruises. Pa was a man who lived recklessly, running straight into trouble all the time. They were never missed."

"It would be good for her to talk about it."

"After all these years? We've managed not to talk about it for so long, to break through that would be so hard for her . . . for both of us. I remember when I first told you how terrible it was to say it all out loud."

"It would be hard. I can feel myself shaking as if I've exposed something terrible to the whole world. As if I've taken a huge risk. As if fear has me in its grip. But I think maybe airing it out to the world has helped."

"And you think Molly should take that risk, too?"

"I think if she doesn't, she's never going to know true freedom. Whatever she witnessed when your parents died, and whatever her part was in it, keeps her chained to the past. She's a solemn young woman who isn't happy here and maybe can't really be happy anywhere until she breaks those chains."

"And if she *does* speak of it, she could hang for murder. That's one brutally heavy chain."

ELEVEN

"The school is closed?" Molly had to force her gaping jaw shut.

"Shhh . . ." Mrs. Brownley took Molly's arm and led her farther from the gathered congregation outside the little log church.

The services were over. The congregation wasn't staying long outside due to the chilly weather.

Molly had packed all her belongings. She intended to stay in town while her family went home without her.

Mrs. Brownley was near the small cemetery behind the church when she glanced around Molly to make sure no one was near enough to overhear. "We are a small town. Not many children in the school. We hoped for twelve, though one family with two children is out of town a fair distance and don't come in during the winter."

Molly looked at the gentle snow swirling down around the tombstones. It was like her dream of independence was blowing away with the dispersing church members. It was October, and winter was as good as here. It would be her first winter in Wyoming, and the rumors of blizzards and bitter cold were frightening.

"If two of the twelve are out, or soon to be, what about the other ten?"

"There are four families here in town." Mrs. Brownley's voice dropped again, though there was no one near. "Someone started talk of your—your, um . . . character, I'm afraid."

She looked into Molly's eyes. Only kindness there.

"My character?" A chill that had nothing to do with the icy breeze slithered down Molly's spine. She thought of how her parents had died and knew if that was being bandied about, then the talk was fair. But no one knew that. No one except Kevin, and Win knew some of it. Well, in truth, Kevin only knew some of it.

"I'm not sure where the talk started, but of course everyone knows of the odd business with the RHR and Clovis Hunt's will. There's talk of you having an improper, um . . . well, uh, connection to that business."

The reason she got fired in Wheatfield, Kansas. Or close enough. Clovis Hunt was here to ruin her life once again.

"But it was my ma and Clovis's marriage that wasn't proper. What's more, my ma had no idea of such. She trusted Clovis. When she heard he'd died, Ma remarried. But the fact that he was already married when he wed her meant her first marriage wasn't legal and her second one was. My birth is perfectly proper."

Mrs. Brownley had her hands clutched together, pressed to her chest, as if she were begging Molly not to be upset. Or maybe it was an attitude of prayer.

"Two of the larger families said they won't be a part of

the school when a scandal follows the teacher across hundreds of miles."

She should have been able to leave it behind, Molly thought grimly. And maybe she would have if they hadn't come straight to Clovis Hunt's hometown, where all this nonsense about his abandoned wives had first come to light.

"That takes the school down to only four students. And that includes the two who come in from out of town. Besides, those unhappy families aren't agreeable to just keeping their children home, they are clamoring for a different teacher. The school is closed until a new teacher is hired."

Molly looked into Mrs. Brownley's eyes. The woman was a bit shorter than her, thin enough Molly worried about the Brownleys losing the income from boarding the teacher. Molly wanted to defend herself. She wanted to find those families and firmly explain her birth was all proper. She wanted to scream that it wasn't fair that she was tarred with a brush she'd had nothing to do with.

One look in Mrs. Brownley's kind eyes told her it would be a waste of time.

Molly's shoulders slumped. "I should move on, head down the trail. Leave the terrible injustice of Clovis Hunt and the RHR behind. If I go without my family, and maybe change my name, no one would look down on me."

Mrs. Brownley's hand settled firmly on Molly's shoulder. "You can't do that. A woman alone can't strike out in the world. It's not safe."

Molly thought of Amelia Bishop. A happy, courageous young woman looking for adventure. Mistreated by Oliver Hawkins. Married to a man who ended up being an outlaw and was now dead. Returning, a more fragile woman, to the safety of her father's home.

And no one would describe Molly as a courageous, adventure-seeking woman. Mrs. Brownley was right that to leave on her own wasn't safe.

Kevin and Win came up to Molly. Win said, "We're ready to unload your things."

"What's wrong?" Kevin knew her so well.

"The job is no longer available." Molly didn't want to go into it. Not here at least, not when she wanted to scream and rant and weep. "I will be coming back to the RHR after all."

Wyatt came to her side. "We want you back at the ranch, but what happened to the job?"

She thought of Clovis and the wreckage he'd left behind.

She thought of Amelia Bishop and what Rachel had said about how frightened she'd been.

She thought of the other vanished housekeepers and Win's dead ma. And Molly's dead ma.

A fury gripped her hard. She kept it in check, but she didn't try to make it go away. Instead, she nurtured it, hugged it close, and thought of a way she could show a little courage.

"I left a few things at the parson's house. Let's get them and go home."

～

Rachel had slipped into the house that first day and never went outside again.

Never stood in front of a window. Never lit a lantern when she was alone in a room.

Not even the cowhands knew she was there. Including Andy.

Now she helped set food on the table. Molly had to admit the meal looked good. "Rachel, you worked for several months at Hawkins's as a housekeeper, didn't you?"

"Yes, I was there over four months."

"I've been thinking, if a Pinkerton agent like you can masquerade as a housekeeper, then maybe a housekeeper like me could masquerade as a Pinkerton agent."

No one else was in the kitchen. They'd gone in different directions to get out of their Sunday best. Molly had rushed to change her dress so she could speak to Rachel in private.

Her hands full, carrying a plate piled high with freshly sliced bread, Rachel cast her a shrewd look. "What happened to teaching school?"

Molly explained in the quickest amount of time possible. "I could get a job as Oliver Hawkins's housekeeper and go in there and snoop around. You were searching for evidence of Amelia Bishop, but now that we know of other missing housekeepers and what happened to his wife, well, a housekeeper is in every room of the house. She dusts shelves, tidies up desk drawers." Molly found the first smile since she'd been fired. She suspected it wasn't a nice smile.

"You don't know how to be a Pinkerton agent, Molly."

Molly came to Rachel's side and clutched her arm. "You could teach me. And I could come to town for supplies or weekly to church and report on anything I'd found. And I could see how Oliver treats me. And between us we could figure out—"

Rachel held up a hand, palm flat, almost in Molly's face.

"Don't tell me no," Molly said desperately. "I need a job. And I need to help."

"Why do you need a job? You've got a good life right here."

"What Oliver did to his wife . . . it makes me sick. I—that is, my ma, well, she suffered at the hands of my pa. I won't stand by and do nothing while a man gets away with that."

Rachel stared at Molly for a long time. Finally, she muttered, "Statute of limitations." Then she went back to getting the meal ready.

"I think we can work together, you and me," Rachel said. "I think you have the skills you need to be an agent and a housekeeper, and maybe we can stop this man from killing again."

Molly touched Rachel's arm. Their eyes met. Molly felt hers brim with tears, but she staved them off. "Thank you."

"I didn't become a Pinkerton because it interested me. I've seen men who needed to be brought to justice in my life, too." Rachel nodded. "There's a lot to it. And it will be a job. You'll earn money from the Pinkerton Agency for this."

Molly hadn't expected that. "Hawkins will be paying me, won't he?"

"Yes, but when you work for me, you get paid by me. We need to talk long and hard. I can tell you Hawkins has a safe I was never able to crack, and I believe he has another hidden, but I was never able to find it. But I did find—"

Wyatt came down from changing. His eyes flicked back and forth between the two women. "Now what's happened?"

Molly looked at the Pinkerton agent, who nodded.

Molly threw her hands wide and said, "I've got another job."

~

"If you really believe he's a murderer, you can't send her in there."

Molly slapped the table, which drew Wyatt's eyes from Hobart. "Stop talking to her. She's not *sending* me anywhere. I'm going. She's going to teach me how to handle things so I can get the evidence we need against Hawkins."

Wyatt's jaw got so tight he was afraid his teeth might crack. "It's not safe."

"I want to do it." Molly, usually quiet, occasionally snippy, but never loud, yelled, "It makes me sick to see a man get away with hurting a woman. Somebody needs to stop him, and there's no one else to do it."

"He won't believe you'd work as a housekeeper. He'll be suspicious."

"I was going to teach school and that fell through. Why would he not believe I'd take a different job?"

Wyatt wasn't going to be able to stop her. He saw a determination in her eyes that was tinged with . . . perhaps a hint of desperation. But the thought of her over there. Defenseless, living with a possible murderer. What's more, winter was coming on.

"The weather is going to turn bad. You won't be able to leave. I won't be able to come if you need help. You're going to get snowed in over there, as everyone does eventually in the Wyoming hills."

"Rachel has already searched as much of the house as she could. She thought of a few more places she should have checked, looking for some proof of what he's done. I'll look there, and I'll find what I need and be out of that house within a matter of days, before winter slams down. And the safe—"

Fists on the tabletop, Wyatt thought frantically. He needed to stop her. He couldn't stop her. So he'd . . . he'd . . .

"Most of Hawkins's hired men were in on the plot against him," Wyatt said. "Nearly all the honest hands had moved on, leaving only the dishonest ones. Ralston was stealing money and cattle, but nearly all the hands stood ready to let Ralston take over when Hawkins was killed. We got a list of names from Wells, to the best he knew them, and all those men were arrested or have run off. Hawkins is shorthanded, I know that. Add to it, he does none of the work himself. I'm coming with you. I'll get a job as a ranch hand."

Molly opened her mouth, closed it, opened it again. It reminded Wyatt of a trout he'd landed last summer.

"Why would Hawkins believe you'd work for him?" she asked. "Why would the owner of the neighboring ranch come looking for a job?"

Wyatt narrowed his eyes as he sorted through a plan. "I might be able to just move into his bunkhouse and never tell Hawkins I'm there."

"The other cowhands would notice," Hobart said, "but they don't talk to Hawkins. If you told them you were hired, whether they believed it or not, they probably wouldn't go to Hawkins. Ralston gave the orders, and Hawkins mostly spent his days in the study with his feet up. I had to dust around the lazy half-wit."

"I could say I'm not living here anymore," Wyatt said. "I could claim to be upset about the new brothers, now married to Win and Cheyenne. That I felt forced out of my own home. Just as Molly does. We could say we got tired of living here and came up with the idea of working for him."

"He made me clean the whole stupid house, except for the third floor, which is kept locked. I felt lucky he didn't insist I go up there and dust, but I wanted to search it if I could figure out how to get in there without flat-out knocking down the door. I couldn't pick the lock and never found a key, but near as I could tell, it was pure empty." Pulling her cup of coffee close, Hobart said, "And he has a safe hidden behind a picture on the wall of his study, but I never got into it. I did sneak down there in the night many times and finally found a combination to the safe. But that was the day you came riding in to accuse Ralston of cattle rustling. I knew when you came that he'd taken off and was probably making a run for it, so I went after him. And that very night, when I should have been opening the safe, I came here to the RHR to question you about what you'd found out about Ralston."

"You were sneaking in," Wyatt said. "Admit it. You were going to search our house and sneak right back out."

Rachel smiled. "Whatever my plans, they were foiled by your sharp-eared brother Falcon."

Falcon had heard her slipping around in the night, or rather, heard someone. He caught her and dragged her inside because they suspected her of shooting Wyatt.

"Then you found Amelia Bishop for me, and I left Hawkins's house for good. I ran out of time to search the combination safe."

"Combination safe?" Molly rested one hand on her chest and looked for all the world like a woman who'd never heard the term. "What is that?"

"Some detective," Wyatt muttered darkly.

He squared his shoulders. He knew he wasn't going to stop her. So he'd try his best to make it safe for her. "We have a combination safe here. You can practice opening it, and we can talk about how the numbers Rachel has will work on a different safe."

"And, Molly," Hobart said, "I told you I also believe he has a second safe. I did some research on the floor plans of his house. A company in Omaha did the construction."

"You can find things like floor plans and look them over?" Molly sounded awestruck. Wyatt sure hoped she didn't abandon teaching and housekeeping for detective work.

"Yes, those things are available if you know where to look. I couldn't find where the safe was installed, but I found that a second one was purchased. It's not uncommon in a grand house, and that monstrosity Hawkins owns qualifies. I suspect it's in his bedroom because I searched the rest of the house from top to bottom many times. Well, not the third floor. You'll have to find a time to search his bedroom for the safe. It's probably behind a clothes chest or behind another picture on the wall or under the floorboards. And there will be a secret switch or lever or something that will have to be used to lift up a section of the floor or move a panel on the wall. You'll have to find it and—"

"This is ridiculous!" Wyatt flung his arms wide. "Now she's got to find a hidden safe with a secret switch? And do you have the combination for that, too?"

Giving him a narrow-eyed look, Rachel smiled faintly. It could almost be called a smirk. "Actually, I do. There was a second number on the piece of paper I found. I copied both, not sure which one would work on the safe in his study. I'm still not sure, so if one doesn't work, you'll have to try the second. At first, I thought maybe he'd changed it and hadn't scratched out the old number. Now I'm sure it's for that second safe."

"And what am I looking for in these safes?" Molly's jaw was firm. "What can he possibly have hidden in there that would tie him to crimes he committed years ago?"

Hobart got very quiet. Her eyes appeared to burn as she studied Molly. It was a long stretch of seconds before she answered with grim regret. "A man who kills a woman because he abuses her is one kind of criminal. He may have a history of battering other women, but often he'll marry, and the wife has no way out of the abuse. Or sometimes a woman can be so worn down by the abuse she thinks she deserves it."

Molly watched Hobart as if she were absorbing every word.

"If Hawkins is that kind of man, we may never prove he killed anyone. But—" Hobart swallowed hard, glanced at Wyatt, then spoke more gently, as if she hated putting this knowledge in Molly's head but felt she had to. "There is another kind of killer. A man who, rather than abusing his wife, is . . . is . . . well, he—" She swallowed again. "He enjoys killing and makes a *habit* of it. There's a form of madness that makes a man kill people for no reason except that's his madness."

"But I've met Hawkins." Molly rubbed her hands up and down, from elbow to shoulder, back and forth as if she were cold. "There is nothing that suggests he's furiously mad."

"There is, Molly, if you know what to look for, and I do.

He has a way of treating women. Amelia and I discussed it, and I think you'll see it, too, when you go to work there."

At the word *when*, Wyatt's jaw clenched in fury and fear for Molly.

"At the start, Hawkins is very charming, engaging, full of compliments and lavish with attention. He'll want to watch you work, be in the same room as you. At first, it's a little strange, but if a woman wasn't suspicious, she wouldn't be afraid. She might even be flattered. Then he'll begin to make demands. Small things at first, reasonable things considering he's your boss. But they struck me as odd, and they will you, too, especially since I've told you to watch for them. He'll ask you to do things he could so obviously do for himself that it's strange he doesn't. Things like asking you to pour his coffee when you've got your hands in dishwater or coated in flour while you're kneading bread. And the coffee-pot is sitting right in front of him. And he'll expect you to do it quickly. He comments on it if you're not grateful and demure. Mostly, he wants you to do as you're told, and if you don't, he expresses displeasure, first mildly, then with increasing severity. He is frightening."

Molly gasped, then clenched her jaw as if to keep her fear tightly under wraps.

"When Amelia began to fear him, she accepted Percy Ralston's offer of a runaway marriage. She really saw Ralston as a savior. And he told her she had to live secretly so Hawkins wouldn't find her. Amelia was frightened enough of Hawkins to believe it. But Ralston's real purpose was to hide that he was a cattle rustler.

"I've done some study of killers like this, the ones who

do it out of some mad need for power over a woman. They often keep a record of those they kill or collect something that belonged to them. A keepsake of some kind. It's part of that need for power. If Hawkins is the kind of man I think he is, he'll have something from each woman. There's a good chance he has it in his secret safe."

Wyatt's stomach twisted at the thought of a man collecting things from women he'd killed. There was no color left in Molly's face. But she also looked determined. Quietly, he reached across the table and rested a hand on Molly's little clenched fist. "You shouldn't do this."

Molly met his gaze. "I probably shouldn't. It's *not* safe. But how many people protect themselves at the expense of another life? How many women die at the hands of brutal men while other people refuse to interfere? Hawkins isn't an elderly man. If he was, maybe we could lie to ourselves that his life is almost over, and God would sort him out in the next life. But he has time to hurt or kill more women. I will not stand by in safety while he goes on his way. Not when I can help."

They looked into each other's eyes for a long moment.

"You're going to have to leave Molly alone, Wyatt."

He snatched his hand away and glared at Hobart.

She didn't even flinch.

Wyatt had to admit, to himself only, that he had a sneaking admiration for Rachel Hobart. He'd made more than one man back down with his glare. She looked right back at him and never wavered.

"If she's to do any true detective work. Part of her job is observing the way Hawkins treats her. He'll move slow, but he will move. He did with me. In some ways it's a shame

Cheyenne found Amelia because Hawkins's behavior was becoming alarming."

"Then why was it a shame you got out of there?" Molly asked.

Hobart's teeth clenched. "Because I wanted him to try to hurt me, so I could make him sorry. I wanted the pleasure of fighting him when he attacked. I'm not some helpless young miss who doesn't know how to protect herself. When he finally acted with violence, I would have come back at him hard, and I would have won. And he'd've hanged by now."

Admiration burned in Molly's eyes. Wyatt had thought Molly might end up married to him. Instead, she looked like she wanted to team up with Rachel Hobart and head east to become a Pinkerton agent.

Wyatt rubbed both hands over his face. "He'll know I'm there with her. He won't bother her."

"That's true if you're showing special interest in Molly or spending time with her. To catch him, you'll have to stay away. And if you do that, I doubt he can stop himself from . . . *bothering* her. I doubt he can stop himself from bothering any woman in his household. If he did it to me and Amelia, and if Win is right about her mother, then it's his way. His habit. And the other two women who went missing—two I've found out about, there could be more—add to my suspicions. I've spent a lot of time on this case with Senator Bishop's full support. He's contacted men he knows in Wyoming, including the territorial governor in Omaha, that's how I got hold of those floor plans and purchase orders. And his associates in Chicago helped me dig into Hawkins's background and found nothing. Nothing is almost as bad as finding something sordid, because I should have been able to trace him right back to infancy. Senator Bishop opened doors I'd have never gotten through so I could look into this. If I'm right, then Oliver Hawkins is a man who badly needs to be stopped."

Molly nodded, looking straight at Hobart as if the woman were writing law right before Molly's eyes. "I'm going to be the one to stop him."

Her voice rang with zeal. As sick with fear as this made Wyatt, he admired her courage. He also knew there was something else going on here. The depth of her fervor, the gleam in her eyes, told him she wasn't doing it for justice. To fight for right and wrong. Nor because Hobart had inspired her. Those things were part of it, but Molly had personal reasons, and they had to be rooted in her past.

Molly had said loud and clear she never intended to marry. She'd said her pa was no great pillar of decency. Molly had been hurt. She was grabbing her chance to fight back.

Wyatt intended to find out who'd hurt her. And while he was learning, he'd be close by to protect her.

TWELVE

*A*re you out of your mind?"

Molly's hair nearly blew back in the face of Kevin's outrage.

"No, Molly." Win leapt from the table. "You can't. This isn't right. You could be harmed." She came around the table and threw her arms around Molly.

Win and Kevin, Wyatt, Rachel Hobart, and Molly were the only ones at the table. Falcon and Cheyenne hadn't come back last night.

Molly had her pretty blue dress on again, the one sprinkled with white flowers. Win wore a neat black riding skirt with a pleated white shirtwaist. Wyatt looked at the two of them. Win with dark curls, blushing pink cheeks, and bright blue eyes brimming with tears. Molly with hair so fair it was more white than yellow. Fine hair she wore in a tidy bun on the top of her head, but with wisps escaping, framing her face, accenting her lighter blue eyes. Studying them, Wyatt hoped they worked things around to make themselves a family. Win and Molly needed one.

Win's arms came around Molly's neck from the side, so

her left arm crossed Molly's chest. Molly reached up and held on to that arm.

Then the crying started. Win only.

Molly wasn't much of a crier, but Win seemed to have a talent for it.

"I'm leaving now." Molly clutched Win's arm. Wyatt thought it looked like her hands were acting the exact opposite of her words. She was leaving, but she really didn't want to.

"I swear to you, Molly"—Kevin, sitting directly across the dinner table from her, jabbed a finger right toward her nose—"I will follow you over there and ruin it."

Win hung on, sniffling.

Molly patted Win's forearm. "Let go, Win. I won't be harmed because—"

"Because I'm going with her." Wyatt had been thinking about it, even talked about it, but until this moment, he hadn't realized his mind was made up.

"What?" Win raised her head and drew a sleeve across her eyes. "That makes no sense. Pa won't believe you would move over there with Molly."

"Your pa lost almost all his hands. His foreman put out the word for more help, but I don't think he's found it. Leastways I'm sure he's still shorthanded. I'll go over and sign on. I plan to tell him I'm fed up with life here." Wyatt loved the RHR, and no one with a functioning brain would believe otherwise. Lucky enough for him that Hawkins didn't seem to use what few brains he had . . . except to harm women.

His jaw tightened. "I'll tell your pa I plan to strike out farther west in the spring, but I don't want to cross the mountains in the winter. I'll say I'm mad as blue blazes about the new broth-ers as good as stealing my land, and I won't spend another hour under the same roof."

"We didn't steal your land though," Kevin said. "We need to . . . to . . . ." He snapped his fingers and pointed at Rachel. "We need to hire one of you Pinkertons! See if you can find the exact date of Falcon's ma's death. If Pa was still married to her when he married Wyatt's ma, the marriage isn't legal and neither is the will."

"We haven't told anyone that yet," Wyatt said. "We settled it amongst ourselves, but the will needs to be struck down legally. I haven't spoken to Carl Preston since you got here, and we probably oughta get his lawyerin' involved. I figured Pa's will being illegal made Ma's legal, and we're just going back to splitting things in half." He stalked out of the room and could be heard thundering up the stairs.

Kevin scowled at Rachel. "This is your fault. You came in here and stirred up trouble for my wife, making her relive an ugly worry she's wanted to escape from. And now you're putting my sister in danger while you hide here in the house."

Molly rose from the table and began clearing breakfast dishes. She'd waited until morning, until right before she left, to announce her plan, in order to lessen the wear on her ears. She knew Kevin wouldn't like it.

"You won't change my mind, Kevin. And you can't ruin it. Come over and make your accusations to Win's pa, and I'll just act like you're lying to keep me from working."

"He'll know we've got suspicions."

"Then I'll be in even more danger. Thanks to you." She made short work of cleaning up the kitchen. Win fell in and helped her. It was a good reminder that all this was going to fall on Win from now on.

"You two move into the house." Wyatt came downstairs with a satchel and bedroll. Then he said grimly, "Maybe we'll be back in a couple of hours. Maybe Hawkins won't hire neither of us. But if anyone talks of it, remember we've had a bad falling out. And ride over to see Cheyenne and Falcon and tell them, so they don't trip up. Tell Cheyenne she's in charge of this place. They'd probably best come back here while I'm gone. I'll tell Rubin I'm leaving. I trust him enough to be at least mostly honest. He'd never believe I'd abandoned the ranch."

Molly went for her things, came back, pulled on her coat, then hugged Kevin goodbye.

Whispering, just for his ears, she said, "You know why I have to do this." She pulled back, meeting his gaze, her heart almost trembling with memories and pain and shame.

He knew how she felt. It was the one great secret they shared, although Kevin had told Win—at least he'd told her all he knew—but it had never gone further.

Molly followed Wyatt out into the early morning of a chilly October day. The wind was mild. The sun was out. Snow had fallen again in the night but not heavily. It danced along the ground, as if the day were joyful.

Molly couldn't say she felt the same.

Wyatt spoke quietly with Rubin. Molly followed him to the barn, and they saddled two horses. Then he and Molly were on the trail.

"I've never applied for a job before," Wyatt said as they rode in the cold.

"He'd be a fool not to hire you, even if he thinks it's strange. It sounds like you're a better cowpoke than anyone he has."

"Do you remember everything Hobart told you?"

"I think you'd better call her Mrs. Hobart, should her name ever come up in front of Hawkins. You'd do well not to sound like you know her enough to be casual."

Molly thought about another way into her soon-to-be new employer's business. "Has Hawkins found someone to take over all the bookwork Ralston did?"

"Not that I know of." Wyatt glanced at her as they galloped along the rocky trail, heading southwest. Hills came up beside them. They rode through a herd of magnificent, shining black cattle. "Do you think he'd let you do his bookkeeping for him?"

"Why not? It sounds like he's a lazy man. I know my arithmetic from teaching school. If I work it right, he'll think he's asking me for help when really he's letting me get a close look at his finances."

"Ralston died without telling much. There's a good chance he was stealing Hawkins's money besides his cattle."

"Has anyone searched the cabin he took Amelia to?"

"Ralston wouldn't have left anything behind. They were clearing out."

Nodding, Molly considered it. "You're right he wouldn't have left any money, but did they search carefully? He might've left some information about what he was up to. And maybe you can search his cabin while I work inside. I might be able to find where he paid himself a special salary. If I get a chance, I'll try to find out how much money

106

Hawkins has. He's been spending his dead wife's money for years."

"His ranch runs, but it's no great success. And with all the hired help, that has to cut into his profits."

"I don't see how finding out about his finances leads me to proving him a murderer, but it will be interesting." Molly felt a cold chill of anger at Hawkins. A deep desire to avenge the deaths of women who'd been harmed by him. A deep desire to turn over every slimy rock that came near Oliver Hawkins and see what kind of worm crawled out.

They fell silent as they rode toward the Hawkins Ranch. Molly, lost in thought, planning what she'd say to get the job. Wyatt might be doing the same thing.

"Molly, about kissing you—"

"There'll be no more of that, Wyatt." Her hands tightened on the reins so suddenly her horse slowed and tossed its head.

Wyatt reached out quick as a rattler and grabbed the reins. He slowed the horse and gave Molly a few seconds to get ahold of herself.

Molly's chin came up, but she didn't look at Wyatt. Instead, she stared straight ahead. "It was a mistake. I have no plans to marry. Because of that, I shouldn't behave as if I have an interest in a man. It's unfair of me. Sinful even."

"A kiss isn't sinful, not when it ends so soon."

Molly remembered the kiss, and it had gone on far too long. "It's sinful if I have no proper intentions toward you. You started that kiss, Wyatt, but I should've called a halt to it immediately. It won't happen again."

"I'm not so sure."

Molly didn't respond to that.

"I remember waking up with you in my arms, Molly. I think about it. Often. I'm not likely to forget how nice it felt to hold you close."

He looked at her, heat in his eyes. Molly only knew he looked because she looked at him. And she couldn't look away. It was long minutes before Wyatt released her reins, and they rode on.

The trail curved around a steep bluff, and the ranch lay before them. Molly saw the house and gasped. "Who built that?"

Wyatt turned to look, then shook his head. "Like everything else, Hawkins hired someone to do the work. And remember, this was nearly twenty years ago. There was no train. There was no sawmill, so no boards. He had the wood shipped in from a lumber mill somewhere. He hired men out of Omaha to travel with the fancy work, the doorknobs, and glass. There are marble fireplaces inside, all sorts of outrageous flounces. When you see it, you'll wonder if Hawkins is a fool or a madman."

"He could be both. If he's killed women, then he's a monster on top of it."

"Be careful in there, Molly. You packed a gun, didn't you?"

"And a knife."

"I'm just a shout or a shot away."

And then they rode into the ranch yard, and there was no more time to talk.

~

"No one's gonna believe Wyatt rode off, mad at everyone, and took a job being a cowpoke at another ranch." Cheyenne dragged her gloves off her hands and slapped her leg with them. She glared at Kevin, wondering who came up with this stupid plan.

Kevin had ridden to the cabin Cheyenne and Falcon had moved to. They had come outside, hearing a rider approach. Then Kevin had told her of Wyatt and Molly. "It's too late to stop him. Wyatt is gone. He's hoping Hawkins is too badly in need of help to ask many questions. And he says you oughta come on home until he gets back. You're who should be running the ranch. I sure enough can't do it."

Win sat on her horse beside Kevin. Cheyenne was struck by the way these two were always together. Of course, she was most always with Falcon, too. But that was different.

She turned to look at Falcon. "We've got the cabin ready to be lived in. I like it here."

He smiled that rugged smile. His hazel eyes sparked humor and more. "Let's go keep your brother's ranch running until he comes home, then we'll get back over here. I like it here, too." Falcon turned to face Kevin. "And Hobart is staying at the house now?"

"Yep. And Win and I were told to move into the big house, but if you're coming back, we'll stay where we are." He turned to his wife and smiled.

She smiled back. "We've gotten settled in there."

Cheyenne was bothered by that private smile. Win and Kevin had gotten the better of the deal, having the ramrod's house to themselves.

It didn't matter if it bothered her or not. She had no choice but to go back. Someone had to run the ranch.

"While we're there"—Cheyenne slapped her gloves into

the palm of her hand—"we can talk to Hobart about what's involved in hiring a Pinkerton to find out the details about your ma's date of death. Or how she thinks we need to proceed. We don't dare talk to anyone local, not while Wyatt and Molly are at Hawkins's place. He might get wind of it and be suspicious of Wyatt's reasons for leaving." She frowned. "I'm sorry I act like I'm overly interested in the date. Losing your ma had to be a terrible thing. I was an adult when my ma died, and it was so sad, so shocking."

Falcon shrugged. "Maybe Hobart could slip out in the night like she slipped in. Ride off a piece, to Casper or farther if we think that's needed, and send a letter or a wire from there to get things started."

"We'll pack up and come along in a bit." Cheyenne half turned, watching Kevin and Win, waiting.

"We'll ride back with you," Kevin said. "We can help if you've got supplies to bring along."

"Nope, not necessary. You go on." Cheyenne decided Kevin was hopeless, so she looked at Win, wondering if her friend could possibly figure out that Cheyenne wanted another hour in her own home. Another chance to be alone with her husband before they gave up their privacy for a while.

Win blushed faintly. "We'll see you at the ranch."

"No, I don't mind waiting," Kevin-the-clueless said.

Falcon rolled his eyes.

"Kevin," Win said sharply, drawing his attention.

"What?"

"Let's go." She turned her horse and rode off. As she'd obviously expected, Kevin came along, never willing to be separated from her.

Falcon laughed softly, probably afraid Kevin would come back and ask what was so funny.

He took her hand and dragged her toward the cabin. "We don't have a single thing that needs to be packed. We even left clothes back at the RHR."

"Just come along quietly, and nobody gets hurt."

He laughed and moved faster toward the house.

THIRTEEN

awkins needed help badly. Wyatt saw that immediately when he led his horse into the barn.

Two men leaned against hay bales. Drinking coffee. While horses stood in dirty straw and cows outside mooed as if hoping for food.

Wyatt couldn't find a clean stall in the whole, huge barn. And the wood was weathered. It looked like, even before so many of his men had been taken away, no one had bothered maintaining it.

"Who's the foreman?"

"There ain't one." The man closest, chewing on a piece of straw, didn't straighten away from where he slouched. Didn't introduce himself. He sure enough didn't have the grace to apologize for the state of things in the barn. "Zeke Bell ran the place until two weeks ago. He stuck it out after all the hands were dragged off. But when Hawkins couldn't find more men and wouldn't come out and work, Zeke got fed up and asked for his time."

112

"And why did you stay?"

One of the loafers shrugged a shoulder. "I don't care if the place runs or not. The boss stays to the house. No one gives me orders. Might as well stay around. Ain't nothing hard about it."

If Wyatt was in charge, the hardest thing might be his fist in this cocky layabout's face. "Are there other men around?"

"A few. Five men besides us, all of 'em riding out to check the herd. But they're grumbling."

Wyatt thought grumbling beat leaning and decided he was going to aim for the foreman job. His first act would be to get these two to clean out this barn, and if they didn't work fast, they'd be heading down the trail.

Wyatt knew Molly was waiting for him near the back door of the house, so they could go in together. He stepped back out into the ranch yard. The pine and snow were the scent of winter to Wyatt. He wanted to be home at the RHR with its massive fireplace. He wanted the winter days, when the cattle were on good grass, and the branding, roundup, and cattle drive were all done.

Instead, he was about to try to talk his way into a job for a possible murderer. Wyatt had probably done more half-witted things, but he couldn't remember when.

~

"You're hired! Both of you!"

Wyatt expected the man to jump up and down clapping.

Hawkins tore his eyes away from Molly to glance at Wyatt. "It'd be great if you'd take the foreman job, Wyatt."

Then he looked back at Molly. "I've had the word out in

town for more men and a few have come in. But no one's applied for the housekeeping job."

Though he didn't say a word wrong, Wyatt didn't like the way Hawkins's eyes lingered on Molly. The idiot seemed more interested in the house than the ranch. And why not? He never spent time working his own land, his own cattle. He probably didn't even know how to judge how things were going.

But the house, well, clearly the man could see dust and feel it when he struggled to get his own meals. The kitchen was filthy, dirty plates and burned-up pans everywhere. Half-eaten meals. Hawkins could clearly see his need for a house-keeper. He might've seen his need for better cowpunchers if he'd ever looked outside.

"I appreciate it, Oliver." Wyatt stuck out his hand, and Oliver Hawkins looked back at Wyatt as if he'd forgotten Wyatt was there.

He narrowed his eyes and said, "I like those working for me to call me Mr. Hawkins."

Wyatt only hesitated a moment. Now wasn't the time to kick up a fuss. But by golly that time would come.

"I'll remember that, Mr. Hawkins."

Hawkins shook Wyatt's hand briefly as if he were grant-ing the help a favor. Yes, sirree, that time would come soon.

When Wyatt had come in asking for work, lacing in his complaints about his family, Hawkins appeared not to have one speck of trouble believing that. He accepted Wyatt's story of being furious about his own ranch being taken over by greedy relatives almost like a man who had that story in his own life.

Of course, that could just be Wyatt being suspicious.

Hawkins was a loud, braying fool. He was always well dressed with neatly clipped brown hair and blue eyes that matched Win's. He leaned toward boasting but usually with a big smile on his face. He had a fair amount of shallow charm that wore out fast. A man very much like Clovis Hunt. Wyatt had never been able to abide Hawkins, and though it'd made him sad because it was his own father, he'd learned early not to trust or abide Clovis.

"I'm going to get to work."

"Excellent. You know which is the foreman's house, don't you?"

"Yes, but would you mind if I take Ralston's house? It's closer to work." Just barely, but Wyatt tossed that out as an excuse. Truth was, he wanted to search Ralston's house, and he wanted to be as close to the big house as possible, to listen for cries for help or gunshots.

"Whichever one you want, it makes no difference to me." Hawkins had turned away from Wyatt and was walking toward Molly, smiling.

Wyatt walked toward the back door to the sound of Hawkins saying, "Let me show you to your room, then give you a tour of the house."

Wyatt and Molly had worked out a way to communicate using a lantern at each of their windows. But that only worked at night.

It took every drop of his self-control to go on outside and leave Molly alone with a man they suspected of murder.

FOURTEEN

Molly set a lamp in the window of her bedroom. She was on the side of the house near the barn, and near where Wyatt would sleep. Win had suggested that. She'd known every bit of the house.

The housekeeper's quarters were two nice-sized rooms. After a week of working for Mr. Hawkins—she'd been just as sternly instructed to call him that as Wyatt had—she'd learned her way around.

He'd ridden out twice: once to town because he carried home a few supplies, and once he said he just liked to ride. He didn't say where, and she didn't ask.

When he was gone, she had the run of the house, and she'd found the safe behind a picture in his office but couldn't find one in his bedroom. There was an entire third floor in the house, and Mr. Hawkins had told her to leave it be. Just as Rachel had said, Molly was so relieved not to have to tackle another full floor of cleaning that she'd just gratefully acquiesced, but if she couldn't find that safe in his room soon, she would have to expand her search to that floor. She was dreading it. She'd heard strange rustling noises from the third floor. She wondered about rats or squirrels being in there, but in truth, it gave the house a haunted feeling.

Despite practicing on Wyatt's safe at the RHR, she couldn't get Mr. Hawkins's office safe open. Last night she'd signaled for help. Wyatt had come to her window, and they'd planned. Tonight, he was coming in to help her.

A lantern light shone back at her, then blinked out, Wyatt's signal that he was coming.

Molly doused her lantern, nervous to let him help with the search. It was worrisome to think of Mr. Hawkins catching her wandering at night, but she'd never be able to explain letting Wyatt in.

And besides that worry, when she'd crept around the house at night, she'd worn her nightgown. In the event that Mr. Hawkins came down and found her, it would be easier to use the excuse of a sleepless night. Tonight, she did the same, but it felt so wrong to greet Wyatt in her nightgown that she wore her dress beneath it and a robe over it. Since the dress barely fit beneath the nightgown, she felt as puffed up as a stuffed turkey.

Wyatt tapped on the glass. Her heart pounding, listening for any sign Mr. Hawkins was awake, she slid open her window and let Wyatt in.

He clambered in, and she shut the window to keep out the cold night air. He took two steps, and his heavy boots creaked loudly on the floor. He froze.

"Take them off and leave them in here," she whispered.

Nodding, he pulled them off and set them under the window.

They slipped out of the room, through the kitchen, down the hall, and into the office.

It stood empty. The fireplace cold, not a spark of light anywhere.

Molly moved carefully around the furniture in the room and closed the heavy drapes, then lit her lantern.

Without speaking, she pushed the painting aside. It swung easily, and she held it there to reveal the safe. The painting was large, a landscape signed by someone named Thomas Moran. Mr. Hawkins had told Molly how valuable the painting was, how important the artist was, he went on and on. But as he did that about near everything, she assumed he was boasting. It was a beautiful picture, but for heaven's sake, no picture could cost that much.

Wyatt had a slip of paper in his hand. The safe combinations Hobart had given them.

Working silently, he turned the dial this way and that, then he reached for a handle and twisted. Something clunked, and the safe began to open.

A board creaked overhead. They both froze.

"Douse the lantern," Wyatt whispered.

Boards creaked again. It might have been the sound of a foot on one of the stair treads.

Wyatt swung the door shut, spinning the dial he'd used to open it, and slid the picture back into place before grabbing her hand and rushing for the study door. "We have to get you back to your room in case he checks on you for some reason."

Molly hurried along on Wyatt's heels. She breathed a prayer of relief that Wyatt had shed his boots. They'd've never been able to move silently and quickly if he had them on. They reached her room as the footsteps on the stairs became steadier. Mr. Hawkins made no attempt to be quiet, and why would he? He wasn't sneaking around anywhere.

"Get in bed."

Wyatt rushed for the window.

"No, he'll notice the cold even if you get out and get it shut."

Wyatt's face was visible in the moonlight, and he took a frantic look at the door.

She took off her robe as the footsteps came steadily for her room, leapt into bed, dragged the blankets over her, and rested her head on the pillow. "Take your boots and hide."

Wyatt grabbed them and dove around her bed. She heard a solid thud, not unlike someone hitting their head on the underside of a bed.

A firm knock sounded at her door, and Wyatt quit moving. Near as she could tell, he quit breathing.

She saw lantern light beneath her door.

The knock sounded again. "Molly, I'm sorry to wake you."

But for all he said he was sorry, he'd sure enough done it. Had he heard her moving around? What could he possibly want?

"I'm afraid I'm having a bit of trouble sleeping."

He snored like a bull. He'd been fully asleep. And why did he think sharing his sleeplessness with her was a good idea?

"I'm coming." She donned the robe again, still over her nightgown-covered dress. She tied the belt in a firm knot and hurried to the door to swing it open just a couple of inches.

"A sleepless night can be upsetting." She didn't know quite

119

what else to say. Was that why he'd shared this news with her? He didn't want to be upset alone?

"I have a tea that helps me sleep. The chamomile in the white tin canister. Brew me a cup, and bring it to my room." He said neither please nor thank you, and he didn't apologize again. Instead, he turned and headed straight back upstairs.

She frowned as he headed away, taking the light with him. She was supposed to brew tea for him? As if he were incapable of that? And bring it to his room?

Molly thought of what Rachel had told her to expect.

"He'll ask you to do things he could so obviously do for himself that it's strange he doesn't. Things like asking you to pour his coffee when the coffeepot is sitting right in front of him. And he'll expect you to do it quickly. He comments on it if you're not grateful and demure. Mostly, he wants you to do as you're told, and if you don't, he expresses displeasure, first mildly, then with increasing severity. He is frightening."

"You're not going up there." Wyatt had somehow gotten up and come to her side. He spoke in a whisper, but that didn't disguise his anger. "You're not going into his room in the middle of the night in your nightclothes."

"No, I am most certainly not." She considered what it might mean to defy Mr. Hawkins. "I'll take it and set it on the table that's just outside his door. I'll knock, tell him it's out there, and leave."

She said it all, outraged at Hawkins's nerve, as she stood there beside Wyatt in her nightclothes in her bedroom.

"You go on. I'll tell you what—"

"I'm not leaving until you're safely back here. And while you brew tea, I'm going to go back and search that safe."

He slipped past her and was gone. She couldn't exactly yell after him.

~

"Molly, I asked you to bring the tea to my room last night." Mr. Hawkins had a chiding way about him.

Shallow charm and the chiding always sounded like he was so sad, so disappointed.

"He wants you to do as you're told, and if you don't, he expresses displeasure, first mildly . . ."

"As I did, Mr. Hawkins." Molly had gone up, set the tray on the table, knocked, and left.

"But you left it outside my room. I find it helps my sleep much more if I'm settled in bed, and the tea is poured and handed to me. I expect my housekeeper to provide such a small service for me."

"Mr. Hawkins, I was glad to make the tea, but it would be the height of impropriety for me to enter your room at night." Molly did her best to sound like a scandalized maiden lady, when she wanted to whack him over the head with the teapot. "If going into your room while it is occupied by you is a requirement of this job, then I will have to leave your employ immediately."

He was eating a cinnamon roll she'd just pulled hot out of the oven. And she'd hit him with her special custard with the crispy caramel topping last night. She had cherry cobbler baking for the noon meal, and the smell filled the kitchen, along with the yeasty, cinnamon scent of his roll.

He might start looking for a new housekeeper, because she was quite sure his intentions weren't honorable, and if she had no interest in him, then he needed a housekeeper who was, but he'd never fire her until her replacement was at hand.

Molly might be here to investigate, but the house was a shambles, just as Wyatt said the ranch was. She'd been working hard to clean it, all the while wondering why. To pass the time and because she had a longing for order. That was the best she could figure. Wyatt said it offended him to see such a poorly run ranch, and the animals were being neglected, which he couldn't abide, so he was trying to run it right, but he, too, wasn't sure why he cared—beyond the livestock. They'd be gone as soon as they got into Hawkins's second safe.

The first safe had held nothing much of interest, except stacks of account books. Wyatt had taken them to her room and gone over them for most of the night. He started with the most recent ones before it occurred to him that information about how Hawkins got the money from Win's mother and how he spent it would be near the beginning.

Molly saw days, even weeks, of work to go through them all.

Wyatt said Hawkins had started with a fortune, but after twenty years of spending it down hard with a loss each year, the large balances in the accounts were dwindling.

It also looked as if Ralston had stolen a nice chunk of money, but Wyatt hadn't gotten to the bottom of all that yet. With serious misgivings, he ended up putting the account ledgers back in the safe, afraid their absence might be noticed. He wanted to come back tonight, but Molly insisted he needed a night's sleep between his investigative forays.

As these thoughts raced through her mind, she saw the way Hawkins looked. His gaze troubled and frustrated.

And beneath that, he was calculating. He didn't like the line she'd drawn, and now he had to decide whether to fire her on the spot or find a new way to get what he wanted.

She hoped he at least gave her time to find and break into his second safe.

Molly had searched his bedroom when she'd gone in daily to make the bed and sweep, dust, whatever was required. She'd looked behind all the pictures and in the closet. She thought the only place it could be was the floor. But she'd started her search with the floor, and there was nothing. Rachel had believed strongly, based on the type of safe he purchased and the blueprints she'd studied of the house, that there was a safe concealed somewhere, and she'd said the floor was a strong possibility, so Molly had to look again. And she was wary of staying in there for too long. Mr. Hawkins was almost always just downstairs, and he'd notice if she lingered. And he'd absolutely notice if she went to the third floor—if she could get into it. For a time-consuming, detailed search she had to wait until he went away.

All of the searching was overwhelming. She hoped Hawkins didn't take her demand to fire her or behave to heart. She needed more time in this house.

Hawkins scowled, then relaxed his expression, back to the charm. It was so easy after a week in his presence to see how false that oily charm was. She shuddered to think of the man being married to Win's poor mother.

He eased back in his chair. She could see he wasn't going to push this now. Not because he knew he was behaving badly, but because of his belief in his own powers of persuasion.

She could also really see him as a man who might have killed someone. Someone who frustrated him, who didn't give in. Or maybe that wasn't even right. Maybe he killed women whether they frustrated him or not.

Maybe he just killed women he had access to.

Molly thought of her father. She knew firsthand that men existed who hurt women, and no one much interfered. At first, she wasn't sure that was Hawkins, who had seemed lazy more than evil. Now she could see a man who would strike out if he was challenged by someone who was inferior to him. And in his twisted mind, that would be every woman. But she'd joined this fight, and she would stop him from ever hurting anyone again.

~

"Kevin, I want to ride over and visit my father."

Kevin, lying beside her in bed, sat up so suddenly her head dropped off his shoulder. "But why? You've never wanted to go see him before. You even hoped he'd heard about our wedding through gossip so we wouldn't have to stop by and see him."

She tugged on his arm, and he came back down beside her. He loved this woman. Loved her beyond reason. Cherished every moment she was in his arms. But right now, he wanted to knock on her head to see if anyone was home.

"Remember we talked one night at the table, all of us, about honoring our parents?"

"Yes, one of the commandments. 'Honor thy father and

mother; which is the first commandment with a promise. That it may be well with thee, and thou mayest live long on the earth.' We talked about having some mighty poor parents to choose from, and how do you honor someone who's lived a long life of cheating and being the worst kind of thief?"

Win moved to rest her head on his shoulder again. She slept close to him every night, and he reveled in it. She filled a lonely place in his heart that he hadn't even known was there. And when he'd told her that, she'd glowed and told him she felt just the same.

No longer alone.

"I've been thinking about that." She settled into his arms. "About how to honor my wretched father. Even if he doesn't turn out to be a murderer, he was never kind. Never wanted me around. He was eager to send me off to live with Cheyenne's family. All while he'd speak ill of them because he didn't consider Cheyenne and her ma to be ladylike. They were working hard outside while Pa sat inside, living off my mother's wealth. So how do I honor a man who never cared about me? Never gave me any time or love or kindness. Was never in any real way a father to me."

"And have you figured it out? Because I'd like to hear it if you have. I can't quite believe it's right to honor a man such as Clovis Hunt."

"Your pa is dead. I think that puts him beyond anything you can do." Win sat up, and Kevin saw her clearly in the moonlight that came through the window. It bathed her in blue, her hair like midnight, her skin mysterious and cool. "But my pa is right here, nearby. All I can think of to honor him is . . . is . . ." Shaking her head, she went on, "It's not enough, maybe it's not even right, but I think I honor him by not being like him. By praying for him. By talking to him if he gives me a chance."

"You'd have to be careful not to warn him or make him suspicious of Molly."

Nodding, Win lay down again. "I can't have a really frank talk with him about how he's hurt me, not now. But I can pray for him. I can be courteous and go see him. And when this is over, assuming he's locked up tight somewhere, I can . . . can treat him like Jesus treated those in prison, those who were lame or sick or hungry. I can confront him with the truth and give him a chance to be honest with me."

"Where's there a prison around here? It might be hard to go visit."

"I can write him letters." She reached over and patted Kevin on the arm. "But before we lock him up, I can begin honoring him as I see fit. And to do that, I have to go see him. You'll get to see Molly, maybe even pull her aside and speak to her, nothing would be more natural than a brother wanting to visit his sister, and it would make sense you'd step away just a bit from Pa to have a quiet talk with her."

"That won't work because I'd never leave you alone with him."

That got Win's attention. "You really think I'm in danger from my own father?"

Kevin hesitated before he said, "I think, that is, I'm *afraid* that, yes, maybe you really are in danger."

"Well, maybe you can step out of the room with me and Pa but not go far."

"Maybe." He pulled her close to sleep, glad he had someone so perfect in his arms.

~

Wyatt dug a pitchfork into a pile of old straw and heaved it into a wheelbarrow to carry outside. He had the stalls all cleaned, and he'd gotten the seven men who worked there to get busy. They were lazy but not so much they wanted to head down the road. He thought he might be able to turn them into real cowhands given time.

The barn was almost cleaned out. The horses and cattle were now being cared for. A chicken coop had eggs being gathered regularly. The place was shaping up. And it burned bad to be clearing things up so well for that lazy half-wit Hawkins.

But he did it. Part of it was simple honesty: he was earning good wages, he'd give an honest day's work. Part of it was caring for the animals. Wyatt couldn't abide seeing an animal in pain or hungry and ailing if it was within his power to help it.

And mostly he did it thinking of Win. This would be hers someday. And seeing as how Wyatt intended to see Hawkins hanged, that day was coming soon.

He was getting the place in shape for a new owner. His friend Win and her husband, Kevin, who still hadn't found a place to live or built a cabin. And that was not their fault. They kept being needed at the RHR.

With Clovis's wedding to Wyatt's ma now strongly suspected by the family to be bigamous, Kevin had no ownership of the RHR. Of course, to break the will, they had to prove the wedding was a sham, and they'd been mighty busy rounding up outlaws and investigating crimes.

Kevin hadn't asked for much. A hundred acres that'd grow a crop. On the RHR, a forty-thousand-acre ranch, they oughta be able to do that. Kevin even said he'd pay rent or buy the place over time. He made it clear staying in the ramrod's house felt like charity. But now that Win was back running the household, and Kevin was being called on to do what could be done to fill in for Wyatt around the ranch, he was more than earning his keep.

Wyatt felt a pang of worry over the RHR. He hoped Cheyenne had moved home. They always worked with a skeleton crew over the winter. So the hands that didn't wander off were hard-pressed to get things done. Cheyenne could handle things. And maybe she'd encourage Falcon to find some cowboy skills. Rubin had trained Andy, and he had several cowpokes to help him. But Kevin was a raw beginner. Jesse, one of the newer hands, had seemed eager to work with Kevin. Wyatt sure hoped someone could teach Kevin to like ranching because he was probably going to be stuck doing it the rest of his life.

It made Wyatt grind his teeth in frustration to wonder how things were going at the RHR. He hadn't heard a word from anyone at home since he'd come over here.

With satisfaction, Wyatt plunged his pitchfork back into the straw, enjoying the crunch of digging out the old to make way for the new. No reason *this* couldn't be Kevin's land. Wyatt intended to see Kevin and Win settled in here.

He worked out the day, keeping at it long after the rest of the hands turned in. He ate with them in the bunkhouse, returned to his work, then finally went to his cabin for the night and waited for the lights to go out in the big house.

~

"We have to wait until Molly and Wyatt get back." Rachel was adamant.

And yes, Cheyenne had gotten to calling her Rachel. Truth was, Cheyenne liked the woman. Rachel was ruthless. She wanted to crush an evil man beneath her bootheels. She wanted to earn a living.

Cheyenne could not find anything in that to object to.

"It'll take a day. That's all," Cheyenne insisted. "You can ride out after dark. You can't send the telegram from Bear Claw Pass nor Casper. Too many people know what's gone on around here. The will, the rustling, the name of my ranch, and they may remember your involvement in all of it, Rachel. Word could get out. It could reach Hawkins, and that would put Molly and Wyatt in danger. You'll have to use White Rock Station, that's the next place east that you can send a telegram. You can reach it by riding overnight. If you send the wire in the morning, include a notice to expect a letter explaining everything in detail. Mail travels fast now, so it should reach your agency in a matter of days. The wire will give them enough information to be ready to move when details arrive. Your agent can get ready to travel, unless they have agents in Tennessee—"

Rachel shook her head. "I've never heard we had agents that far south, but I'm not sure. There may be other private investigating agencies we can work with. But even if no agents are there, they will have some closer to Tennessee than Chicago."

With a nod of satisfaction, Cheyenne said, "Good. An agent will have time to pack and prepare to travel as soon as the letter arrives."

"If Wyatt comes running on that day, saying they have what they need to arrest Hawkins, and I'm not here—"

"This can wait, Cheyenne." Kevin would not cooperate. "There's no rush to settle the estate."

"There'd be no rush to set the investigation in motion before winter crashes down, if I could just go to Bear Claw Pass," Rachel said. "But until we have evidence to take to the sheriff about Clovis, I don't dare trust the telegraph operator not to talk. And in Casper, with Randall Kingston, that lawyer Clovis hired to make sure his will was airtight, living there, I don't trust him not to hear about it. Any news about the RHR would draw his interest. Word could get back to Hawkins."

Cheyenne couldn't believe she'd considered marrying that man. She felt embarrassment creeping every time the memory swept over her. She was fairly dark skinned, so she hoped a blush didn't show. But she was tired of the back of her neck getting hot.

"So we'll do it in the spring." Kevin acted like it was all settled.

Rachel shook her head. "By spring we'll have let almost a year go by. Especially when you add the time it might take to run our investigation. When these legal matters have dragged on that long, a judge might consider them settled and not overrule it. Possession is nine-tenths of the law, and the ownership will have stood for a decent amount of time. I don't think we should let this go on that long. Falcon, do you think we can track down the date of your mother's death?"

He nodded. "The circuit rider wrote down things like births and deaths. He'd have the exact dates, in the church in Chickahoochi Cove. And I know the parson came out. It's hard to say how he'd heard about Ma passin', but word seemed to spread up and down the holler like it was carried on the wind. He didn't make it for the buryin', but he came along soon after and prayed over Ma's grave and talked to me about coming out with him. He offered to let me live with him."

"And you didn't go?" Cheyenne asked. "You were so young, and you chose to live alone?"

Falcon shrugged. "The parson was a fine man, but he was married and had six kids, in a one-bedroom cabin not much bigger'n mine. I should've probably offered to take some of his young'uns in with me. He sure enough didn't need another."

Cheyenne patted him on the shoulder but didn't comment.

"I probably knew enough to say, 'Ma died last week,' or, 'Ma's been gone three days.' Something that'd give him a decent guess at the date. He'd've written it down. Send someone to Chickahoochi Cove to look at the church papers."

"I'll ride out tonight." Rachel stood from the table. "I'll gather a few things to take. Are you sure the town on past Casper is far enough?"

"It's White Rock Station. It's off the train route, but it has a telegraph office," Cheyenne said.

"Cheyenne and I will ride along," Falcon added.

Kevin and Win didn't argue. No one liked it, but Rachel was determined and had said so loud and clear. She'd planned to go alone.

"The whole idea is for no one to notice anything going on. No one even knows I'm here, so they won't miss me. No one knows me in any town around here, so no reason my wire will draw attention. If I'm with a group, it changes everything."

"You can't ride in the night alone. It ain't safe," Falcon said.

"I rode out here alone."

Narrowing his eyes, Falcon said, "That don't mean you should've."

"Rachel, I agree with Falcon," Cheyenne said. "And not because I doubt you're tough, but we really need you to make it, and we need you to get back here. When Wyatt gets evidence against Hawkins, unless he just shoots him or drags him to the sheriff, we need someone who knows the details of your investigation and how you've tied him to the deaths of three women. We can explain it, but Sheriff Corly isn't likely to take our secondhand account of things. We need you here."

"Didn't you take off alone in the wilderness a few weeks ago?" Rachel arched a brow at Cheyenne. "And apparently Wyatt didn't think twice about it except regretting you were upset."

"That's different."

Shaking her head, Rachel said, "That's the same."

"Kevin, just tell Rubin I've gone back to my cabin with Falcon." Cheyenne looked at Rachel. "But I can't be gone one minute more than necessary. We'll ride out as soon as the ranch settles for the night."

"You'll reach White Rock by morning," Win said. "Then

send the wire and turn around and ride back. It'll be after dark by the time you get home. One day. Rachel shouldn't be gone a minute longer than necessary, either. And if you've got a letter to write, you'd better write it now."

~

The man listened at the window, noting every detail. Then he slipped away and got a message sent as he'd been instructed.

They thought their trip would be made in secret. They thought that stranger hiding in their house was still a secret. But he knew everything, and so did the man who was paying him.

~

Finally, Molly set her lantern in the window, her signal for Wyatt to come, and he hurried across the shadows on the snow-covered yard and climbed in through Molly's window.

After his first night examining the account books, and after the way Hawkins had tried to get Molly to come to his room, Wyatt came over every night as soon as the lights went out.

He wasn't leaving Molly alone in that house—it was hard enough in the daytime but impossible at night.

He couldn't search every night. It was too exhausting, considering the long, hard days he was working, trying to clean up the horrible mess around the ranch. But he came over and slept.

The ridiculous house was so large, he could've taken over the whole third floor, half the second, and the cellar if he'd wanted. Hawkins never went in most of the house. But Wyatt picked a place close to Molly. He'd picked a pantry near Molly's rooms, laid a pallet of blankets on the floor, and slept in there.

She greeted him at the window in her ridiculous robe-nightgown-dress getup. She looked to weigh about twenty pounds more than usual, and he wanted to tell her how cute she was, all properly bound into three layers of clothes.

He didn't because tonight she had news.

"I found a loose floorboard in Mr. Hawkins's bedroom when he went out riding today. I'm sure there's something strange about it, but I couldn't get it lifted out. I'm afraid to take time to work on opening it when he's here, even if he's in his study. He's so aware of where I am all the time, and he tends to come and ask me questions. I'm being extra careful not to be in his bedroom when he comes around."

Wyatt's jaw went tight to think of a fine woman like Molly having to put up with such unpleasant behavior. And *unpleasant* described it only if Hawkins wasn't something far worse than unpleasant.

Wyatt couldn't figure out a way to be in the house during the day. He had a few excuses lined up, things to talk to Hawkins about, but he needed to save them for when Molly needed time to get into the safe. But maybe . . . "The men say he rides out quite often."

"He's done it a few times since I've been here. Now that I've found the floorboard, I'm afraid we'll just have to wait until he goes out again."

Thankful their whispered conversation was covered by the distant sound of Hawkins's snoring, Wyatt said, "We'll be patient, then. I wasn't around when he saddled up and left, so I didn't know about it and didn't come in to help."

"You couldn't come in anyway, the men would talk."

"I don't care about gossip."

"You would if they told Mr. Hawkins."

"They have nothing to do with the man." Wyatt hesitated. "One of them saddled his horse today. So maybe you're right."

"At least now, if I'm right about that loose floorboard, the next chance I get, I should be able to open it. That's progress."

"Should we try and get him out of the house again soon? I could tell him I've got questions, or I want him to inspect something. I've been hunting around inside my head, thinking up questions I could ask. Now I'm afraid to even go and do normal cattle chores. I should've known he'd gone off."

"I think sooner is better," Molly said. "He's starting to scare me. I don't want to stay here any longer than I have to. Come to the house tomorrow and get him out of here. I may not get into the safe in one try, but having more time will help—even if it just helps me eliminate wrong ways to get that floorboard up."

"Can you handle the combination?"

"I've practiced, like you told me, on the safe in his office."

Wyatt thought of those account books they'd found in the office safe. He'd been going through them when he could stay awake, but tonight his head almost buzzed with fatigue.

"I've got it figured out now. I hope."

Nodding, Wyatt touched her shoulder. "If he ever lays a hand on you, I will protect you. Even if that means we *don't* prove he committed a crime, and we both get kicked out."

"Agreed. If for any reason he fires you, I'm going too. I won't stay here without you."

He hesitated. His hand tightened on her arm. He wanted to talk to her of the future. Talk to her about staying at the RHR as his wife. Kiss her again. Wake up with her again.

It was all so impossible when he was in her room in the night. He didn't dare begin anything until they could see each other in an open and honorable way. He'd be as guilty of mistreating a fine woman as Hawkins.

Well, maybe not that bad. At least his intentions were honorable and, he hoped, welcome.

So far, Wyatt had been able to keep his mouth shut and his hands away from her. But every night it was harder. Every day it worked on his mind as he cleaned the barns and herded cattle. Ordered the men around and put the ranch to rights.

He'd been up most of the night last night combing through account books. Tonight he had to sleep. As he went to the pantry, he listened to that layabout Hawkins snore, that man who preyed on women in his employ, and wondered if he'd even be able to sleep.

A possible murderer overhead.

A beautiful woman next door.

A few thousand underweight cattle who needed help to survive the winter.

Worry circled in his head, but he'd been up all last night and the night before. Worry chased him into sleep.

FIFTEEN

They rode hard all night.

The sun broke over the eastern sky, and Cheyenne, near to falling asleep on her horse, knew they'd make it.

They hadn't followed the main trail, which would have taken them to Casper.

Cheyenne wanted to stay well clear of it. Her riding into Casper wouldn't matter much, nor Falcon, that could all be explained somehow.

But Rachel was unknown, and people would wonder about her. They'd ask the telegraph operator, who would know too much and share it all.

There was still a good stretch to ride, but sunlight helped keep her head from nodding. Cheyenne was in the middle. Once she'd found the right trail, she'd let Falcon lead. Looking back, she smiled at Rachel. A hardy woman, who seemed tireless. Rachel smiled back, her blue eyes flashing in the rising sun.

Looking on past her, Cheyenne enjoyed the sight of her beloved mountains rising up in the distance. They were on a narrow path that wound around a steep, uphill grade. Trees rose up on the right side, a solid wall of rock on the left.

Cheyenne turned to face forward to see Falcon dive off his horse toward the wooded side. Cheyenne didn't even think. She just moved, taking her rifle with her. The gunfire split the air as she hit the ground rolling to a crouch.

Falcon was running for her. He saw her down and alive, then they both spun to warn Rachel, only to see her slam backward off her horse, who crow-hopped, spooked by the shot.

They reached her as she landed on her back in a puff of dust, a bright crimson star blooming on her chest.

Her horse startled the others, and they reared. Enough ahead that Cheyenne didn't have to dodge hooves.

One hard look at Rachel made her turn to Falcon. He saw the same thing she did. Rachel was hit dead center in the heart. No one survived a shot like this.

The rifle took up firing and rained bullets down as fast as someone could cock it and pull the trigger. A branch inches over Cheyenne's head was shredded by bullets.

"We're out of his sight down low." Falcon crouched and dragged Rachel around the curve of the trail. Farther out of range.

The shooting stopped. Falcon got all three of them up against the rock wall. He pressed his back to it, gun drawn. Cheyenne left him to guard and turned to Rachel. She was shocked to see Rachel open her eyes. Not dead yet, but she couldn't last long.

"T-take this." Rachel dragged a letter out of her coat pocket and shoved it into Cheyenne's hand, then a piece of paper. "Th-the code. Contact Pinkertons. D-don't put my name in the telegram. They'll know I'm dead or in terrible trouble. Someone will come."

Her eyes fell shut. Her grip on the letter and paper trembled, then her hand went slack, and she released both.

"She passed out." Cheyenne pulled back Rachel's thick coat, then opened the top buttons of Rachel's dark red shirtwaist. The bullet was high on her chest. Better than Cheyenne had feared. It had missed her heart, probably missed her lungs. Maybe it wasn't deep enough to sever her spine. Maybe Rachel had a chance. Taking frantic assessment of the bleeding wound, Cheyenne dragged her knife out of the sheath at her waist, cut a strip off Rachel's black riding skirt, and formed a large pad. She pressed it to the wound and felt the hard lump of the bullet. It wasn't in deep.

Looking away from the trail, Falcon's eyes flashed with fury. "I didn't see anyone until a rifle moved, aimed. They hit exactly who they wanted to hit. I think they'd've killed us, too, and not minded when they were firing after that first shot, but we weren't the targets. She was. Even knowing that, we don't dare round that corner. We have to go back."

With one jerking nod, Cheyenne said, "Bring me your knife. It's got a better edge on it. I can feel the bullet. I can almost judge the distance that dry-gulcher was from here because that sounded like a Henry rifle. I know its range, and this had to be near the end of it for the bullet not to have gone in farther."

Falcon whipped out his knife and extended it to Cheyenne.

She took it and probed the wound. And heard the sickening scrape of metal on metal. "It's barely beneath the skin.

Falcon, she may make it." Cheyenne was surprised by the sigh of relief. "Hold her still, in case she takes a notion to wake up while I'm doing my ham-handed doctoring."

They were both silent while Cheyenne gritted her teeth and dug the bullet out. Rachel groaned once and tried to roll away from the pain. Falcon held her in place.

The bullet came free, and the wound bled faster. Cheyenne pressed the pad of cloth hard against the entrance wound. While she worked, she glanced up at Falcon, who wasn't looking at her. Instead, he kept his eyes on the trail and the woods around them. On guard, as wary as a wild creature.

Quietly, using more torn cloth to tie the bandage on, Cheyenne said with grim certainty, "This has to be connected to Hawkins somehow, doesn't it? There's no other reason to want her dead."

"He didn't know she was here."

Cheyenne's eyes flickered up, then back to her doctoring. "Someone did. And someone knew we were heading for White Rock."

"They even knew we were taking a route to avoid Casper. And no one knew that."

"Unless someone listened while we planned it."

"Another traitor on the RHR?" Falcon came to crouch beside Rachel, regret shining in his eyes.

"But who?" Cheyenne gripped the letter in one gloved hand.

"I don't know." Falcon's jaw tightened. "But someone sure enough did. And Wyatt is over there."

"Wyatt?" Cheyenne, already so tense she nearly snapped, heard his tone, and it was worse. "What about him?"

"It strikes me that whoever did this managed it in the same way Wyatt was shot. Right down to him being with us."

"We figured one of the men who died when we went after Ralston and brought in his gang had done it."

Falcon glanced at the horses, which had trotted off but were now skittishly coming back. He looked at the trail they'd been heading down and now had to go back on.

Then he looked at Rachel Hobart. A tough woman who'd insisted she could ride to town in the dark alone, but nope. She needed the protection of a savvy Tennessee mountain man and feisty lady rancher. Rachel Hobart now lying unconscious and bleeding on the ground.

At last his eyes came to Cheyenne's. "I'd say we figured wrong. And I'd say now is our chance to find out who did this before he does it again. It's time to stop him once and for all."

"We're not going back?" Cheyenne could feel fire flashing in her dark eyes. As if the fire came from inside, burning right out of her core.

"Nope." Falcon turned to face the direction of the gunfire. "We're going forward."

"Good."

~

Mr. Hawkins—Molly was careful to always call him that, to his face, to Wyatt, even in her thoughts, in an effort to behave in a respectful way that wouldn't alert him to her suspicions or her contempt—dawdled at the kitchen table, drinking a third cup of coffee while she cleaned up after breakfast.

He liked to watch her. She had to force herself to keep working and not glance over her shoulder to try to catch him leering.

A hard knock sounded at the door as she dried the last pot.

Hiding a sigh of relief, she glanced at Mr. Hawkins. "Do you want me to get that?"

Without anyone getting the door, it swung open, and Wyatt walked in. She saw Mr. Hawkins scowl briefly before his wide smile appeared.

"Wyatt, nice to see you. Join me for coffee?"

"No, not now. Thank you, but I've got a few questions, and a report on the cattle. Can you come out to the barn?"

The scowl returned. "I'm sure however you want to do the work is fine. You're a skilled rancher, Wyatt. I won't meddle in your way of doing things."

Molly turned back to hang up the pans on hooks over the stove. Mainly so Mr. Hawkins wouldn't see her roll her eyes. Meddle? It was his ranch. He was *supposed* to meddle. And it wasn't meddling to run your own property.

"I can't make this decision without you, Oliver."

Mr. Hawkins narrowed his eyes as Molly turned back around.

"Please remember that I prefer to be called Mr. Hawkins by people who work for me."

"Yes, sir." Wyatt's jaw tensed.

And why? Wyatt's foreman called him Wyatt. Rubin Walsh came to the ranch house door often enough, and Molly had heard him call his boss by his first name. She'd never seen anyone give it a second thought.

Wyatt had been the owner of a ranch just as big as the

Hawkins spread and called him Oliver when he visited the RHR. Oliver liked to drop in for meals. He seemed to be eager to talk to Win, but Molly suspected he was mighty sick of his own cooking.

And Wyatt's family had found out cattle were being stolen from Hawkins and put a stop to it, ridding his ranch of traitorous cowboys. Insisting on being called Mr. Hawkins didn't smack of much gratitude.

Add to that, Wyatt had been shot helping Mr. Hawkins.

Clearly, none of that was as important as putting Wyatt on a lower rung than before. Mr. Hawkins felt the need to do that, and it told Molly a lot about the kind of man he was—none of it good. Molly's already low opinion of the man sank lower. She hadn't known it was possible.

With some grumbling, Mr. Hawkins stood and took his coffee cup to the sink, which brought him too close to Molly, deliberately she was sure, then he headed for the back door. There was a huge entry, and Mr. Hawkins slowly put his coat and boots on, almost as if to test Wyatt's patience.

Wyatt held the door to let Mr. Hawkins go out ahead of him. Wyatt looked over his shoulder at Molly and grinned like he was a kid getting away with a handful of candy. He was getting his surly boss out of the house. His hazel eyes flashed, and she remembered their kiss. She remembered waking up with his strong arms around her.

Then he was gone, but the memories stayed with her.

Molly waited for a few seconds, watching them head for the barn, to make sure Mr. Hawkins didn't forget something and come back. But she was worried about how long Wyatt could keep him busy, so before more than a few seconds had passed, she grabbed a knife out of the kitchen drawer and ran for that loose floorboard.

Pounding up the stairs, she dashed into Mr. Hawkins's bedroom and noted she'd yet to tidy it, so she had an excuse to be in there, then she dropped to her knees beside a chest of drawers. There were two boards that slid up just a bit and weren't flush with the other boards. They should have been nailed down. She tried prying with her fingernails.

Running her hands all along both sides, she felt for anything out of the ordinary. What she wanted was a lever, but surely that would be visible.

She felt as if a clock ticked in her head as she gave up on any button to push or lever to pull. She slid the knife between the boards and heard a metallic click as the knife sank through where it should have hit wood.

Dragging the knife along the side of the floorboard, careful not to nick anything, suddenly something gave and four floorboards, in an uneven rectangle, swung open on some kind of hinge.

With a gasp of excitement, she leaned down and saw the second safe. Topped by a round combination lock.

She quickly pulled the slip of paper with the two combinations on it out of her pocket. Molly carried it with her at all times, afraid if she left it somewhere, even in her room, Mr. Hawkins might find it, or she might need it—just like now.

She carefully followed the same set of turns, forward and backward, turning the dial a different number of times for each of the three numbers. A lock clicked inside. Her hand trembling, she lifted the lid of the safe. It was about a foot square, but made of heavy iron, and she needed both hands to lift the small lid. Opening it wide, she tipped it up until it rested against the floorboards.

Inside she saw several packets, mostly envelopes or other folded paper. They weren't completely flat like they'd be if they only contained letters.

"I'll be sure to check on that, Mr. Hawkins." The kitchen door slammed.

Slammed deliberately. Wyatt was warning her.

Then footsteps pounded on the stairs. Mr. Hawkins was back and coming fast. Desperate to find out what she'd discovered, Molly plunged her hand past the top envelope and grabbed three from below, hoping if Mr. Hawkins checked the safe, he wouldn't notice they were gone.

She swung the lid closed, spun the dial, and put the floorboards in place. They wouldn't fit.

~

"Stay off the trail." Falcon led the way, not back but down. Into the woods. On foot. With that gunman possibly still up there, the only way forward was off the trail.

Cheyenne came right along. Not as quiet as she could be but enough to make a man proud.

Rachel Hobart was good, too. Tough, savvy. They had no choice but to leave her, unconscious, the bleeding staunched. She needed care.

They had to find whoever did this, do it fast, and get her help.

And they had to do it without being shot down themselves. Good as they both were in the woods, no one was good enough to dodge a bullet fired from cover, but they could sure enough try to keep trees between themselves and that vicious would-be killer.

The forest swallowed them up. The way was slow. Scrub brush to slip past. Downed trees tangled up in vines and standing trees. Tumbled stones cropping up randomly. The leaves still fluttered down, but they were nearly done. All that plus leaves left piled and rotted from the beginning of time turned the forest floor into a nearly impassable tangle.

Falcon was used to that. A glance back showed his wife keeping up with no trouble. Where had that shot come from? Falcon had seen movement. Late, far too late, but he'd thrown himself off the horse and sprinted for Cheyenne even as the gun fired. And he had one moment to fear the most important person in the world to him might have died.

Then he had her, alive and unhurt. And Rachel hit the ground, bleeding. Now he sorted through all those rapid-fire thoughts and knew right where he'd go to find this evil dry-gulcher.

Forging on, each step chosen carefully, his eyes never resting, Falcon kept trees between him and any gunman who might be coming or waiting.

He reached a point where he thought the gunman, should he still be in place, might be visible. Falcon doubted the killer was still there. It was the way of people who fired from cover to run after the deed was done. But he might think the trail was covered from where he sat. He might be content to watch and wait and kill again given a chance.

Reaching from behind, Cheyenne's hand came into his. He looked back and tipped his head toward the massive oak tree right in front of him.

Cheyenne nodded and stayed still. Falcon eased forward, considered. Saw himself peeking around the trunk of this tree and getting his head blown off. Nothing to like in this situation. Instead, he looked overhead and saw a heavy branch within grabbing distance. He had to launch himself upward, but that was no problem.

Catching hold, he swung himself up, hooked his knees around the branch, then swung around to sit. He climbed to his feet. The branches were thicker, closer together up here, and stout enough they didn't shake under a man's weight. Hopefully, even if the shooter was still out there, he wouldn't be looking for trouble coming from the treetop. Falcon fetched his rifle around and, with his hand on the trigger, pointed it up so the muzzle wouldn't be visible, then leaned enough to get one eye around the tree.

Studying the area with eyes as strong as a flock of hawks, he searched back and forth, up and down.

There! Maybe fifty paces up the mountain slope.

Falcon fought down the surge of triumph and rage. Calm. Steady. He didn't want this man dead. There were too many questions. But he wanted him stopped, and stopped hard.

The man was on the ground, behind a waist-high boulder, his rifle resting on the rock. He was sheltered and all but hidden from the trail, but from where Falcon was, his whole left side was exposed.

Falcon faltered as he realized who the man was. What could he have to do with the Pinkerton investigation of Oliver Hawkins? His thoughts chasing themselves around did no good, not right now. Right now, he had a would-be murderer to catch.

An inch at a time, Falcon brought his rifle down. Movement drew the eye, and he didn't want the man's intent focus on the trail diverted.

Falcon aimed, considering where to hit him to stop him.

His finger pressed on the trigger, as far as he dared. He breathed in deep and let the breath out halfway. Waiting for a second, going completely still, he fired. A bright bloom of scarlet exploded on the dry-gulcher's shoulder. Very close to the spot where he'd hit Wyatt.

The man slammed backward onto the ground. His rifle flew over his head. The killer shouted and crawled toward the long gun. Falcon fired again and hit him in the leg, then again and blew the rifle to pieces. The man clawed at his pistol. Falcon smashed a bullet into the holster and the six-shooter snapped in two. The man's fingers were stained with blood.

"Go." He hissed down at Cheyenne.

She tore up the hill toward the man. Falcon was on the ground and after her, his rifle again slung over his shoulder.

"Knife!" Cheyenne hollered.

The man slashed at her, the knife held awkwardly in his left hand. She leapt away and landed on her backside.

Falcon, pushing hard, felt every second like an hour as the man came at his wife with a knife. He remembered his ma calling him a berserker and knew that was in him right now. He roared as the man staggered to his feet.

Jerking his head up at the sound as if he feared an approaching grizzly, the killer's gunshot leg went out from under him.

Cheyenne, flat on her back, kicked the blade aside. He lost

his grip, and fumbled at his right sleeve. Cheyenne twisted with the grace of a hunting wildcat, regained her feet, and stomped on the wrist he was trying for.

Then Falcon was there. He pounded a fist into the man's face. Falcon grabbed his left arm as Cheyenne dragged a derringer out of his sleeve. Falcon slugged him again, and the man slumped to the ground.

"Don't trust him," Cheyenne said. "He acts like he's passed out, but I don't believe it."

She held up the tiny, two-shot firearm. "Nice gun. Maybe I can keep it."

Cheyenne pulled a length of leather off her belt.

"I must say I admire a woman who is always prepared to tie up a prisoner."

She grinned at Falcon, but it didn't last. "You really think this man might've shot Wyatt?"

Falcon studied him. "We'd just be guessing unless we can get a confession out of him. But he sure as certain shot Rachel and fired at us. And came at you with a knife. At-tempted murder on two women oughta be enough to hang him. If they do, or if they just lock him up, we'll count it for Wyatt, too."

"Who in the world is he?" Cheyenne threw him onto his stomach and pulled his hands together behind his back.

"I know him."

"Really?" Cheyenne stopped tying.

The man made a sudden wild leap forward.

Cheyenne brought the derringer down hard on the back of his head, and he went still. This time he was really out. She tied him up tight anyway.

"Remember when I came out west, I stopped in Casper to talk to the lawyer who sent me the information about Pa's will?"

Cheyenne shrugged as she finished binding. "I can't remember you saying that, but we got a wire from him, telling us you'd be on that morning's train."

"This is that lawyer. His name is Randall Kingston. He sent that wire."

Cheyenne, already kneeling beside their prisoner, dropped to fully sit on the ground. "But he knows all the details of Pa's will. Our lawyer in Bear Claw Pass said he was handling contacting you. And Rachel had nothing to do with Clovis's will. She was out here searching for Amelia Bishop. Why did he shoot Rachel?"

Falcon finished with the feet. "Randall Kingston's name was on the wire I received back in Tennessee informing me of the inheritance. And I didn't know where you lived. Didn't know Bear Claw Pass from a hole in the ground, much less how to get to the RHR. But I had Kingston's name, so I got off the train in Casper and hunted him up to ask where to head next."

It had about killed him to ask for directions, but he'd done it. Not being able to read. Not knowing a soul out here. With no idea hardly what a ranch even was, he'd wanted some answers before he just showed up at Bear Claw Pass.

"The train had left before I finished with the questions, so I was stranded for a bit. This man was mighty friendly. He helped me find the schedule for the next train."

"So he knew exactly when you'd get to town."

"Yep, but he never acted like he had any interest in me beyond doing his job as a lawyer."

"If he shot Rachel, he must have some connection to Hawkins." Cheyenne reached down and flipped the unconscious man onto his back. Studied him.

"They're connected somehow. And connected to Pa, too."

Cheyenne hunkered down beside Kingston and tugged gently on one of his eyelids. And stared into brown eyes shot through with gold. "His eyes are the same color as Clovis's." Cheyenne looked up. "The same color as yours."

"Brothers?" Falcon looked at his wife.

Cheyenne shrugged. "Some kind of kin, I reckon."

They both crouched there across from Kingston for a long time, not talking, Falcon sorting it out in his head, and he could tell Cheyenne was doing the same.

"We can't figure it out here and now. We've got to get Rachel to the doctor," he finally said. "Let's bind up his wounds so he doesn't bleed out before we get him to the sheriff. I'm going to toss him over his saddle, but I think we need to build a travois for Rachel. Is there a sheriff in White Rock?"

"I don't think so, but we're not that far from Casper. Some of our questions might get answered there."

"It's his town, will the sheriff take his word over ours?"

Cheyenne rose. "My family is a respected one in the territory. They'll take what I say seriously."

Falcon nodded at a horse standing back in the woods a distance. "You watch over him. I'll use his horse to round up ours and get Rachel. And while we're in Casper, we can mail that letter and send our wire to the Pinkertons. No more worrying about a talkative telegraph operator. I've got a feeling the one person in Casper we wouldn't want to hear about the wire is this man."

"Rachel said someone would come. I s'pect when they get here, they'll be looking for Kingston as well as Hawkins, and they'll want some answers."

Sixteen

The raised piece of floorboard wouldn't fit.

The footsteps came fast.

She pushed, lifted, then pressed down and sideways. It clicked into place.

Mr. Hawkins was almost to the door.

Molly looked at the unmade bed. An excuse to be in here. She had no pockets. She slid the envelopes and knife deep under Mr. Hawkins's dresser, leapt to her feet, dashed to the bed, and pulled up one side of the covers.

The door slammed open hard enough it hit the wall behind it. Mr. Hawkins stood, breathing hard, something . . . frightening . . . glinting in his eyes.

"Mr. Hawkins, you're back." She sounded false and cleared her throat, fought to conceal her pounding heart. "Did you find out what Wyatt needed?"

He studied her. Could he know? What exactly had Wyatt said?

It flickered through her mind as she smoothed the covers that all the times he'd come looking for her, especially when she was in the bedroom, she had assumed improper motives.

But maybe Molly saw personal motives when that wasn't it at all. Maybe he was watching her because of what was in the safe. Maybe the moment she was out of here, he'd open that safe, find things missing, and come for her.

"Wyatt Hunt is not long for this ranch if he wastes my time like that again."

Molly plumped the pillow and rounded the bed so she was on the opposite side from her boss. "He didn't need anything important?" Her heart rate, already too high, sped up. Fear swept over her to see Mr. Hawkins in whatever mood this was.

She struggled to appear calm as she finished with the bed. She tried to act as if today were the same as any other day. All the while knowing she was one false move away from being caught in an act of thievery. She hadn't thought of it like that. She'd considered herself to be an investigator, searching for evidence of a crime. But what if those envelopes were completely innocent? Or what if they contained money?

He could haul her in to the sheriff, accuse her of stealing, and be completely right. She'd be guilty. She could go to prison.

Worse, what if there *was* evidence in them that would show him to be a killer?

There'd be no sheriff. No, he'd silence her permanently, and Wyatt was too far away to stop him.

She walked to the chest of drawers and picked up the pitcher resting in a bowl on top of it. She filled it with fresh water daily. And right now, it was a barrier between her and Mr. Hawkins.

She headed for the door. She had to walk near him. He

154

stood between her and the only way out. As she came even with him, his hand flashed out and caught her upper arm. His grip was tight. Too tight. He smiled, but it was more a baring of teeth.

"I need to get started with dinner." She spoke brightly, as if he weren't holding her arm to the point of pain. "We're having cherry pie. I found more canned cherries in your cellar, and my cherry pie is delicious."

He was almost as greedy for food as he was for standing too close to her. She saw him weigh whether to release her or not. Her hands tightened on the pitcher. A dousing with cold water might calm him down. And if not, a crack on the head with the heavy pitcher would be next. She was tempted to just get on with whacking him, but if she did, all the cherry pie in the world wouldn't save her job, and there were those envelopes under the dresser. She needed to see what she had there. If they were nothing, she'd really prefer to return them to the safe rather than explain what they were doing out of it.

Mr. Hawkins's grip tightened even more. Molly would have bruises tomorrow from the crushing grip. His fingernails dug into her arm until she wondered if he'd tear her dress and leave claw marks on her skin.

Then he released her so suddenly she stumbled back. Steadying herself, she nodded as if nothing untoward had happened and rushed out. If she had a chance, she'd get those envelopes yet today because they were the only way she was going to prove anything. She'd get them, and either they'd contain evidence she could somehow use, or she'd admit defeat, because she was getting out of here.

He didn't follow her. Was he opening the safe?

Her heart thudding, she knew there was nothing she could do about it, not right now. She rushed to the kitchen, refilled the pitcher, then looked at it. Her excuse.

She had to take it back up.

At some point.

Her heart pounded with fear as she pictured herself in that room again. She certainly wasn't going to do it while he was in there. But later. She only needed a moment. Whisk in, grab those envelopes, get out.

And maybe . . .

She sloshed the pitcher so the front of her dress was wet.

Then went to her room and changed into one she had with good-sized pockets. Hanging the wet dress from a peg in her room, Molly admitted she was so worried about Mr. Hawkins she wanted proof she'd gotten her dress wet, lest he check and catch her in a lie.

She heard him coming down the stairs. As she pulled on her dress, she looked at a red, swollen spot on her upper arm. Her skin was broken but not bleeding, all courtesy of Mr. Hawkins. She quickly finished dressing and left her room. As worried about Mr. Hawkins catching her in *her* bedroom as his.

She was in the kitchen measuring flour into a bowl when he came in. Silently, she swore she would put vinegar in the pie if he so much as touched her.

He stood in the doorway. She heard him but didn't look up from her work. His presence there was like a looming vulture.

As she measured in lard, she felt the vulture leave.

With a sigh of relief, she focused on preparing the noon meal.

And wondered when she'd have her chance at those letters. He closed the door on his study, and it occurred to her she ought to go up with the pitcher right now.

~

"Why'd you shoot Lawyer Kingston?" Sheriff Greg Gatlin studied the unconscious form of Randall Kingston. They'd stopped at the doctor's office to leave Rachel and Kingston. Falcon stayed holding a gun on the unconscious lawyer while Cheyenne fetched the sheriff.

Cheyenne had brought him over to the doctor's office.

"He shot Rachel Hobart." Cheyenne pointed to the Pinkerton agent. "Shot her from cover."

"Did you see him shoot the woman?"

Falcon's stomach twisted. He'd been afraid there might be trouble in Casper. Kingston was a known man in this town. Falcon was a stranger.

"Greg, you know how good a tracker I am," Cheyenne cut in.

Falcon did have a hideout weapon though. His wife.

The sheriff nodded.

"We were riding along, strung out on a narrow trail. Rachel third in line," Cheyenne said. "He picked her to kill. It was deliberate, and the bullet hit her chest dead center. Only because of the distance and Rachel's layers of clothes is she still alive. We ducked for cover and then worked out where the shot came from. And Falcon is an even better tracker than I am."

Gatlin glanced at Falcon, looking impressed.

Falcon didn't smile, but it made a man feel mighty fine to

hear his woman speak highly of him. And Cheyenne didn't like admitting anyone could out-track her, so it was a real compliment.

It seemed Sheriff Gatlin knew that, too. "Really? He's better'n you?" He pulled off a dirty white Stetson and scratched a thatch of gray hair. Then his eyes turned to Falcon. "That's sayin' something, mister."

"We slipped around and found him. Still aiming at the trail. After that first shot hit Rachel, Cheyenne and I made for the forest while he fired more times. I think he stayed there, covering the trail just in case he got another chance at us, but Rachel Hobart was clearly his main target."

"He needs to be patched up some." The sheriff went over and clipped one handcuff on the prisoner and one on a leg of the bed. He was nice enough to cuff the hand that wasn't bleeding. That seemed considerate of him. Or maybe he just thought he couldn't cause much trouble with a shot-up hand.

Falcon took it as a sign Gatlin trusted them, or at least he trusted Cheyenne.

The doctor was leaving the lawyer till last and working on Rachel. He straightened from where he'd been working on her chest and held up a small, round object.

"This saved her life."

Falcon, Cheyenne, and the sheriff all leaned closer.

"Is that a . . . button?" Cheyenne asked.

"Yep, a good-sized metal button was inside the wound. The bullet hit it and drove it into her chest. But it slowed down the bullet. The button was flat, not as easy to embed in the skin. God was watching out for her today."

Cheyenne looked at Falcon and smiled. Neither of them had done much smiling since Rachel was hit.

"She's still knocked cold. There's a bump on the back of her head. I'd say she hit a stone or the knot of a tree root when she fell. No bleeding but she's knocked into a good solid sleep. I'll put in a few stitches here, and it's just as well she be unconscious for that part. But she'll be fine."

Falcon reached out and caught Cheyenne's hand. "I didn't like her much at first. Now I'm real happy she's gonna be okay."

"I reckon we still oughta hang Kingston," Sheriff Gatlin said. "And if we're gonna, it seems like a waste of your time to patch him up, Doc Reynolds. But he probably oughta be able to get out of bed to stand trial, so it has to be done."

"Got no other cases once I finish with Miss Hobart, here," Reynolds said with a shrug. "I don't mind a few more stitches."

"Can we go look through his office?" Cheyenne asked. "We have no idea why he wanted Rachel dead. We're hoping we can find a reason he turned murderer."

"I oughta come along, but I don't want to leave Doc alone with this varmint, even with the shackles on. You're gonna find Kingston isn't well liked in Casper. A sharp character who's cheated more than a few. Shooting someone from cover don't surprise me overly. Finding his reasons don't make no never mind. Can you look around without my help?"

"Be pleased to, Sheriff Gatlin," Falcon said.

The sheriff reached in Kingston's pocket and pulled out a key ring holding three keys. "Seen him with this clutch of keys plenty of times. He had a habit of tossing them up and catching them while he'd stand talking. His office, the rooms abovestairs where he lived, and the third one I don't know. His house is the nicest one in town, on the north side, just up at the end of the street outside. You won't miss it. Town's too humble for such a house. Never was sure why Kingston settled here. Bring the keys back, and let me know what you find."

Nodding, Falcon went out, Cheyenne right behind him.

They didn't bother to untie their horses. It wasn't far to the north end of a town barely clinging to life after the fort left.

"Let's send the telegram first and post the letter," Cheyenne said. "Asking the Pinkertons to look into your ma's death doesn't seem so important anymore, but it needs to be done. And the Pinkertons need to know what happened to Rachel."

Cheyenne thought a moment. "She told us not to mention her name, but I think she was afraid she was dying. With the man who shot her arrested, do we still keep the details a secret?"

Considering it carefully, Falcon said, "I'd say we'd better do as she asked. If we don't hear anything from the Pinkertons, we can wire them again, tell them straight out what happened."

They sent the wire and posted the letter, then headed for Kingston's office.

It stood off by itself, looking more like a house than an office. A mighty grand building for a small town. They walked up five majestic steps to a porch that stretched across the front. The biggest key fit perfectly.

SEVENTEEN

Molly picked up the pitcher and walked upstairs, making as little sound as possible without actually tiptoeing, for fear Mr. Hawkins would notice *that*. She recognized that she was making mental excuses, practicing explanations, in case Mr. Hawkins asked her what she was doing.

This was how a fearful woman behaved. Young as she'd been, she remembered her ma acting this way. Trying to avoid her husband's wrath. In the end, Ma hadn't been able to.

Molly walked straight to his room and set the pitcher in place. Moving fast and listening for Mr. Hawkins to come upstairs and bother her, or worse, she crouched and saw the envelopes still in place with the kitchen knife beside them. She grabbed all of it, tucking the envelopes deep into her pocket and hiding the knife in the folds of her skirt. Then she rushed out of the room. She caught herself before she broke into a run.

Back in the kitchen, she replaced the knife and continued cooking, trying to decide if she needed to peek at the envelopes first or just flat out quit. Walk out now, find Wyatt, and ride for home. Open the envelopes when they were safe.

LOVE ON THE RANGE

She wished Wyatt would come to the back door again. Talk to her, make a plan. He would come to her window tonight. If she didn't just up and leave before then, she'd wait for Wyatt, check what she had, then they'd leave together in the night after Mr. Hawkins went to sleep. Evidence or not, she was done here.

She agonized over whether to keep the envelopes in hand, and fear the crinkle of paper as she moved, or hide them in her satchel. She didn't want to let them out of her sight. She found a solution she could live with. She hid the envelopes in a place Mr. Hawkins could expect a fat lip if he touched her.

Then she went back to her baking, slid the pie in the oven—no vinegar because she planned to have some herself—got potatoes on and sliced ham to fry. She couldn't do much of anything fancy because her hands tended to start shaking.

Mr. Hawkins came to the kitchen early for dinner as usual. To watch her work.

She smiled as she poured him a cup of coffee. She'd learned his preferences: bring the cup to the table, then get the pot and bring it to the table, and pour. He said he liked it piping hot and that helped, but in truth he liked her standing near him.

While he sipped coffee, she got the table set. Next the pie was out of the oven, the potatoes were mashed, and the ham was keeping warm on a platter on the back of the stove.

Setting the table, she was surprised when Mr. Hawkins rose. He seemed to like to sit and be served. She half expected him to ask her to cut his meat and fork it into his mouth.

"Everything's ready, Mr. Hawkins. I'm just bringing the coffeepot over." She reached for the big pot on the back of the stove, thinking of how she'd liked the idea of having the big water pitcher between them. Even better to have the boiling hot coffeepot.

Before she got hold of it, Mr. Hawkins caught her arm and pulled her away from the stove.

Startled, she squeaked as he turned her to face him. "Molly, I think it's time we talked of things other than food and drink."

This was it, then. Whatever he said right now, she'd have to leave. Assuming he allowed it. There'd be no staying for another day once words came out of his mouth that suggested they be more than employer and employee.

"I've enjoyed having your help here. You're the best housekeeper I've ever had. But my feelings—"

A sharp rap on the back door made him back up a few steps just as the door swung open.

Molly looked, hopeful it would be Wyatt but glad for any interruption.

"Hi, Pa, Kevin and I thought we'd stop in for dinner." Win waved with a big, if somewhat phony, smile on her face. She came on in and headed for the table.

Kevin was right behind her.

"Oliver, good to see you and Molly." Kevin walked straight to her, his expression mild, pleasant, but his eyes were sharp, and he clearly wanted to know how she was doing.

"Kevin." She lost all control of herself and threw her arms around her big brother.

Catching her by the waist, Kevin lifted her to her toes. "I've missed you, little sister."

He gave her too tight a squeeze, and close to her like this, he whispered, "I want a chance to talk to you before we go."

She hid the flinch when his squeeze hurt her arm. But maybe she didn't hide it well enough because his eyes narrowed.

Molly got ahold of herself and said brightly, "I've made plenty of food. Let me add plates to the table."

With the first genuine smile she'd managed while Mr. Hawkins was in the room, she hurried around, setting places for them. Mr. Hawkins was at the head of the table as always, and Molly sat at the foot, closest to the stove should she need to fetch anything.

Win got busy pouring coffee and talking lightly with her father.

Knowing how Win felt about her pa, for them to come for a visit gave Molly a sweet rush of love for her sister-in-law. She had to stop mourning the loss of a brother and start celebrating that she'd gained a sister.

The food was dished up. Mr. Hawkins was doing his usual wide smiles and charm. Something Molly knew was only skin deep—and his skin was extremely thin.

The meal was eaten, the pie served. Win and Kevin remarked on the wonderful food. Mr. Hawkins now talked favorably about her cooking, too, instead of acting like he was entitled to hard work and fine cooking from his servant.

They talked about general things while they ate, but after the pie was finished, Win said, "I'd like to stay awhile, Pa."

She took a sip of her coffee. "I've realized since I married Kevin and we've talked about our families that I don't know that much about Ma or you or how you grew up."

"Well, you can hardly fault me for not telling you stories, Winona." His voice had a sarcastic edge. "You left before you were old enough to remember much, and since you've come home, you're never here."

"You're right, but I'd like to change all that." Color bloomed high in Win's cheeks, but she clung to a smile and a pleasant tone. "Now, as an adult woman, a married woman, I'd like to learn more about your childhood and Ma's. I'd like to better understand where I came from. I have faint memories of Ma's mother, and I knew of Grandpa, but I can barely remember their names. I know we came from Chicago to here, but what did Grandpa do in Chicago? What work did you do back there? And I'm sure I've never heard a thing about your family. I would like to know more. What were Grandma and Grandpa Hawkins's names? What did Grandpa Hawkins work at? Do you have any pictures?"

Molly watched Mr. Hawkins during Win's friendly chatter. She saw a glint in his eyes that reminded Molly of how he'd looked at her upstairs, while he'd held her arm tight enough to bruise it. She remembered Rachel saying he could be frightening.

As Win's questions went on, he calmed down—or maybe he just got himself under control. He said in his usual falsely charming voice, "Well, now, you're right. We've never spoken much of my family. It's odd to think of that. Strange that you don't know about either of your sets of grandparents at all."

Mr. Hawkins rubbed his chin as if thinking of old memories, but it struck Molly that instead, he was thinking whether to tell the truth or lie. Or maybe he didn't hesitate over it at all. Maybe he was concocting the lie.

"I don't have pictures of them, nor pictures of myself or your mother." He fell silent for too long. At last he said, "I may have some of your mother's parents. I haven't had them out in a long time. I might be a while finding them, but come into my study. That's where they'd have to be. We'll have a look."

"Oliver, I'd like to visit with my sister, catch up. I haven't seen her in a while. I'll be right in to look at pictures though."

The way he said it, letting Mr. Hawkins know he wouldn't be alone with Win for long, sounded almost like a threat, for sure a warning.

Mr. Hawkins left the room with Win, the two of them talking as if they'd always enjoyed each other's company. As soon as they left, Molly frantically unbuttoned the top three buttons of her dress, pulled out the envelopes, and hissed, "Hide these. Check on them with Wyatt before you leave the property."

Kevin arched a brow as Molly, quickly rebuttoning her dress, looked past his shoulder to make sure Mr. Hawkins hadn't come back. Kevin had a coat hanging in the entryway. He strode to it, thrust her small collection of evidence deep in a pocket, then came back.

She hissed, "It might be something to use against . . ." Her eyes shifted to the door Mr. Hawkins had just walked out of. "If it's not, then I have turned thief, and I want a chance to put those envelopes back in the safe in his bedroom."

Then, on an impulse, she threw her arms around Kevin's neck and said, speaking normally, "I've missed you."

He hugged her gently. Then, setting her back so their eyes met, he asked, "Are you safe here?"

There was only silence. Molly couldn't lie and claim she was safe. But neither could she say the words that would make Kevin yank her out of here. But her very silence was an answer.

"You're leaving with Win and me."

"No, not yet. I want those envelopes opened, without them looking like they've been opened if possible. There may be something in them that, once I see it, would lead me to something else here in this house. Once I leave, we'll never get anyone back in here."

She held up the flat of her hand. "I'm leaving very soon. I very much doubt I'll still be here tomorrow morning. I don't like being here and"—she barely moved her lips, hoping not to be overheard—"Rachel was right. Mr. Hawkins is frightening. Open the envelopes so I know what's in there. I intended to do that after Mr. Hawkins went to sleep tonight. Wyatt comes to my bedroom every night and—"

"He does *what*?" Kevin's voice wasn't a bit quiet on that question.

"Hush." Molly shoved Kevin's shoulders. "Nothing wrong is happening between us. He comes to my window to see if I've found anything, then he sneaks through my room." She checked for Mr. Hawkins again. "And sleeps in a nearby pantry, so he's close enough to hear me if I need help. But today I decided I'm done."

She gripped Kevin's wrist tightly and thought of how Mr. Hawkins had gripped her arm. And what had he been about to say when Win and Kevin had arrived? Yes, there was no more decision to make. Her time here was up. "I haven't been hurt, but he's a frightening man."

"I'm going to go find Wyatt and give him these envelopes. We'll look at them right now. Can you go into the study with Win and Hawkins? I don't want her alone with him."

"He won't like me in there. I'd be forgetting my place. He's very particular about how he treats servants." Her eyes grew wide. "You should hear how he talks to Wyatt."

Kevin's brows arched. "And Wyatt puts up with it?"

"Go. And get back here. I'll take coffee in. I think he'll accept me coming in to serve him."

Kevin kissed her on the cheek. "I'll be back in five minutes. I didn't see Wyatt when we rode in. If he's not to hand, I'm not going hunting." He ran out of the kitchen.

Molly picked up the coffeepot and set it on a tray. She added delicate china cups and saucers, white with blue flowers, as pretty as anything Molly had ever seen. Then she headed for the study, determined to interrupt even if nothing was going on.

~

"Pa, can I have these pictures?" Win looked at the small portraits of her grandmother and grandfather. She recognized her grandmother. It shocked her to realize she'd held the memory of the fine old lady all these years. Her heart warmed until it was nearly hot.

"Yes, of course you can. I should have given them to you years ago."

"How about Ma? Do you have pictures of her?"

"I don't remember having any. I'd be willing to sort through more old papers to see if they turn up, but I'm not sure where to start. Maybe that's a task I can give myself in the near future."

At least Win was sure she remembered her mother. A picture would have been a cherished possession, but her memory was keen. "Tell me about yourself, Pa. Your childhood. Where did you grow up?"

Her father's eyes sharpened. He smiled easily enough, but it went no further than his lips. "I grew up in Chicago. Lived there all my life until your ma and I headed west."

"Tell me about your parents."

She saw his gaze shift. He looked down to the left, and she could almost feel him creating a story. She knew what he'd say next was a lie.

He talked of his father, a lawyer. A successful one. And his mother, a lovely society matron. He was an only child.

Since Win assumed it was all a lie, she wondered for the first time if her father wasn't an only child. Did she have aunts and uncles? How could she find out?

He went on, talking about a happy childhood. A fine school that made him want a finishing-school education for Win.

On he went, and Win prayed as she listened to a made-up life so grand and pretty it was only fit for a fairy tale.

Lord, how do I honor my father? Is there a rule in the commandments that allows a believer to abandon this one commandment if there is only dishonor in the parent?

She'd told Kevin that honoring was not to let her father's lies and mistreatment, possibly even to the extent of murder, go on to the next generation. She would honor him by not living as he did. And she would honor him by being honest. That was the hard part. To honor him by speaking truth to him and giving him a chance. He might change his life. He might become worthy of honor. But she couldn't do that as long as Molly was in his house.

God, is that right? It has to be right. Because there is no way, as honor is traditionally understood, to honor such a man.

Her pa talked of meeting Ma, and she wondered if there was truth in that. Even if he wasn't the well-connected young man he pretended, he might have lied his way into Ma's social circle. Charmed a pretty young woman. Married her while keeping the falsehoods alive. These lies might be of long-standing, lies he'd told in his youth and clung to even now.

As she wondered what to say, what to do, what to believe, words pressed to be spoken. The truth. She needed to speak the truth. She'd be honest, then she'd leave here, Molly and Wyatt with her. She had to challenge his stories, and she felt God goading her to speak right here, right now.

She opened her mouth to do it.

Molly walked in, and Win's mouth snapped shut. Had God been goading her? Or had God sent Molly just in time?

"I thought coffee might be welcome. Kevin will join you soon, but I didn't wait for him." Molly got very busy setting the tray up, pouring the coffee. She didn't sit down.

Molly was as good as a sister now. And yet, Pa didn't invite her to join them. And Molly hadn't brought a third cup. She knew she wouldn't be welcome. She hadn't brought a cup for Kevin, either. Win wasn't sure what that meant.

"M-Molly." Win ransacked her mind for some topic of conversation beyond the only one Win could think of: *Have you proved my father is a killer yet?* "Look at these pictures Pa gave me."

Molly came and looked. Win felt her father stiffen at the invitation. He'd been able to accept the intrusion when it was nothing but a servant bringing coffee. But to join the conversation annoyed him.

What's more, Molly knew. Win saw a slight tremble to

Molly's hand as she reached for the pictures of Win's grandparents. They were small, and Win knew two prominent, wealthy Chicagoans would have had full-sized portraits painted. Large, well-done portraits. And there should be paintings of her mother, too. Possibly even one of Win as a small child. Where were all those pictures? Had Pa burned them? He'd dug deep for these in a book in a forgotten corner of his study. Possibly he'd meant to burn them and neglected these small portraits and had only remembered them when Win asked.

A poor family setting off across the continent hoping to homestead eighty or one hundred sixty acres might be forced to leave valuable family heirlooms like portraits behind. But a wealthy man like her father? Who had moved luxuries across four states?

If those portraits were gone, it was an act of spite. Win couldn't help but wonder if he'd forced Ma to watch him burn them. It seemed like the kind of thing her pa might do. Maybe she couldn't speak truth to her father today, but she could demonstrate right and wrong, at least as Win saw it.

"Molly, go get another coffee cup. Get two, one for Kevin and one for you, and join us."

"Now, Win . . ." her pa began.

"Molly is my sister." Win cut him off before he could say whatever unkind thing he was preparing to say.

"Sister-in-law," he corrected her. "And she's my housekeeper. You can't expect me—"

"I do expect it, Pa." Win met his gaze. As their eyes met, she realized how rarely she'd done it. Every lifelong reflex she possessed pushed her to look down, look away, and mind her father. Don't provoke his wrath. But in this way, she could truly honor him. By expecting honor *of* him.

"I lived with Molly so I know what a hard worker she is, what a fine cook." Win looked at Molly and then reached out to grab her hand and hold on when Molly might've left the room. "You are blessed to have such a fine housekeeper. But that doesn't mean she's not my sister. We *will* include her. I'm sure when Kevin comes in, he'd be shocked not to find Molly with us. He'd find it terribly wrong, and so do I."

"Don't take that tone with me, Winona." Something burned in Pa's eyes that Win knew, as an adult woman, was frightening. She'd always known this was part of him, but before, she'd looked at him with the eyes of a child. She'd avoided him and been polite and lived away from him as much as she could manage.

She squared her shoulders and stood to face her father. "The only tone was to ask you to treat Molly as my sister. I expect it of you, and what's more, I demand it of you. I won't slight her."

"You'll do as I say. You're my daughter, and my word is law around here."

"Your word isn't above God's, Pa." She softened her voice, wishing she could reach him. She doubted it was possible but honor demanded she try. "Pa, God calls me to honor you. But the only way to do that is nearly the same word, *honesty*. I have to tell you honestly that you need to humble yourself before God. I need a father who is worthy of honor, and you are not."

The burn in his eyes turned to a raging fire. Win braced herself to be slapped.

EIGHTEEN

Look at this, Falcon." Cheyenne held up a picture she'd found buried in a drawer in Kingston's bedroom.

Falcon came to her side and stared at the picture.

Cheyenne tapped on a mostly grown boy in the front row. "That's your pa."

Falcon leaned close. "It's like looking at a picture of myself. That has to be Pa."

"And look at who he's standing behind."

"That has to be Randall Kingston."

"Yep. And they look alike. I wouldn't have thought of it if he didn't have your eyes." She stared at the group of young men. "They're so young."

"Just boys."

"Some kind of school picture. There are . . ." She counted swiftly, then she quit counting as a jolt went through her that felt like lightning. She tapped her finger on a young man in the back row. "Wait, look who's standing behind Kingston."

"That's Oliver Hawkins."

With a grim nod, Cheyenne said, "They knew each other.

Or is he another brother? Hawkins doesn't have your eyes, and it seems to run strong in your family."

Falcon shook his head. "So Kingston, who I shot today, is my uncle? And maybe Hawkins is another uncle?"

"I'd say for sure with Kingston. With Hawkins, an uncle or a very old friend." She flipped the picture over. "Jeffers House of Refuge for Young Men." She looked up at Falcon. "What is a house of refuge?"

Falcon shrugged.

Then she tapped another line of words. "Jeffers, Tennessee. 1839. I've never thought I heard a single note of Tennessee in Oliver's voice. He sounded nothing like Clovis."

"Can I look at the picture again?"

Cheyenne handed it to Falcon, wondering what it felt like to have a pa with such a twisted past. "Your Bible says Clovis married your ma in 1840. He looks old enough here to be nearly out of school, if this was a school."

"Never heard tell of no little brother for my pa. But Kingston might have changed his name, or Pa did, or both. Whatever made 'em do that, they didn't end up, all three of them, out here by happenstance."

"I don't know when Kingston moved out here, but Hawkins was definitely here ahead of Clovis."

"Pa and his little brother must've followed Hawkins out. If they knew he hit the mother lode marrying Win's rich ma in Chicago, then headed west to escape any harsh judgments from his wife's friends, the others might've come hoping to get in on the money."

"Kingston sets up as a cheating lawyer, and Clovis sees what a smart move it is to marry for money and latches on to my ma. You know, I told you Hawkins was Clovis's only friend out here. I always just thought they met and got on well. Instead, they knew each other from before."

"Jeffers House of Refuge for Young Men. That sounds strange," Falcon said. "Refuge from what? What kind of school is it? I don't reckon it matters, but this connects three men at the center of a lot of trouble."

Falcon reached out and caught Cheyenne's arm. "And if Kingston knew about Rachel, then Hawkins does, too. And if he knows about her, he's likely to know Molly and Wyatt are up to something in his house."

Cheyenne's eyes locked on Falcon's. "We've got to get them out of there."

~

"She found something?" Wyatt's eyes flashed with excitement, and maybe relief, when Kevin handed him the envelopes.

"She said to open them carefully. If there's nothing criminal in them, then she'll try and slip them back in his—"

Wyatt tore open an envelope, shredding it in his hurry. Then he looked up at Kevin and grinned. "Sorry, big brother. I can't get too upset about how I treat Hawkins." While he talked, he dragged out a white, embroidered handkerchief. "Spending time over here has been a mighty fine lesson in how to treat animals, hired hands, women, and probably God. Just do the exact opposite of Oliver Hawkins." He handed the handkerchief to Kevin and looked in to find a single sheet of paper.

Wyatt read it aloud. "'Dear Hannah, too many days have

passed since I last saw you. No better woman has filled my days, and no one can take your place. If only you had been as good to me as I was to you. Now I must go on alone.'"

Kevin held up the handkerchief. A delicate, lacy thing with an embroidered corner. A single letter *H*.

"Who's Hannah?" Kevin glanced nervously at the house. "I've got to get back in there."

"Maybe one of those other housekeepers Rachel said was missing. She said a killer of the type Hawkins might be would keep some token or memento from a victim. That kerchief would qualify." Wyatt tore the second packet open. This one made of brown paper like that used to wrap parcels at the general store. A jeweled pin fell out, like the kind that could be fastened to a woman's dress bodice. There was another note. This one read, "'Dear Lydia, with your vibrant red hair, you called out to me from the first moment.'" Wyatt jerked his head up. "There's more here but the end is the same. 'Now I must go on alone.'"

Kevin had the third and final envelope open. This one flat and lightweight. There was nothing in it but a sheet of unlined paper. He read, "'Dear Amelia . . .' That's all it says. It must be a note he began to Amelia Bishop before she vanished."

Kevin's eyes met Wyatt's for a single grim second.

"I'm going to pack my things," Wyatt said. "This isn't much, but I'm through here and so is Molly. I'll saddle the horses Molly and I brought over, then I'll come to the house and tell Hawkins I quit. We're taking Molly with us whether she agrees or not."

They'd already next thing to kidnapped her from the parson's house. They were getting good at it.

"I think she'll agree. She wants out." Kevin handed his letter to Wyatt. "You hold on to all of these. I'm going in."

Wyatt wished they had better evidence than odd poems, only one of them with the name of a woman they knew had worked for Hawkins. "I'd like to have more proof to take to the sheriff but . . ."

"We'll show these to Rachel." Kevin clapped him on the shoulder.

"That's right, she knows the names of the two missing women. These poems, along with what evidence Rachel has, might be enough to bring Hawkins in for questioning, then the sheriff can go through that safe. Having left any other letters in there might be better proof than if we have them and the sheriff has only Molly's word where they came from."

"I'll be ready to leave with the women when you get up there." Kevin turned for the house.

Wyatt watched him go at a run. Wyatt's heart sped up as he thought of how close they were to stopping a murderer, and if they didn't accomplish that, at least they'd be getting out of here.

NINETEEN

Cheyenne didn't want Rachel alone with Kingston, even if *alone* included the sheriff and the doctor. They might not be suspicious enough.

She was running by the time she reached the doctor's office. Rachel lay unconscious, a good bandage covering her dress that the doctor had cut open. Her coat hung next to her. Blood soaked, too, but it would serve for modesty.

"As soon as she wakes up, we're going home," Cheyenne said. "Kingston has connections back near Bear Claw Pass and my brother and sister may be in danger."

The doctor stopped working over Kingston and turned to listen to every word.

The sheriff came up out of his chair, his brow furrowed. "Tell me what you've found that's upset you so much."

Cheyenne took turns with Falcon telling them every detail. She'd brought the picture along, too.

"I'm going to send a few wires," Gatlin said. "Track down this school. If you're right about him being a brother to Clovis, then that school oughta be able to tell me his real name. I can see if there are any wanted posters. I can also see if there's any proof he ever studied the law. And maybe that'll help me figure out how he paid for that big house. He had to've come in here with money because he sure as certain never made enough working here in Casper to pay for it."

Cheyenne went to Rachel's side. Her face was pale as milk. Her eyes remained closed. She breathed steadily. "You stitched her up, right, Doc?"

"Yep, she's really not bad hurt except for that bump on the head." The doctor abandoned Kingston. Cheyenne got a strong feeling the doctor, like the sheriff, had little use for the man. He bent over Rachel and tugged on one of her eyes to lift the lid. He stared for a few seconds, then shook his head. "She's out stone cold. We just have to wait."

Cheyenne saw Falcon rub the back of his head. He'd been clipped by a bullet there, and it'd knocked him out hard enough he woke up without any memory. Win had heard of such a thing and said it was called amnesia. Falcon knew a knock on the head could do plenty of damage.

"We can't wait." Cheyenne couldn't stand to.

"Doc Reynolds," Falcon said, "would it be dangerous for her to come along with us? We don't have a wagon, but—" A train whistle cut him off.

"That's it." Cheyenne looked out the window in the door to the doctor's office. "We can catch the train. Load our horses. We'll be home in an hour. Can she make it, Doc? We have a decent doctor now living at the RHR."

"I suppose." Dr. Reynolds didn't sound that happy about it.

"And will Kingston stay locked up?" Falcon asked. "We can come back in a few days, but he's dangerous."

"I take Cheyenne's word for what happened. You're a second witness, Falcon, and I saw Miss Hobart brought in. Yes, that's enough to keep him locked up. I'm going to investigate him a bit, and I'll wait for you to come back and testify."

"I'll go buy three tickets, arrange for the horses to get on board, and send another telegram to the Pinkerton Agency about the Jeffers House of Refuge." Cheyenne turned for the door. "You bring Rachel. The train usually doesn't stay in the station long, especially not in a town this small."

Cheyenne was gone, running for the train station, trusting her husband to handle Rachel. She enjoyed the sweet feeling of having a husband she could fully trust.

~

Kevin burst into the study just as Mr. Hawkins slapped Win across the face.

Win cried out and clutched her cheek. Molly rushed to her and pulled her away from Mr. Hawkins's fury, and his hand raised to strike Molly.

Kevin charged at Mr. Hawkins and slammed a fist into his face, knocking him back hard enough he fell over the arm of his overstuffed chair. Hawkins's feet caught under the low table holding the china cups and coffee, and it went flying.

Kevin kept coming.

"No, stop." Win grabbed his arm and threw all her weight against him.

Molly jumped in and grabbed Kevin's other arm. Not because she particularly wanted him to stop. She thought a few more solid fists to the face were just what Mr. Hawkins needed.

"Let's go, Kevin." Win sounded shaky, near tears. Her face had a red splotch on it the size and shape of an open hand.

"I'm going with you." Molly had had enough. She wasn't staying in this house another minute.

"No, don't leave me, Molly." Mr. Hawkins dragged himself to his feet. Holding one hand to his jaw, he kept the chair between him and Kevin.

"You're just going to have to hire a new housekeeper. I didn't like the way you treated me, *Mr.* Hawkins." Molly made sure to load that formal name he'd always insisted she use with scorn. "But I would *never* stay working for a man who'd *hit my sister*!"

At that moment, Wyatt came in. "He hit Win?"

Win gave Molly a desperate look across the breadth of Kevin's chest. Molly let go and plowed into Wyatt as he strode toward Mr. Hawkins.

They collided hard enough she almost went over backward. She clung to him, face-to-face, her arms tight around his waist.

"I just quit. I'm leaving with Kevin and Win. Maybe you'd like to join us?" Her eyes met his and though they flashed with anger, a tiny flicker of humor shone. He shook his head a few times. His fist relaxed.

"Molly, who will feed me?" Mr. Hawkins acted like the slap had never happened. "And I thought, that is, I had hopes that we might . . . might be more—"

He quit talking when Wyatt slipped around Molly and clamped a hand on his throat. Wyatt had gotten away, and Molly had to admit she'd wanted someone to stop Mr. Hawkins's horrible words.

Mr. Hawkins clawed at Wyatt's hand. His face turned an alarming shade of red. A gurgling noise was the only sound he could make.

"Did you really just slap your daughter's face?" Wyatt released his grip.

Wheezing, Mr. Hawkins said, "I'm her father. A father's got a right to discipline his child."

Wyatt's hand clamped again.

Molly tugged on Wyatt's arm, not the one he was choking Mr. Hawkins with. And she reckoned if she were really serious about stopping him, she'd've grabbed that one.

Wyatt escaped her grip and caught her by her upper arm. She gasped and flinched.

Wyatt, still strangling Mr. Hawkins, noticed and looked away from his current victim. "Did I hurt you?"

His brow furrowed. His eyes shone with regret.

"No, it's nothing." She couldn't quite control her eyes, which slipped to Mr. Hawkins, then away.

Wyatt ran a hand up her arm, gently. He felt the swelling.

"Did *he* hurt you?" Wyatt jerked his head at Mr. Hawkins.

"I'm not going to discuss it," she said.

"That means yes." Wyatt's regret turned to fury.

"Let him go, Wyatt." She admitted privately she wasn't doing her best to pull him off the man.

"A father might swat a child's backside for disobedience. But your daughter is a married woman. You lost any right to *discipline* her long ago. And slapping her so hard you left a mark on her face doesn't count as discipline by anyone's reckoning."

Then, speaking slowly, as if addressing a very stupid, and

slightly deaf, man, Wyatt said, "And as for Molly, there is no time *ever* when it's right to leave bruises on your housekeeper."

Wyatt shook him just a little. "You and Molly are not now, nor are you ever gonna be *more* to each other. You should abandon all your hopes, Oliver."

Wyatt let him go with a tight shove that made him stumble back.

Mr. Hawkins coughed and covered his neck with his own hands. He backed farther away until the couch was between him and the rest of the room. He didn't speak. Didn't protest or try to grab anyone again.

But his eyes . . . all pretense of having hopes for something between them, all pretense of a boss treating his employee correctly, was gone, replaced by pure hatred. Molly would see his loathing for the rest of her life. The only real trouble was that he wasn't looking at her with loathing. He was looking at Wyatt.

This man who lived near where Wyatt had been shot. Controlling a shudder, Molly tore away from watching him.

"Molly, do you have things to gather?" Wyatt asked, never looking away from Mr. Hawkins.

Molly was almost completely packed, having had plans to slip away tonight. "I won't be but a minute."

She rushed out of the room, partly hurrying to get her things. Partly running away from the deadly glare in Mr. Hawkins's eyes. She grabbed her satchel, stuffed the few things in it that were still left out, and met her family in the kitchen. Her family. Kevin, yes. Win, after only a second of hesitation she thought, *Yes, Win is my sister.*

Wyatt?

Her heart warmed as she thought of how he'd cut off what might have been humiliating words from Mr. Hawkins.

And that's when she realized something that made her eyes spark with pleasure.

Kevin was ahead of her ushering Win out the back door. Wyatt was behind her, but close enough he noticed the spark.

"What can you possibly find to like in this mess?"

Then they were outside. Wyatt had four horses tied at a hitching post only steps from the door. They were mounted up and moving before Molly got a chance to answer.

"Molly thinks something's funny?" Kevin scowled at her, then looked at Win's swollen, red cheek.

"Not funny." She held the reins in her left hand and ran her fingers gently over the swollen spot on her arm. "Not one thing funny about that man."

And still, she smiled. "It just made me happy to realize I'm never going to have to call that man Mr. Hawkins again."

The four of them lined up. Win rode between Kevin and Molly with Wyatt on Molly's right. Win looked at Molly and gave a firm nod of her chin. "And I'm never going to call him Pa, either."

She reached out her hand, and Molly clasped it as they rode along.

"How far were we from this place when Wyatt was shot?" Trust Kevin to think of something to worry about.

"Not that far." Wyatt rubbed his shoulder and started looking behind him. "Let's pick up the pace."

TWENTY

The conductor called Bear Claw Pass, and Cheyenne gave Rachel, who was groggily sitting up, a worried look. "How are you feeling?"

Rachel blinked at her owlishly and didn't answer.

"The doctor told me before I left that she needs quiet. A blow to the head like that can make the brain swell up inside her skull. She could feel poorly for a week."

"A week?" Cheyenne gave her head a violent shake.

"I told Doc Reynolds when she came around that sounded too long. He said we have to keep an eye on her, make sure she eats and drinks if she's too addled to do it for herself. Mostly, she needs rest."

"Hogback at the diner has a wagon that doesn't get much use. I'll go ask if we can borrow it. Better yet, maybe he could drive us out to the RHR and then he could take his wagon back."

The train slowed. Cheyenne was on her feet the second it stopped, heading for the door, Falcon right behind her with his armload of injured woman.

They descended and tried to arrange with Hogback, who had just closed the diner after the noon meal, to drive them home with Rachel tucked in blankets in the back. He refused, apparently fond of his idle time, but let Cheyenne borrow it, on the condition she bring it back tomorrow.

"I don't need to lie down. I can sit on a horse," Rachel said.

Cheyenne ignored the unsteady woman and got her into the back. The fact that Rachel didn't fight over it told Cheyenne how bad the poor agent was feeling.

Cheyenne drove the wagon hitched to Hogback's sway-backed mare. A horse by all appearances as fond of idle time as her master. Falcon rode his horse so he could keep an eye on Rachel and lead the other critters stretched out behind the wagon.

They made slow time because Cheyenne was taking great care.

She was also half expecting gunfire to ring out. She had to wonder if this was all somehow connected. They'd decided the attacks on Kevin and Falcon were related to rustling and a devious plan to kill off the heirs in the midst of the confusion over Clovis's will. But there were too many dry-gulchings. Too many cowards involved in this mess. It seemed like they'd wandered into a gang of outlaws who'd all learned the lowest of skills from each other.

Could Hawkins have known about the thieving? Could he somehow have been involved in it? Could those rustled cattle, a mix of his own Herefords and the Angus from the RHR, have been sent to that canyon with Hawkins's knowledge?

It was too much to get in order right now. She had to get

Rachel home, set Kevin up to guard her, then ride to find Wyatt and Molly and get them out of the Hawkins Ranch before something terrible happened.

Because whatever lies Wyatt had told to get the job, it was almost certain Hawkins knew there was suspicion cast on him. The attempt on Rachel's life by Hawkins's old friend Randall Kingston proved that.

They were a good stretch of the way home when they heard thundering hoofbeats approaching.

"That's the direction of the Hawkins Ranch. Be alert."

Falcon flashed her a huge smile, which was a simple reminder that her husband was always alert. Then he produced his gun with lightning speed and turned to watch who was coming up beside them.

"It's Wyatt and Molly." Falcon holstered his gun. "And Kevin and Win."

Cheyenne, the reins of a plodding single horse well in hand, twisted around to look, and a huge smile broke over her face. "They're leaving the Hawkins Ranch. They must be."

The foursome caught up to Cheyenne.

"Rachel?" Win looked in the wagon, which never stopped its steady forward march.

Win's brow furrowed with worry as Rachel struggled to sit up, then resigned herself to making the trip flat on her back. "What happened? Is she badly hurt?"

"We've got a lot to tell. We were going to get Rachel home, then come and get Wyatt and Molly out of Oliver's clutches. Rachel's been knocked unconscious, but she's coming out of it, somewhat. We hope she'll be all right."

"And shot," Falcon added.

"What?" Win shouted.

Grimly, Wyatt watched their back trail.

"Rachel had to write down the names of the missing women somewhere," Molly said.

Falcon rode up beside her. "She didn't carry much with her. But maybe she's got notes tucked in her satchel."

"We'll look," Wyatt said. "But unless we can find something, until we know names, and hopefully they're the same names as what we found in Hawkins's safe, I'm not sure what to do next."

"You got in the safe?" Cheyenne kept driving.

Nodding, Molly said, "We've got a lot to tell, too. And then we've got a lot to sort out. We're going to need a lot of good luck to put it all together."

"What we *need*," Wyatt said, studying Rachel, "is a Pinkerton agent."

They all looked at Rachel for a time, but she'd settled in to sleep.

Cheyenne was relieved to have all three brothers watching all around. Three skilled men, feeling fully threatened, watching out for trouble. They eased up some when they reached a wide spot in the trail, the forests far enough back no coyote looking for an easy kill would be lying in wait for them here.

"Like I said, there's a lot to tell." Cheyenne set out to tell what had happened, including the connection from Kingston to Clovis to Hawkins.

Wyatt told the tale of what had gone on at the Hawkins Ranch.

Cheyenne eyed the shadow of a bruise forming on Win's face and scowled. "Let me see your arm, Molly."

"Not out here for heaven's sake. I can't pull my sleeve up far enough to show so you're just going to have to wait."

Cheyenne didn't like to admit it, but Molly had a point. It stewed and boiled inside her to see how bad hurt Molly was, and Cheyenne wanted to hurt Oliver Hawkins even more.

"But you got word to the Pinkertons?" Molly picked up the story Cheyenne had spun.

"Yes, according to Rachel, what we sent will let them know she's in trouble. So they should send help. And we've set in motion the investigation of Falcon's ma." Cheyenne looked at Falcon regretfully. The importance of knowing the date she died seemed unfeeling, all about land and money and ownership. But she thought of how young he had been, left alone in a cabin. His ma needing to be buried. It didn't bear thinking of. She wanted to hold him and offer him comfort.

The RHR came in sight, and Cheyenne's heart lifted. So much going on, and now she was home. Home. The law might not say so at the moment, but in her heart this would always be home.

"I think I've figured out what God meant when he said honor your father and mother." Win pressed her hand over her swollen cheek.

They all turned to look at her. It was a question they'd all wrestled with.

"I think God calls us to honor them. But He's given us the Ten Commandments all at the same time. When you consider how many of those commandments our fathers have broken.

Have sneered at every day of their lives. God, well, He wants honor. He wants a soul turned to Him and a life lived faithfully and honorably. I will pray about this, and I will continue to show honor to my father, but only as an example to him. I will live with honor myself. I hope it's with God's understanding and support that I admit I will never trust him. I know him too well."

Kevin reached out. He was on the same side as the bruised cheek, so she had to uncover the bruise to take his hand.

Their hands clutched each other. Their eyes met with love and trust.

It was a private moment, an intimate one. Cheyenne felt as if she was intruding by watching them.

She turned back to her driving, glad to be home.

Glad to have her family together.

TWENTY-ONE

want to see that arm." Wyatt stood in front of Molly like a couple hundred pounds of stubborn.

"Wyatt, I am *not* going to expose—"

"Go upstairs and put something on so you're not exposed. Cheyenne has a short-sleeved shirtwaist if you don't. Put hers on." Wyatt crossed his arms. "We do nothing more until I see how bad he hurt you. And you haven't told us what he did, either."

Wyatt's eyes narrowed as he studied her. "I can see he said or did something that really frightened you. We're trying to be honest here, to clear this up. Molly, don't keep secrets from me."

Molly thought of the terrible secret she was keeping from everyone, even Kevin, secrets that had nothing to do with Oliver Hawkins. A tiny niggling deep inside whispered that maybe, just maybe, this family would help her find a way past the guilt, the nightmares that still jerked her awake at night.

If ever there were people who knew what it was to have trouble with a father, it was this group.

Rachel had stirred when they were lifting her out of the wagon. She insisted on walking up to bed on her own. Falcon humored her until her knees gave out, then he carried her upstairs. Cheyenne had gone up with him, and Molly followed. Cheyenne and Falcon went back down, and Win came up. She stayed with Rachel while Molly decided what needed doing and went downstairs for supplies, only to face a formidable group all lined up.

Kevin, whom she trusted completely, which made her years of lying worse because he deserved better. But honestly her deepest lie was in part to protect him.

Falcon, a wild man, the easiest going of the group, or it might be more accurate to say he was the one who didn't let much upset him. He'd also be the first to tear someone's throat out.

Cheyenne, a dangerous woman, and that's what Molly liked best about her, since she seemed to be on the same side as Molly.

And Wyatt. As soon as she stepped in the kitchen, Wyatt said, "I want to see your arm and hear what Hawkins did to you. Now."

Giving in, since she had little choice, she said, "I've got a dress with buttoned cuffs on the sleeves. I can push those sleeves up high enough. I feel ashamed that he hurt me, and my impulse is not to talk about it. Pretend it didn't happen. But I will. I know this isn't my fault. I'll run up and change."

She was back in a few moments, wearing her blue calico dress sprinkled with white flowers. She came into the room to find them all standing there, muttering to each other. No doubt planning to bury Mr. Hawkins—no, Hawkins, his mister days were over.

They all turned, four in a row, to face her when she came in.

Cheyenne with her arms crossed, angry on Molly's behalf. Wyatt with his fists clenched, with only one person he wanted to punch. Falcon with both hands shoved in his front pockets. Looking mild mannered, a complete deception. Kevin, his lips moving silently, she hoped it was in prayer. This mess could use some prayer.

"It just happened this morning, and he's never put his hands on me before," Molly said. "I can tell you straight out, I was holding a heavy glass pitcher of water in my hands when he grabbed my arm, and I was fully prepared to smash him over the head with it if he didn't let go."

She'd left the buttons of her sleeve undone. She slowly rolled it up, revealing a bruise just above her elbow. Black in the exact shape of Hawkins's fingers. The skin so swollen it was shiny. Four curved slits had broken the skin. They oozed clear liquid. No blood but they were ugly.

Cheyenne growled. Kevin gasped. Falcon's eyes narrowed. Wyatt took two long strides to reach her and gently cradled her arm. His hands, so much bigger than Hawkins's, so much stronger, and yet Wyatt had never touched her except with gentleness.

"It looks awful, doesn't it?" She'd seen it while changing, and frankly, she'd been shocked.

"I'm going to kill him." Wyatt slid one hand gently over the ugly bruise.

"Let's see if we can hang him instead. I'd like the law to

handle this." Molly spoke lightly, hoping to calm Wyatt's savage anger.

"It looks worse than awful." Cheyenne's lips formed a grim line. "You're the doctor. Is there anything we can do to treat this? Or at least reduce the pain?"

"I'll put some ice on it later. I need to see to Rachel."

"Win is with her. Let's get that ice on it now." Wyatt let her go. "I'll get it." He turned and ran outside.

Kevin was next. He slid an arm around her waist. "Molly, tell us what happened. Are there other bruises? Did you fight him? Did he try—try to—to . . ." Kevin gave her a helpless, furious look.

Molly was glad Win was out of the room. This was hard enough to talk about without her knowing her father had done it.

Wyatt came storming back in with what looked like a snowball, which was a pretty good idea.

Cheyenne got a towel. Wyatt put the snow in the towel and spread it into a flat layer. He folded the towel over the snow.

As they worked, Molly said, "He grabbed me but nothing more, which doesn't mean I need more than this to judge him as a brute. There are no more bruises, but believe me, this one is enough."

She thought of how Hawkins had begun to talk to her before Kevin and Win came in. She didn't mention that.

"After he released me, I went and changed my dress because I wanted one with pockets so I could hide those envelopes I found." She'd told them how she'd found them in the safe. "I'd stuck them under the dresser in his room when I heard him coming. When I changed, I saw that my upper arm was red and swollen. The bruise hadn't started to form yet. I was already disgusted with him and frightened of him before I saw how much damage he'd done. I'd already decided not to spend one more night in that house. I intended to leave, whether Kevin and Win had come or not."

She looked at Kevin. "But you came at just the right time. Delivered to me by our faithful heavenly Father. Just as Wyatt came in earlier and lured him away to give me a chance to find that safe in his room."

Wyatt brought the wrapped snow pack to her and pressed it around the bruising until her arm was wrapped. Only then did she realize her arm wasn't just sore, it was hot.

"That really helps." She looked up and met his eyes. "I-I think I'd like to sit for a while and let the ice soothe the pain. Then there's so much to do. I need to get dinner and see to Rachel, then—"

Wyatt rested the tips of his fingers on her lips. After a long moment of silence, he tore his gaze from hers and looked at the witnesses all around them.

"Can you let me talk to Molly alone for just a few minutes?"

"Why?" Kevin's brows lowered into one straight line.

Cheyenne grabbed him by the arm, nice and tight, but Molly knew there would be no bruising. Cheyenne dragged Kevin out of the room. When he resisted, Falcon helped by shoving him, then muttering something to him Molly couldn't hear.

Kevin stretched to look over Falcon's broad shoulder and gave her a shocked look, then he was out of the room.

She turned back to Wyatt.

Still holding the wrap on her arm, he slid his hand along her back and urged her toward the table. "Sit down. Please. I had no idea he'd hurt you so bad, Molly."

She sat, and Wyatt crouched beside her.

"You're not really going to kill him, are you?"

Wyatt's jaw went tight. "No man should harm a woman. In the West, we know that a woman is a rare and wonderful thing. A precious thing. That he would do this to you—" His chin moved as if the words he wanted to say were fighting to get out.

"I want the law to handle this, Wyatt. And not just because I don't want you killing anyone, but because Hawkins deserves to be punished by the law for his crimes." She rested her palm on his cheek. "And killing someone leaves a scar on your soul, Wyatt. I don't want that for you."

Wyatt leaned his head to press his cheek to her hand and closed his eyes. She saw him battle to control his anger, and she saw him win.

Finally, he opened his eyes. He looked calm and kind. "Molly, I've come to your bedroom window night after night."

"Knowing you were coming made the days bearable."

A faint smile curved his lips, but his expression remained solemn. "I've wanted to talk to you of how I feel."

"I know you've wanted to find proof against Hawkins. You didn't need to tell me."

"Hush." He kissed her. It shocked her into silence, which was no doubt his goal.

"Not how I feel about the investigation, or Hawkins, how I feel about you."

She thought of the kiss they'd shared. Thought of waking up in his arms.

She had feelings, too.

"It wasn't right. It wasn't *proper* to have such a talk when we were, well, when we were—were there . . . alone . . . in the night. With you taking such risks, and me just leaving you there in danger all day."

"I wasn't in danger, not really. Not until today. Rachel lived there much longer than I did, and he didn't leave a mark on her. I wonder why he hurt me so much sooner?"

"I think he was getting scared that after she left his home and found Amelia Bishop, the truth of Amelia's fear of him had come out. Then somehow he found out Rachel came back. He must've known, or that lawyer from Casper wouldn't have waylaid her. Hawkins is cruel to women all the time, but it just came out meaner and faster when he was under so much pressure."

Wyatt leaned close and kissed her again.

She really had to tell him to stop doing that. But maybe not just now.

"Every night I controlled the urge to speak of how much I care about you."

"You did?" She cared so much it was frightening, and wonderful.

"Yes, but you can see it was impossible at night, alone as we were, can't you? I didn't want to treat you so disrespectfully."

Molly's heart was feeling as warm as her poor bruised arm. But with her heart, it was a nice kind of warm that she didn't ever want to go away.

Wyatt leaned forward and dropped to his knees. He might

have lost his balance just a bit, but he seemed like he was coming to her as a humble man, a man who wanted something desperately.

"Molly." He was close enough he could have kissed her, but instead, he asked, "Will you marry me?"

She gasped. After a wild surge of hope, common sense returned. "No. I've decided to never marry."

"You said your pa was unkind to your ma, and you didn't want a man to rule over you. But, Molly, I would be good to you. You've known me long enough to believe that, don't you? And if I ever overstepped into unkindness, well, Kevin's right here to beat on me until I behave better."

A laugh escaped her lips, which trembled with the longing to say yes.

"And if I ever overstep into unkindness toward you"— Molly reached out and took his hands—"Cheyenne is here to beat on me until I behave better."

Wyatt grinned.

Their smiles matched for a time, then Molly's faded. "You don't know me, Wyatt. You don't know the woman you are proposing to."

"I don't believe there is anything I could find out about you that would make me change my mind."

She reached a hand to brush the dark hair off his forehead. Her fingers shook. "There are things you should know about me before we decide to marry."

"I'll listen. We can talk about anything you want."

Closing her eyes, Molly drew in a deep breath, let it out, and looked at him again. "Now isn't a good time to talk with everyone one room away and probably listening at the door."

"Then we'll talk later." Nodding, Wyatt added, "We don't have to run to town and get married tomorrow. Just because everyone else around here went from not even courting to deciding to marry to the wedding in about one day doesn't mean we have to."

"Thank you for doing me the honor of asking me. It really is a fine thing to be asked by such a good man. We do need to know each other better. And not because I hesitate to say yes to you, but be-because I'm afraid that once you know me better, you might regret asking."

Hope leapt into his eyes when she said she wanted to say yes. "That's not going to happen, but if you fear it might, then we need to talk everything out. Maybe we can even have the wedding in an orderly way. We could set a date in advance, invite the family, and have a nice meal afterward. You could even have a ring and a bouquet of posies if you had a little notice."

Molly smiled.

"Although posies in Wyoming deep in the fall would be a hard trick." He rose, adjusted the snowy-cold wrap on her arm, and said, "You're not feeding this crew tonight. You are going to rest."

That made her grin, then whisper, "The trouble with that is then I'll have to eat someone else's cooking."

"Falcon said he'd roast a possum if we didn't mind waiting until he went hunting and fetched one around for us."

Molly shuddered.

Then Wyatt whispered, "It'd probably be better than whatever Cheyenne would cook."

"Hey, stop talking about me that way." Cheyenne charged into the room.

Molly smirked at Wyatt. "That's why I'd like time to talk to you in private."

"Don't know why it's so hard for you to fetch a wife around, little brother." Falcon came in and slapped Wyatt on the shoulder. "Easiest thing in the world. I've done it twice now without a speck of trouble."

Cheyenne nodded. "You must be doing something wrong."

Kevin came in and stood at Molly's side. "You need to rest."

"House is gettin' crowded with me and Cheyenne living here." Falcon crossed his arms and looked up like he could see through the ceiling to the upstairs and was counting bedrooms. "You'd have a place to stay if you'd just get hitched to Wyatt and slept in his room."

Molly felt her face heating up, no doubt turning pink.

"There's still a spare room, but it doesn't matter, I'll be up watching over Rachel."

Since Molly didn't get all that much sleep in this house, especially when someone was wounded—and it seemed like there always was someone—she couldn't worry overly about it.

TWENTY-TWO

*I*t'd been four days.

"Why is she so addled?" Win asked as Molly came in with a tray carrying a small bowl of broth. She kept it warm on the stove at all times, ready for Rachel, in one of her wakeful moments, to take even a sip.

Win shook her head. By now they worked well as a team. Win sat on one side of the bed, slid an arm behind Rachel's back, and lifted until she nearly sat up straight. Molly spooned broth into her mouth. Rachel had spells where she was more awake than asleep. Molly stayed with her day and night, because it was during these moments they could get a sip of water into her or a few swallows of broth.

Molly and Wyatt hadn't yet found time for that badly needed talk. She had to make sure he understood that marrying her could ruin his life. They hadn't even found time for less important things. Nothing passed between them that could be called any sort of courtship.

There just wasn't time.

Wyatt had hovered around for two days. Finally, Cheyenne

201

had dragged him off to get some ranching done. Falcon went along. He said he was curious about what there was to the job.

Kevin stayed close because Win did. Right now, he was downstairs making the evening meal as the short days of October faded to an early dusk.

Molly and Win had gotten a ham roasting and a baking of bread ready to slide in the oven, but Kevin was handling everything else. Although they all requested Molly come in at the end and make the gravy. Kevin leaned overly toward lumps.

Molly had several nice visits with Win, and she was coming to respect and enjoy her new sister. She loved that, but honestly that wasn't the person she cared to talk with most.

They'd heard nothing from the Pinkertons. And they'd heard nothing from Oliver Hawkins.

Molly could set her gut to burning just tormenting herself over whether Hawkins had found those envelopes missing. And she'd rage at herself for not taking more of them. The fitful sleep she was getting on a pallet on the floor beside Rachel was haunted by dreams of digging through that safe and Hawkins bursting into the room. Over and over. Sometimes she'd find awful, ugly things in that safe. Her father was there a few times. Her mother once.

Sometimes she'd find custard.

Any of those jerked her out of sleep. And each time she woke up, she was grateful. Exhausted but grateful.

Her arm was feeling better. The bruising was still tender, but the swelling had mostly gone down.

Win's face had been a dull shade of red, now faded to yellow.

"We're quite a pair, aren't we?" Win eased Rachel down after Molly quit forcing liquid into the woman.

"At least my bruises are hidden away." Molly rubbed the bruised arm gently.

"Yes, yours was worse than mine, yet I hesitate to say you are the lucky one of us."

"If only I'd grabbed more of those packets in his safe. I got enough to confirm some of our suspicions, but nothing that comes close to proof. If only—"

"Hush." Win's hand came up. "I'm doing the same thing, so don't get me started. 'If only, if only, if only.' The truth is, Molly, we both did the best we could. You certainly more than me."

"Your father was, I'm very much afraid, getting ready to say something all wrong to me when you and Kevin came in." Molly rubbed her arm again. "The kind of thing that would've forced me to leave right then and there. So I'm just torturing myself by wishing I'd had more time. There was no more time."

Molly suddenly rounded the bed and pulled Win to her feet. She wrapped both arms around her new sister. "I've never been so happy to see anyone in my life as when you and Kevin came to visit."

Win hesitated, then her arms came around Molly. "And I have a family, after a whole lifetime of feeling like an outcast. Avoiding my pa, scared to death he killed my ma. Afraid to say anything." Win's voice broke, and her arms tightened.

There were similarities in Molly's deep secret and Win's. For a moment, Molly teetered on opening her mouth and spilling all her ugly secrets on poor Win.

She might've even done it. She thought Win would understand. But Wyatt had to be first.

The hug lasted longer than any in Molly's life. She whispered, "I've always wanted a sister. Brothers can get to be a
bother sometimes."

For some reason, that set Win to giggling. She pulled back,
and Molly saw tears on her face while she fought down the
laughter.

Molly joined in. No tears, she wasn't prone to them. But
a hug and laughter. There'd been too little of both in her
life for a long time.

They got a hold of themselves and turned to look at their
sleeping patient.

"Why won't she wake up?" Win straightened Rachel's
blanket.

"I don't know, and for all the broth and water we've
forced on her, she's losing weight. I don't know how long
she can go on like this." Molly felt her throat swell a bit,
almost like she could shed a tear. Instead, she cleared her
throat and rounded the bed to pick up the small glass pitcher
that stood empty.

"I'm going to go check on supper. Call if you need anything." Molly wondered if she'd ever get a chance to talk
to Wyatt.

~

Another day passed and another. The lump on the back of
Rachel's head had gone down. She was awake longer but very
confused. She was seeing two of everything, and she couldn't
gather her thoughts enough to discuss the information she

had about the women who had disappeared after working for Hawkins.

Her cheeks were hollow, and her skin had a gray tone that grew worse by the hour. The wound on her chest was healing, and Molly removed the stitches.

Midafternoon on the seventh day since Rachel had been brought home, Molly was in the kitchen while Win and Kevin sat with Rachel. She looked out the window when she heard hooves clopping softly in the deep snow.

A man came riding in on the cold, windswept trail from Bear Claw Pass. Someone she'd never seen before. He was dressed in a buffalo robe and rode a sturdy, high-stepping brown stallion. He led his horse to the barn, and a cowhand came out to meet him. They talked a bit, and the newcomer handed his horse over, then came to the house.

Calling upstairs, she said, "Kevin, someone's here, a stranger."

Her brother's heavy boots pounded down the stairs. She stepped aside, and Kevin went straight to the door and had it open before the stranger could knock.

Without bothering with polite greetings, the man said, "I've come because of the telegram we received from Rachel Hobart. I'm a Pinkerton agent. I'm John McCall from Nevada."

Molly stepped up behind Kevin and looked around his shoulder. She saw cool competence in the man's ice blue eyes.

"Come in," Kevin said. "We were hoping the agency would send some help."

"Is Rachel dead?" From McCall's tone, Molly was sure he knew Rachel and felt grief over the question he'd asked.

"She's not dead." Molly stepped back as McCall came in.

A wave of relief crossed his face that made it hard for her to tell him the rest.

"But we're worried sick about her."

~

Molly poured coffee while Kevin got the notebook they'd found among Rachel's things.

"Her notes are in some kind of code," he said. "We couldn't make much out of them, and she's somewhat addled from a blow to the head."

McCall took the pages and studied them. "It's a type of shorthand. We're all taught it at the Pinkerton Agency, though often an agent only uses it on certain cases when they are undercover."

"So you can read it?"

"Yes."

"Here are the letters I stole from Hawkins's floor safe, the one Rachel told me to search for," Molly said. "She found evidence it existed while she was there. She'd narrowed her search and told me where she suspected it was. Hawkins was coming, so I grabbed a few, hoping he wouldn't notice they were gone."

McCall nodded, intent on listening, then he took the envelopes, read the odd poetry, and switched to reading Rachel's notes.

Before he was done, Wyatt came charging into the house.

When he saw Molly and Kevin sitting at the table with Agent McCall, he stopped so suddenly he skidded.

McCall whirled around. A man ready for trouble, it seemed.

"This is the agent the Pinkertons sent out, John McCall," Molly said. "Agent McCall, this is Wyatt Hunt. He was living at the Hawkins Ranch, working foreman while I worked as Hawkins's housekeeper."

Wyatt blinked. "You got here that fast?"

"Wyatt Hunt." McCall nodded brusquely. "I was told the Hunt family was at the root of this. I live in Nevada, and I work very select jobs out near Virginia City. And I get sent to cases that are near me. The code Rachel had you include in her telegram to the Pinkerton Agency was something an agent would only send through someone else. And only if they were dying. Or too badly hurt to send the wire themselves. They wired me instructions, and I came here afraid I'd find Rachel had died. She's an old friend and a solid agent. It's not like her to run into this kind of trouble."

"It came from a very unexpected direction." Wyatt stepped back into the entry, hung up his coat and hat, tossed his gloves on the floor under them, and came back in.

Molly was up pouring him coffee. He always came in deeply chilled after long hours riding his land, working his herd.

"Have you shown McCall your arm?" Wyatt asked.

McCall's blue eyes went sharp. "What's this?"

"Hawkins hurt her and Win. He grabbed Molly's arm bad enough it was swollen and bruised. After a week, I'd reckon it still looks bad."

Molly refilled everyone's coffee cup as Wyatt told about Hawkins's treatment of her and the connection between Hawkins, Clovis Hunt, and Randall Kingston.

"Your telegram to the agency mentioned that connection

and the school. The Pinkertons notified me that the Jeffers House of Refuge for Young Men is a prison."

"What?" Molly almost dropped the boiling hot coffeepot on Wyatt's lap.

He dodged the pot, took it from her, and set it firmly on the stove.

"Tennessee, like a lot of states, started opening special prisons to keep the younger criminals separated from the adults. The rule had been to just toss them all in together, but it's an ugly business putting youngsters in with adult men. Often boys who might be reformed end up as hardened criminals before they've served their sentences."

"Do you know what they did? How they ended up there?" Kevin asked.

"The details are supposed to reach me in a letter. I had a whole packet of information waiting for me in Bear Claw Pass, and they'll send more as they find it."

McCall looked out the window at the swirling snow. "I hope it comes soon because I need to solve this and get out of here. My wife, Penny, is expecting our second child, and if I have to spend the winter on this side of the Rocky Mountains, snowed in away from her, she's going to make me regret it for years." Then he grinned. "The only reason she didn't come with me is because she's about seven months gone on a baby. She's worked as a Pinkerton agent, too, from time to time. She enjoys tracking down bad men."

The grin convinced Molly he wasn't all that afraid of his wife.

"Can I study Rachel's notes for a while? If there's enough here, we can go arrest Hawkins, dig through his safe for the rest of his rotten poetry, and hang him high. Then I'll send Rachel back to Chicago and go home."

He made it sound like he could accomplish it all today. Molly was glad to keep quiet, hoping he could manage that.

McCall read Rachel's notes quickly, taking notes himself. Then he read them again more slowly and reread the poetry from Hawkins, studying the contents of each packet.

Cheyenne and Falcon came in just as McCall set the notes aside. They stared suspiciously at the newcomer while Wyatt introduced them and caught them up on the Jeffers House of Refuge.

"It's time to bring the sheriff in on it and arrest Hawkins," McCall said. "We can do it tomorrow morning, and anyone who wants to ride along is welcome."

Everyone wanted to come.

TWENTY-THREE

*T*he weather, colder every day, gave everyone an appetite, so they ate supper before they continued talking about the case.

Molly set the cobbler and a stack of small bowls on the table, then she got a small pitcher of cream.

McCall ate a bite of the cobbler, closed his eyes as a look of bliss crossed his face, and sighed with delight. "My wife is a fine cook, Miss Garner. But this is the best cobbler I've ever had."

"You should taste her custard," Wyatt said. "There's nothing else like it in this world."

Molly smiled.

McCall ate a few more bites. "I was an experienced agent long before Rachel joined the Pinkertons. I worked with her a few times before I moved out west. We have very few women as agents, and we are protective of them. When they feared Rachel might be dead, I was closest, and they wired me and asked me to come. The telegram had a few particulars about the case, and Mr. Pinkerton himself sent a packet by the first train headed west in hopes it would arrive by the time I did. I picked it up in Bear Claw Pass before I came out to the ranch. It contained every fact they had, including the information about the Jeffers school, which was new, and the information Rachel had dug up about the other missing housekeepers. But we didn't have the pieces of the puzzle you found, Miss Garner, or Rachel's exact notes."

"Rachel told me what to look for." Molly felt her cheeks turning pink. It was wrong to take credit while Rachel lay upstairs unconscious.

"And you said there are more packets? Can you guess how many more?"

Molly thought hard, then lifted her hands helplessly. "I just grabbed those you have and shut the safe. I don't know how deep the safe is, so there's no way to guess how many packets he had. He was coming fast. I should have gotten more. I should have—"

"No, you did exactly right. Taking just a few increases our chances that your investigating hasn't been detected by Hawkins. According to Rachel's notes, the two new names you found are of his former housekeepers. And the objects he kept are mementos of those women. The poems about missing them, written as they are, this is the kind of thing we sometimes see in men who seem to live a fairly normal life, then kill for . . . well, for pleasure."

Cheyenne scowled. Win moaned and buried her face against Kevin's arm.

Molly gasped. "That's just sickening. I can't believe there are such people."

"One of the things that is off about this case is that men who do that don't usually let years pass between victims,"

McCall said. "That's why I asked about the number of packets. If he is that kind of sick killer, then it's very unlikely he's
killed only three women."

"Only?" Wyatt's brows shot up.

"Yes, according to this, we have multiple women who
died or went missing while they were involved in some way
with Hawkins." McCall nodded at Win. "That includes your
mother, Mrs. Hunt. I'm sorry to discuss such things in front
of you."

Kevin's arm came around Win. She turned, her face now
resting on his shoulder, and said, "If it's true, then I want
him found out. I want him to pay for killing my mother."

McCall studied her expression for a few seconds then,
reluctantly, nodded. "The Hannah he mentions most likely
refers to Hannah Monroe, a woman who worked as a housekeeper for your father right after he sent you off to school,
Mrs. Hunt."

"Please, call me Win. There are too many Mr. and Mrs.
Hunts at this table."

With a quick smile, McCall said, "That's true. Everyone,
actually, except Miss Garner."

"Make it Molly," Molly offered.

"Then it's John." John referred to his notes. "She worked
there until she moved on, according to Rachel, but there was
no record of her after her time there."

"Then Lydia was employed there, too?" Win asked, her
voice quiet but steady.

"Yes, Rachel found a record of a Lydia Trenear. She was
known a bit around town. A faithful church attender, and
she wrote steadily to an elderly uncle back east. When her

letters stopped, the uncle was in failing health, and though he made some inquiries, he died before he could find out what became of her. He talked with the police. He was sure she'd come to a bad end somehow, or else she would have written. He made enough noise there was a record of her connection to Hawkins.

"Rachel has very thorough notes, including information from Amelia Bishop and from her own experience. Amelia most certainly believed she was in danger. Now we have your information, Molly, and the injury to your arm."

"I'm mostly healed." Molly heard herself trying to diminish how badly she'd been hurt. She still felt ashamed. Trying to study that strange truth, she remembered how her ma had tried to have the house and meals just so to keep Pa happy. As if his violent treatment were her fault. Ma had felt ashamed, too. Molly knew it wasn't right. This was not her shame, so she squared her shoulders and refused to take any blame.

John looked as if he could read all that flashed through her mind. "If your bruises aren't healed after a week, then that tells us a lot about how bad they were. And we have an eyewitness account from your family of how serious they were. Yes, I've got enough to ask the sheriff to arrest him, and if the sheriff hesitates, then I'll take him into custody myself. Through the influence of Amelia's father, we have the support of the Wyoming territorial governor in this, and I've been sworn in to work with the authority of the US Marshal's office. So I can make an arrest myself. Then we'll search that safe, see what other evidence we find. That will bolster our case."

Molly's spirits lifted. John McCall was going to handle this, and Hawkins would pay for his crimes.

She looked forward to the day.

"I didn't ask questions in Bear Claw Pass. I thought it was wise to come out here first and talk to all of you, find out who I could trust. I'd like to get Hawkins arrested tomorrow. I'll head home as soon as I'm sure Rachel is all right."

"I'm better every minute."

Everyone whirled to look at the door to the stairway. Rachel, pale and wobbly, stood there in her nightgown. It should have been outrageous for her to appear dressed as she was, but instead the whole room broke into motion.

Molly charged forward to lend an arm. John was up and at Rachel's side in seconds.

"John McCall, our agent from the Wild West. They sent you?"

"Yep." He slid an arm across her back. "Are you up to sitting?"

Rachel nodded, but neither Molly nor John quit supporting her.

John guided her forward. "Come join us at the table."

"The food smells wonderful, Molly. If you think I dare risk it, I'd love some."

"You're long overdue for a good meal." Molly smiled. Her relief was matched only by her delight. "Come and join us. We had chicken stew, which is just a bit up from chicken soup. I think you can have some."

Rachel sat down in the chair John had been sitting in.

"I've been on a train and now at the table for so long it feels good to stand," he said. He quickly ran through all he'd found again.

Rachel listened and added a few details that she hadn't yet written down, especially about Randall Kingston.

"He's being held in Casper," Cheyenne said. "They already arrested him for shooting you, but they were waiting to see if the charges would rise to the level of murder."

Rachel paused her eating and scowled for a bit. "Glad I couldn't accommodate them about the murder. But I'd like to know how much he knew about Hawkins. We might be able to question Kingston in a way that makes it possible to charge him as aiding in all of Hawkins's crimes, including murder."

Silence fell as Rachel ate. John retrieved his cobbler and leaned against the kitchen wall.

Into the silence, Molly asked, "So which one of those men shot Wyatt?"

That got everyone's attention.

"I've sort of figured it was one of the outlaws Cheyenne and Falcon shot," Wyatt said. "Two men died when they brought those rustlers in. They weren't all accounted for when we were hunting Ralston."

"I thought so, too," Cheyenne said. "It'd be real tidy if the man who shot you was dead. But the way Kingston shot Rachel was so similar to how you were shot, it really made us wonder."

"If Kingston and Clovis are brothers, Kingston should have been loyal to Wyatt," John said. "Clovis managed to have three sons, and he cared enough about you all to leave you land. Why would his brother try to kill you?"

"Did Pa really care?" Kevin asked quietly. "Or did he want to flaunt how he'd fooled everyone? What better way than, after he was dead, to let his big secret out of the bag. It was a way to hurt Cheyenne, too, and take a big old gouge outa Katherine Hunt, his third and final wife, who made no secret of her contempt for him."

"So Clovis left the land to his young'uns," John said. "That still doesn't explain why they'd hurt Wyatt. Or which one of them did it."

"My dislike of my pa was no secret. Could that be enough?" Wyatt asked.

John came to Rachel's side of the table. "You're one of the best agents we have. How do you read this?"

"Kingston might admit to my shooting under questioning. Shooting a woman is a serious business out west and nowhere more so than in Wyoming Territory, where women have the right to vote. If we convince him he's going to hang, he might be willing to admit to a second shooting—again with no one dying—to escape the noose."

"Especially if we can prove he knew about Hawkins being a murderer and covered it up. Those would be hanging offenses." John took his last bite of cobbler.

"He might turn on Hawkins to keep from having his neck stretched." Falcon looked at Wyatt. At Kevin. "We've all been shot in this mess."

"But you and Kevin were shot by the rustlers."

That gained another lengthy silence.

"Hawkins couldn't have been in on rustling his own cattle, could he?" John asked.

"Except, *did* he rustle his own cattle, or were the bulk of them from the RHR, and he just ran some of his cattle in with them?" Wyatt asked. "Or maybe turned a blind eye when his men did it, as long as they left his main herd alone?"

Shaking his head at all the pieces that needed to fit together, John said, "We'll arrest Hawkins tomorrow and see about bringing Kingston over here to face charges. While Hawkins is in jail, we'll search his house and see what else is in that safe."

Rachel finished her chicken stew and managed a small bowl of cobbler. Then she said, "After a week in bed it feels foolish, but I need to get some rest."

"Let me help you back upstairs," John said. "I'd like a moment of time talking in private."

Kevin and Win began washing the dishes. Molly cleared the table and wondered what John McCall didn't think he could say in front of all of them.

TWENTY-FOUR

*W*yatt hitched up the buggy the next morning. They didn't use it often because they usually either rode horseback or needed a wagon to bring home supplies. But Rachel, worn down but determined to go, needed the easiest ride they could find for her.

When they arrived at Sheriff Corly's office, Wyatt was surprised to find him talking to Sheriff Gatlin from Casper.

Both men greeted them in a friendly way, but whatever they were talking about ended.

"We've got an investigation going that concerns Randall Kingston, the man who shot Rachel Hobart," Sherriff Corly said.

Gatlin's eyes shifted to Rachel. "I'm glad you're doing well, miss. Real glad."

"How's Kingston?" she asked.

"That's what I'm over here for." Gatlin nodded at the jail cell. Stretched out, sleeping like an innocent child, was Randall Kingston.

"We would've come back to talk to you, Greg. You didn't

need to haul him over here." Cheyenne stepped forward and offered her hand to Gatlin. "But I'm glad you did. We've got some serious questions for Kingston, and they concern our interest in having Oliver Hawkins arrested."

Wyatt noticed both John McCall and Rachel eased back and let Cheyenne do the talking. It was smart of them. Let the locals, who were well known to both sheriffs, open this ball.

"Hawkins?" Corly leaned forward and placed both hands flat on his desk. "What did he do?"

Cheyenne did some fast talking to explain why they were after Hawkins. She showed them the notes Molly had found.

Wyatt noticed the word *found*. Which skipped over some important details.

Corly had some sharp questions for Rachel, and she took over. Wyatt noticed her clear, calm way of talking about all she'd found. She produced her notes and talked about the Jeffers House of Refuge.

"And Kingston is connected because we've found proof he, Clovis, and Hawkins knew each other, might even be brothers. They've been real careful to keep that a secret," Cheyenne said.

"I can tell you right now, Hawkins was a regular visitor to Kingston and so was Clovis," Gatlin said. "I never thought much of it, but now that Kingston shot someone, and with your suspicions about a connection between them, brothers makes sense. A connection they kept quiet."

"We're expecting a letter with more details about Jeffers, but it's not here yet," Rachel said.

"We haven't checked this morning. I'll go." John darted out of the building.

"The letter will tell us what sent them to prison as youngsters. What we do know is that they filtered into this country one at a time. Hawkins first with his young wife and child." Rachel gestured at Win. "Then Clovis, who took up with Katherine Brewster and married her faster than was wise. And a while later, Randall Kingston with his wealth and no real ability to explain where it came from. Their goal was to cheat people, and all three of them have been real successful at it."

"Kingston wasn't much liked in Casper," Sheriff Gatlin said. "Finding out he's gotten his money in a dishonest way wouldn't surprise none of us."

John came in carrying a packet of papers. "I've been reading as I walked and found out Clovis and Randall Hunt and Jethro Pervis were brothers sent to the boys' prison—and make no mistake, that's what it was, not some school for orphans or such."

"Pervis?" Wyatt asked. "One of the brothers had a different name?"

"Looks like it. It doesn't say why."

"Jethro must've changed his name to Oliver," Falcon said.

"You said Randall had eyes that matched Pa's and ours," Kevin said. "I bet we'll find out their pa married a woman with a son. Oliver doesn't look like the other two."

"Randall was a known thief in his small town." John went on reading. "Clovis had cheated a few honest folks, and they'd forgiven him. But all three of them got arrested at once when it was . . . was . . ."

John looked up. His eyes locked on Win.

"Go ahead." Win squared her shoulders. "I already believe the worst about him."

"Your pa killed his parents."

Win turned away. Kevin pulled her against his chest and held on tight.

A line of furrows appeared on John's brow as he looked between Win and the letter.

"We need to hear the rest of it," Kevin said quietly.

John nodded. "Their pa had a mean temper and was given to taking a fist to them. Their ma was quick with a switch, too. The townsfolk knew it, and that's why they let the boys get away with small crimes many times, felt sorry for them. But when their parents went missing, folks noticed because their pa was always at the saloon. He swept up in there and kept his family fed but only just."

"How long were they missing?" Sheriff Corly asked.

"About a week. Finally, a sheriff came to the house, and the boys all claimed their parents had run off, abandoning them. But the sheriff didn't believe it. It didn't take long to find two graves dug in the root cellar. The boys' story changed, and they claimed their folks killed each other, and the boys' only part in it was burying them. But the questioning went on until Randall confessed that Oliver had killed them in their sleep. They all three got sent to Jeffers. But they were young, and there was some sympathy for them, so they stayed a few years, finished growing up, got fed better than they had at home, and learned to read and cipher. Then they were let loose."

John looked up. "Clovis had been out a year when he

married your ma, Falcon. Randall and Oliver left the area. I suspect they headed north, got rid of their Tennessee accents, and set out to get rich however they could."

"Oliver was always the worst of us." A voice turned them all around. They watched Randall Kingston sit up on the cot in the jailhouse. He rubbed both hands over his face. "I was a thief. Clovis a liar and a cheat. Oliver a killer. A fine lot we were. The one thing we came away from our childhood with was loyalty to each other. That's why I've kept quiet about Oliver all these years. I had my doubts about how his wife died, but I wasn't around and didn't really know about it. I could let myself believe she'd died birthing a child. I never heard tell of the housekeepers."

Wyatt wondered how long Randall had been awake. And he wondered how good a liar he was. Good enough to talk his way out of that jail cell by turning on his brother? "Why'd you shoot Rachel?"

Randall's eyes came to Wyatt. Cold eyes. The same golden brown as his. Only Randall's were cold as the grave.

"Oliver told me she'd shot you. And tried to kill him. He'd heard she was back around."

"How'd he hear? She slipped in at night and stayed to the house."

Randall's jaw tightened. "We have someone who keeps an eye out at your place. Youngster named Jesse."

Cheyenne and Wyatt had matching expressions of rage.

"He looks in the windows when he can. He saw her. Heard your plan to ride to White Rock Station and the trail you'd use. Jesse told Oliver. Oliver told me she was coming back to kill him. I set out to stop her."

"We've got a hand we need to fire." Cheyenne's voice could out-cold Randall's eyes any day of the week.

"I'm glad you survived it, Miss Rachel. I know a few other things, but I'm not saying another word until I'm sure I'm not going to hang for what I done. And I don't want to spend any more time in a cell."

Wyatt looked around the group. A lot of purely suspicious expressions in this room. None of them believed Randall was all that innocent.

"What's more . . . I know . . . well, no." Randall's eyes went flinty. "I'm not saying another word. Except you're going to need my help, and you're not going to get it unless I can walk free from this jail cell." Randall glared at Sheriff Gatlin for a long minute, then he turned sideways to lie down on the cot.

Despite questions, he refused to say another word.

TWENTY-FIVE

*T*hey didn't all go charging out to the Hawkins Ranch.

Molly had to go because she knew exactly where the safe was. Win stayed behind because she couldn't stand to be part of it. Kevin stayed behind because he couldn't leave Win alone and unprotected, and he didn't count Sheriff Gatlin, who stayed behind to guard Kingston and protect Win. Rachel stayed because the ride to town had worn her out.

Wyatt knew exactly how many hands were working out there, and the caliber of men they were. He'd assured everyone there'd be no shooting trouble from the cowhands. They were too lazy to fight for the brand. None from Hawkins, either, unless there was a chance to do some back-shooting.

Molly bent low over the saddle, the horse's hooves pounding as they galloped at full speed. Wyatt had gained the lead because he had a fine stallion to ride, McCall right with him, but the rest of them were close behind. Everyone wanted to be a part of bringing Hawkins to justice.

He was a killer. That's what his older brother had called him.

"I was a thief. Clovis a liar and a cheat. Oliver a killer."

Kingston had said that. And he'd been so calm about it. *"I was a thief."* A hard thing to say about yourself, especially when you want to get out of jail. But compared to being a killer, he probably thought it sounded decent. Even knowing he'd shot Rachel—and there she'd stood, looking him in the eye—the man thought he had something they'd bargain for.

"Clovis a liar and a cheat." Well, seeing as how three brothers had lived a life created through Clovis's lying and cheating, they had to agree with that description.

"Oliver a killer." Those words had come out as if it was a childhood chant that he'd known all his life.

Thief, cheat, killer. A dark legacy for one family to dole out into the world.

Molly wondered what Kingston had meant by "you're going to need my help." What did that man know?

Even as they galloped toward the Hawkins Ranch, Molly felt like they were too late. Kingston had an ominous attitude, as if he was sure they didn't know everything.

"Be on the lookout for someone shooting from cover," Wyatt shouted. "That'd be Hawkins's way."

Wyatt and Falcon rode side by side. They were busy, looking at any spot where boulders and woodlands came close to the trail. Molly smelled dirt from the trail and the cold damp of snow, kicked up by the horses in front of her. They rode southeast away from town, and the wind kicked swirls of snow across the trail. Wind bit at her cheeks, and they felt pink and chapped.

Despite the cold and their terrible mission, it was a day of breathtaking beauty. The mountains rose up before them, and the sun, fully risen but still low in the eastern sky, painted snowcapped mountains in shades of orange and pink, against a sky so blue it made her heart ache.

A magnificent land, Wyoming Territory. One she'd like to have for a home. If they could just get all the danger settled. Not counting blizzards, of course. Or cattle stampedes or rattlesnake bites. But those she'd face. It was the danger that came from evil men targeting her family that she wanted to end.

With the thundering hoofbeats as the music to drive them along, she thought of secrets from her own past and urged more speed from her horse, as if running away from the truth. She heightened her vigilance, looking all around for danger. She'd ridden to the Hawkins Ranch from the RHR when she'd gone there to work. She'd never ridden there from town. She knew nothing of the dangerous parts of this trail, so all she could do was keep her eyes open, keep up, and keep praying.

The trail was wide, and she suspected they didn't take the shortest route, so they could avoid certain spots.

One thing she did know, Wyatt had been riding for town when he'd been shot. He'd split up from Falcon and Cheyenne, who had followed Ralston's trail. Wyatt had chased after Rachel, thinking she was part of the gang with Ralston. Now they were riding from town to the Hawkins Ranch. The place Wyatt had been shot was around here somewhere.

They kept moving fast and were going at a full gallop when they charged into Hawkins's ranch yard. No one had

226

attacked them along the way. And now that they'd arrived, no one poked a head out of the barn or bunkhouse.

The whole place had an abandoned look about it.

Wyatt swung down and hitched his horse by the back door. By the time Molly dismounted, Wyatt had the door open and was inside, shouting Hawkins's name.

"Falcon, Cheyenne." Molly rushed after Wyatt. "Hawkins is usually in his office. Check there. I'm going to look at his safe."

There were unwashed dishes in the sink. Dried, burnt food in pans on the stove. It looked a lot like it had when she'd started as a housekeeper here.

Pounding up the stairs with Wyatt on her heels, she found a mess. Clothes strewn about. The bed unmade. Ignoring all that, she went straight to the safe, dropped to her knees beside the dresser, and flipped open the cunningly hidden floorboard.

Sheriff Corly came into the room behind Wyatt, and Molly was glad he was here. She wanted a witness to what was in the safe. Someone who didn't have a grudge against Hawkins, as she knew every member of the family did.

John was a step behind him.

Reaching in, she dialed the combination and opened the iron safe. It was still full of packets. Whatever had happened, Oliver hadn't taken time to clean it out.

"Sheriff, you take these out. I want you to know I haven't done a thing to tamper with them."

The sheriff knelt beside her and drew out envelope after envelope.

"Did he create a packet and write a poem for each woman he killed?" Wyatt crouched beside the sheriff.

"B-but there are a dozen or more of them." Molly eased

back. She pressed her hand to her twisting stomach. To think of so many murders.

"The top one says your name, Miss Garner." The sheriff held it up for her to read. "And there's one for Miss Hobart. Those show he intended harm but didn't do murder."

"Because we got away," Molly said grimly.

The sheriff nodded. "Let's hope more of these packets are the same." He got everything out of the safe, then lifted all the contents up to spread them across the top of the dresser.

"This is the one down the farthest," the sheriff said. "It's got two names on it. A man and a woman. Last name Hunt."

"He kept a record of his parents' murders?" Molly didn't look anymore. The rest of them, save Falcon and Cheyenne, who hadn't come up yet, began combing through what they'd found.

"The next one has his wife's name on it." Wyatt tore open the sealed letter and pulled a small painting out. He held it up, a small oval painting about two inches wide and maybe three high. "The woman in this picture looks a lot like Win. And there's a poem.

"*My beloved wife, my betrayer.*
 My heart aches for what she made me do.
 No greater serpent have I nurtured to my bosom,
 save my own mother.
 Do not ask my forgiveness for you are not worthy.
 Now I must go on alone."

"He's blaming her." John reread the poem with a cynical scowl on his face. "In my work, I've found it's typical that an abusive man blames the woman. Whatever he did, however she ended up dead, he blames her for it."

"Hawkins makes no mention of his wife dying birthing a child," Wyatt added.

The sheriff said grimly, "I consider this poem as good as a confession." He looked at John.

Molly felt the lawmen banding together. It was a little annoying considering she'd been something of a lawman herself while in Hawkins's house. Plus, she'd found the safe and now opened it.

She wasn't going to be left out. "We should search the house. I've always wondered what's on the third floor."

"And we should take his account books." Wyatt sounded like he didn't like being left out, either.

"If he's run away, where would he go?" Molly wondered out loud. "Could he have a hideout right here in the house?"

"Rachel looked at the floor plans and talked to one of the men who helped build it," John said. "She hasn't specifically said there isn't a hidden room, but she'd've mentioned it if there was something like that on the plans. And she found both safes, so they knew she was wondering what he might be hiding."

"I'm surprised the builders talked that much," Sheriff Corly said.

"I asked Rachel about that, and she said Hawkins was tightfisted, slow to pay his bills, and, in the end, cut back on what he paid by complaining about shoddy workmanship."

Everyone took a moment to look around the oversized bedroom. The house was splendid and still standing in very good shape twenty years after it was built.

"Yep," Wyatt muttered, "I'll bet they didn't mind gossiping about him."

"The account books are a good idea, Wyatt," John said. "I'm going down to fetch them."

Wyatt handed him a strip of paper. "The top number is the combination to the downstairs safe, and there was more in there than just account books."

"I'll bring everything. I'll look through his desk, too."

Wyatt told John which picture to look behind.

John went downstairs. The rest of them went to the door to the third floor. Molly remembered the sounds she'd heard from up there, the feeling of the house being haunted. Could Hawkins be upstairs? Molly, more curious than honestly believing Hawkins was there, tried the door. It was locked.

After fiddling for a few seconds, Wyatt pulled his gun and shot the lock off. The door opened on a narrow flight of stairs. As her head rose to the level of the next floor, she heard a strange sound coming straight for her and ducked so hard she fell backward. She shrieked, then Wyatt's strong arms clamped around her, steadying her.

Glancing over her shoulder, she said, "There's something up there."

He plunked her on her feet, drew his gun again, stared up into the stairwell for a long moment, and then holstered his gun. "It's a pigeon."

Molly was a step above him. They were the only two that had come up this far. "He's got a pigeon in a house this well built?"

"Maybe there's a broken window."

There was no wind, but the small peaked attic was cold. Of course, it was unheated in Wyoming in October.

Wyatt slipped past her and went on upstairs.

John McCall appeared at a run at the base of the closed staircase. "I heard a gunshot, then a scream. Trouble?"

Molly smiled down to see him putting his gun away. "No, the door was locked, and Wyatt shot it open. There's a pigeon up here. It startled me. I'm sure it's—"

"A pigeon." John came up the stairs at a jog. Molly heard the distinctive coo of a pigeon. Wings continued to flutter in the space overhead.

Molly hustled to get to the top of the stairs because John was coming fast. He seemed fascinated.

Molly had no fondness for birds diving at her head.

"One got out of its cage, but there are more." Wyatt pointed at the window in the east wall.

John strode toward an elaborate wire birdcage with many small coops sized for one bird.

Once Molly looked there, she saw several more pigeons. Then she looked around the attic and saw crates and trunks, stacks of unidentifiable things. What looked like massive shrouded pictures leaned against a wall. Molly wondered if Win knew these things were here.

A light pattering sound drew Molly's attention from the stacks of things lining the attic to see John throw something. The pigeons got very busy eating.

"He had pet birds." Molly glared at the poor things. "And he just abandoned them when he ran? That's awful."

John tossed what must be feed on the floor, and the flying pigeon went for it fast. As hungry as the others.

"It's awful for that rattlesnake Hawkins but good for us."
John rubbed his hands together. "We'll use them to find
Hawkins without letting Kingston out of jail. It doesn't suit
me to let a man shoot Rachel in the heart and him not go to
jail and stay there."

"Aw, now, John, don't be fussing about it," Wyatt said sar-
castically. "She got over that shot to the heart mighty fast."

"You're right." John went to study the coop and the
frantically eating birds with a mean smile on his face. "I'm
petty and spiteful. One little old bullet to the heart of my
coworker, and I'm holding a grudge."

"I think it's a little strange that I lived in this house for
two weeks and never knew he had pets, was never asked to
feed them. He made me do everything and never lifted a
finger to help. I wondered why he wasn't making me dust
up here. But I didn't ask about it. I just thought the house
was so large he'd closed part of it off. All I felt was relief."

She looked again at the stacks of things stuffed in here. Glad
she hadn't been set to the task of dusting all of it. "I realize
now he was *insistent* that I leave the third floor alone. He made
it sound like he was easing my work, but I'd say, he didn't want
me to see he had pigeons. I heard rustling up here, too. It was
spooky, but I thought maybe the house creaked in the wind
or he had rats. Why would he keep these birds a secret? And
how in the world can pigeons help us keep Kingston in jail?"

"They can help," John said with cool satisfaction, "because they're not regular pigeons, they're homing pigeons.
I'd bet anything if I let one of these birds out of that cage
and shooed it out the open window, it'd guide us straight
to Hawkins's hideout."

232

"You're assuming he's got a hideout and these birds would know to fly there." Wyatt looked skeptical.

"What I'm assuming"—John crouched by the pigeons, studying them—"is that if three brothers lived within a few miles of each other and no one ever realized they were connected, they had to have a place to meet."

"Sheriff Gatlin said they were seen together in Casper," Wyatt reminded him.

"Yes, and the fact that no one mentioned them being brothers when they got together over there is all the more proof that they had some other way to communicate."

"It makes sense, I guess." Molly tried to fit it all together. "If this madness could ever make sense."

"Communicating with homing pigeons explains how Kingston knew which trail Rachel would be on," John said. "I'll bet the Hunt family talked about it at the house the night before they left. Someone overheard it and let Hawkins know. He sent a message to Kingston."

"Homing pigeons?" Molly scratched her head. "I've never heard of such a thing."

"We sometimes called them war pigeons."

"War pigeons?"

"Yes, they were used in the war," John said. "The Pinkertons have used them to communicate over long distances when there's no telegraph available."

"If we let them out, you say they'll fly to some hideout, but won't they fly to Casper instead?" Molly asked.

"My guess is these men have trained some to do one thing, some another." John kept feeding the birds. "You let them nest somewhere for a while, and they claim it as their home, then you take them a great distance away and release them. They'll fly back and forth. I'm not sure of all the training because I never did that part, but once they are trained, you can tie a small message to their legs. They can fly a message as far as a hundred miles, and they can make the trips more than once a day, depending on how far they have to travel. I spent a lot of time at sea, and we could take the pigeons and send messages to headquarters. No matter where the ship went to that pigeon would go home to head-quarters."

Molly came to his side and started helping toss handfuls of grain in the coop. "Six of them. You think we can follow them?"

"Yes, I hope so, if we release one at a time. Watch it, do our best to keep up, then if we lose it, we release another one. Most likely there are pigeons in Kingston's house, too. We'll need to go to Casper and take care of them."

"Falcon can probably figure out which direction Hawkins headed."

Falcon came in just as Wyatt offered his services, Cheyenne right behind. "We'll get started searching out which tracks are Hawkins's."

The sheriff looked skeptically at the pigeons and said, "I'm a fair hand at tracking. I'll help find Hawkins's trail."

"Let's take all of the birds. We even have something to haul them in." John pointed to a small wooden crate in one corner. "We'll let the sheriff and Falcon lead us down Hawkins's trail for as long as we can follow it, then let one pigeon go and just see. If they all head straight for Casper, then I don't suppose they'll be of any use. But if some go another direction, we'll follow until we lose sight of it. If there are enough pigeons, we can keep releasing them until we reach our man."

"Wyatt, is there a wagon here?" Falcon asked. "We can haul the crate more easily in that. If he's got horses and livestock and he's on the run, we'll need to tend his critters."

"He's got chickens and a few pigs besides the horses and cattle. It doesn't look like there's a hired man on the place. Either they left when they realized Hawkins did, or he fired them all and abandoned his animals to starve in their pens." Wyatt scowled. "I'll see to a wagon, and Hawkins favors a chestnut mare. I should be able to tell if he chose that horse and can pick out her tracks."

Wyatt, Cheyenne, and Falcon followed the sheriff as he left the attic, leaving Molly alone with John.

"A man like that, who hurts women"—Molly crouched down to pet one of the hungry birds—"he's not going to be concerned with the animals God gave him to care for. Just the opposite. He may enjoy knowing he left them behind to suffer."

"We've got work to do, and we need to be on our way soon." John opened the crate and caught the pigeon that'd been loose. It was frantically pecking at the grain he'd tossed on the floor. He caged it and dropped in more grain. Though he closed the lid of the crate, Molly felt certain the tame and hungry bird would have stayed in the cage, lid open or not.

Gently, he transferred each of the birds from their neatly built coop to the crate. And with the bottom of the crate solid, he could pick it up and let them eat. A couple of them fluttered their wings, and there were some of the pigeons' familiar coos. But they were more pets than wild, and they accepted the transfer as if it'd happened many times before.

Molly grabbed the other end of the crate.

Every few steps, Molly squeaked, but she kept coming. They went down three flights of stairs.

"Are the pigeons pecking your fingers?" John did the hard part, backing down the stairs, bearing most of the weight, though it was more awkward than heavy.

Molly grinned. "I've been ignoring it the best I can. I'm sorry about the squeaking. But my first reaction was to drop the crate, and I didn't. Consider yourself lucky."

"I wanted to drop it, too," John said with a smile. "But I managed not to drop it or squeak so I'm feeling pretty good about myself."

Molly laughed. She liked the Pinkerton agent and wondered about his family. How did they all manage such an unusual career?

They got outside just as Wyatt pulled a small buckboard up in front of the door.

Falcon came running in from the north, silent in his handmade moccasins. "The chestnut mare Wyatt mentioned headed northwest. Away from Bear Claw Pass and Casper. We can follow Hawkins's tracks for now and only release the pigeons if we lose the trail."

TWENTY-SIX

A bullet crashed through the window of the jailhouse. Sheriff Gatlin flew backward, slammed into the wall, and sank to the floor, a bright patch of crimson blood blooming on his chest.

Kevin grabbed Win as another bullet exploded. Spinning to protect her, he felt the bullet hit. Thinking only of her, he dragged her to the floor as Rachel dove behind the sheriff's desk.

Falling, he covered Win to protect her, but his weight was out of his control, everything was. Then blood trickled past his face as it dripped from somewhere. He was foggy. He clawed at his pistol, dragged it out of the holster, and fumbled so it slid under the sheriff's desk.

His eyes dropped shut. He sagged on top of Win.

The jailhouse door crashed open and thudding footsteps rushed in. Echoing as if from a long distance.

Kevin heard Win scream. He fought the odd weakness, but he couldn't move, couldn't think. Then Win was gone, jerked out from under him. He heard the prisoner holler, a happy sound for someone locked up.

"You got 'em both."

"Move fast." Kevin recognized Oliver Hawkins's voice. "Folks in town heard the shots. Bring the women. No one'll shoot through them."

Kevin faded away to the sound of his wife screaming his name. Darkness pulled him under.

～

"Pure rock." Falcon scowled at the ground.

"We've got a direction," Wyatt said, "and it figures there's a trail up."

They'd been pushing hard all morning. Molly had watched a mountain loom closer with every mile. Her stomach twisting with dread that they'd have to somehow climb the monster. But if Hawkins rode through here, then it stood to reason there must be a way. But it was all sheer rock, steep and treacherous.

"If we release a pigeon, it's just gonna fly straight over the mountain. It won't help us at all." The sheriff tore his hat off his head and whacked his leg.

"It'll tell us if we've got mountain climbing to do." John dismounted and came for the crate.

"Whatever else is ahead, there's no trail a buckboard can handle." Wyatt climbed down off the seat.

John opened the crate lid just a crack, reached in, and gently eased out one of the homing pigeons, then closed the lid quickly. He looked around. "Falcon, start up the mountain as far as a horse will take you before I release the bird."

"I think I'm about as far as my horse will take me now."

"Let's give them their heads and see if they can pick out a

trail," Cheyenne said. "This horse I'm riding is a mountain-bred mustang, and he can climb almost like a mountain goat."

She loosened her reins and kicked the horse, and it surprised her by turning to its left. Not down like a horse might go when it could no longer climb.

Cheyenne looked behind her at Wyatt. Molly saw him nod. He said, "Give the critter its head for a while."

The horse wandered along, so surefooted Molly marveled at it.

Then it chose a spot Molly certainly couldn't see as a trail and headed up.

"I'm following her." Falcon rode after his wife. Sheriff Corly went next.

"Wyatt, go tuck that buckboard off the trail somewhere, unhitch it, and bring the crate."

Wyatt rolled his eyes at John's bossy ways, but John didn't notice. Instead, bird in hand, he swung up onto his horse and followed Falcon.

Wyatt was a while getting going, so Molly waited, thinking it only polite. She also didn't think they should leave him behind.

They'd known they might end up leaving the wagon, so Wyatt came back into sight on his saddled and bridled stallion, the crate awkwardly balancing on his lap.

He smiled at her. A warm kind of smile that she was learning was just for her.

Wyatt drew up beside her. "We still need to have a talk."

"Yes, we do."

With a little shake of his head, he said, "Now's not the time. You go ahead. I'll bring up the rear."

Molly turned to follow John. To her surprise all three lead riders had vanished from sight.

Her horse went along as if he could see them. He picked steps out of rough spots on a trail that looked sheer. The horse was calm and didn't hesitate at all, as if the trail were wide and smooth. Molly did her best not to distract the horse by doing anything with the reins. The horse was definitely better left in charge.

From behind her, Wyatt said, "You knew where to find that safe, Molly. We really needed you, but I wish we'd left you back in Bear Claw Pass where it was safer."

Molly smiled. "I always feel safe with you, Wyatt."

~

Kevin came awake on a shout. He lurched to his feet. His head spun until he grabbed at the desk in the jailhouse to keep from falling back to the floor.

A man charged into the jail holding a rifle. The rifle made Kevin think of his gun. Hanging on to the desk, he bent low and fetched it from under the desk, then turned, ready to fight Hawkins and Kingston for his wife.

The man who came in was neither. The newcomer said, "I'll send for a doctor. We're gathering a posse to go after them." The man wheeled around and was gone before Kevin got his gun leveled.

Then he saw the empty jail cell, door swung wide. He heard a moan behind him and looked around, still clinging to the desk, to see Sheriff Gatlin unconscious on the floor but alive. No sign of Win or Rachel anywhere.

Kevin straightened. Found his knees could hold him and

staggered for the door. A posse was a great idea. But he wasn't waiting for anyone to gather anything.

Outside, he yelled, "Which way did they go?"

One man pointed northwest. "Been gone a few minutes is all."

Someone else said, "You're bleeding bad, mister. Better let the doc fix you up."

"They've got my wife." He ripped the reins loose from the hitching post, swung up on his horse, and kicked the tough critter into a gallop from the first leap.

He bent low over his saddle, almost lying down. It helped the horse make good time and kept him from falling off. He needed both.

Storming out of town, his mind was wild with fear. Win, he had to get to Win. Her father had kidnapped her. The man was using his own child as a hostage. They'd known he was evil, but this twisted Kevin's belly into a knot.

Groping for the source of the blood, he found a bullet crease in the back of his head. He'd had one of those before in this stupid territory. He tugged the kerchief off his neck and pressed it to the fast-bleeding wound. The pressure hurt so bad it nearly made him pass out. He clung to the horse, fighting for his vision to clear.

At last it did. He was a decent tracker and saw two horses that'd veered off the main trail he'd taken out of town. Fresh tracks, deep. They had Win and Rachel. Two men, each riding double, which would tire the critters out faster.

Dead ahead was one of the roughest stretches Kevin had seen since coming to Wyoming Territory. Honestly, Wyoming was shaping up to be little improvement over Kansas.

And then he thought of his wife. That was something he'd never had back home. He had to get to her, had to save her before her father did something no father should ever be able to do.

He'd've been flat out sick if he had the time.

~

Wyatt reached the top of a steep climb. The winter wind battered at him as he studied more steep climbing ahead, some down, some up. The wildest land he'd ever known. And he'd known plenty.

He realized he'd never been in this area before. The rocks they just climbed had seemed unclimbable by a horse.

Falcon and Cheyenne were both afoot, studying the rocks, hoping for any sign of a trail.

Looking up from where she'd hunkered down, Cheyenne said, "My horse just stopped. I hoped it'd keep going, maybe follow the scent of another horse that'd passed this way. Instead, it balked, and I knew not to push it. I might get it going in the wrong direction."

Falcon rose, shaking his head. "It's solid rock in every direction, the snow swept clear."

"We're going to have to release a pigeon." John lifted the bird, which had settled contentedly on his lap for the whole climb.

"Are we ready?" John asked. "We all watch, pick up its direction, and go after it as fast as we can until we can't see it anymore."

Wyatt looked around at the rugged land. Straight ahead it went down some, then climbed again. To the left and right, they'd be skimming along some invisible trail, hoping their horses could walk on tiptoes.

Wyatt gave his chin a jerk of agreement. "Let it go."

John released the pigeon, and it just stood there, content with the ride. "Hmmm . . . We might have a defective pigeon."

John picked it up and tossed it in the air. It fluttered a bit, then took off like an arrow, straight ahead.

"It might not be far as the crow flies," Wyatt said, watching the bird. Cheyenne and Falcon were after it, John next, their horses picking their way. They weren't going to do any galloping, that was for sure.

"We couldn't be less like crows." Molly gave her horse a gentle kick, just enough to tell it to get going.

The pigeon crested the highest peak ahead and vanished. Wyatt made very careful note of where the critter was headed.

One of the crated pigeons in his lap cooed. Another fluttered. Wyatt looked down at them. Five more birds. Figuring some had been trained to go wherever the one they'd already released had headed and some would fly east toward Casper, they'd be real lucky, no . . . real *blessed*, if they found Hawkins before they ran plumb out of birds.

~

Was Kevin dead?

It'd happened so fast. Win had seen the sheriff fly backward. She'd heard a second shot as Kevin tackled her. Then her pa had dragged her out from under Kevin.

Win saw blood. She was frantic to help her precious husband, but her father dragged her away.

Was he dead?

No. No, she refused to give up hope. He'd survive, and he'd come for her. He'd bring the rest of his very tough family with him.

She just had to stay alive. Surely her own father wasn't planning to kill her. But he'd given her to Kingston. Maybe that was his way of saying he didn't want to kill her himself, but he'd stand by while his brother did.

Her pa held Rachel, who'd gone gray and slumped back against him. She looked unconscious. She hadn't been out of bed long enough for this harsh, pounding ride.

Win had no idea how to help herself. Try to snatch Kingston's gun? Throw herself to the ground?

That might work, but not now, not while Kingston was so alert and on edge. But she'd be prepared and take any opportunity that opened. Maybe she could find out where they were going.

A prison break . . . two men shot . . . there would be help coming. A posse if Kevin wasn't able to come. The thought sent a sob from deep in her chest, and she fought it. No time to cry. Now was the time to be alert and be ready.

Maybe talking would help. At least she might find out what was going on.

"So you're my uncle. Is that right?" Win asked. All she could think of was that the blood of outlaws flowed in her veins. Her father a killer. Her uncle a thief. "And was Cl-Clovis Hunt my uncle, too?"

Sick, she realized that made her and Kevin first cousins. Was a marriage between first cousins even legal? Was it wise?

"Clovis is my brother, but Oliver isn't blood kin to us."

"Th-that's why my father doesn't have the same hazel eyes."

"Yep, them brown eyes with the stripes of gold run strong in our family. Clovis had 'em, and me. Your pa, the youngest of us, is the son of one of my pa's friends. When his friend died and our ma had died, Pa married his friend's widow and took her boy, Oliver, in. I should've told him to run, risk starving and dying in the cold, but I wasn't smart enough to spare him a new family.

"Oliver was the same as a brother to us. Clovis did his best to protect Oliver and me from Pa when he was sideways from the drink. Both of us looked up to Clovis."

"Your accent is getting stronger as we ride. How did you and my father lose that Southern accent when Clovis had it so strong?"

"We were making a new life. We headed for Chicago, but Clovis met a woman and stayed behind. Oliver and me, we didn't want anyone to know we'd spent time in that boys' prison. And Oliver had plans to marry a fancy, rich woman. Not sure where he got that notion, but it was a good one. He said he'd never fetch one around if'n she knew he was a mountain boy. So we made ourselves into city toffs, invented an education and a background. While we were at it, we didn't mention being brothers."

"Is your name really Kingston or Hunt or Hawkins?"

"Clovis and I were named Hunt. We were half grown when our pa took Oliver in. Your pa's real name is Jethro Pervis. We both chose new names, wanting to sound more like city folks."

"And because there were records of you being in prison under your real names."

Kingston grunted. "If I was going to name myself, by golly, I'd pick a royal name. I kept Randall and settled on Kingston. But Oliver's name was Jethro." With a shake of his head, Randall said, "Jethro Pervis. He was never gonna get a fine woman to marry him with that name. So he went about calling himself Oliver Hawkins."

"So I'm really Winona Pervis?" The name made her want to cringe, but she brightened a bit as she thought, no, she was really Winona Hunt. And that name went with Kevin, not Clovis. And Kevin, with his strong, decent brothers, had made it a name to hold with pride.

"You grabbed Rachel and me because you needed hostages to hold off the townspeople. Now you've gotten free, so let us go. Just set us down on the ground. Your horses will go faster and for longer without the extra load."

"Not how your pa wants it done. He's all het up about Rachel. How she's the one who brought him to this. Drove him from a fine home."

Win thought of the account books Wyatt had talked about. "He was going to have to give up that fine home soon enough. The money is all gone. My father has squandered all my mother's wealth. He married her for it. Killed her for it. And now that it's gone, he'd've lost the place anyway."

Good old kidnapping Uncle Randall blinked at her, then his head flew up to glare at his brother. His voice a great deal louder, he said, "Is that right, Oliver? Is the money gone?"

Pa turned his head so fast Win almost heard it snap. "Of course not. She's lying to you."

"You were going to fund our getaway." Randall didn't seem to even consider believing his brother. "I left my home behind. I should have headed back to Casper when I broke jail. We still could. I've got some cash money. It'd keep us until I find something to steal, or you find a new woman to marry." Randall laughed, but there was no humor in it, only cruelty.

"I've got plenty with me. We head west. I'll find a new wife. I'll have to be easy with a woman until she marries me."

Win had already known her father was a killer. Known it from the evidence that'd been gathered. But now she heard him confess it. Or close enough for her. It made her sick. It made her want to cry and scream and claw his eyes out.

She knew of all the people in the Hunt family, she was considered the softest, with her finishing school education and all the years back east.

But she was a strong woman inside where it counted. And with the deepest, most heartfelt prayers of her life, she asked God to give her a chance. To let her bring her father to justice. To give her the courage, wits, and opportunity to make him pay for killing her mother.

And she prayed it knowing that in the end, her father very likely planned to kill her, and certainly Rachel. Oh, he might think to let Win live somehow, but if she died in the middle of the madness he'd wrought, he wouldn't care.

He might even write her a poem that said, "And now I must go on alone."

She shuddered to think of it.

Win opened herself to every glance, every move on Randall's part. She thought of where his gun was, and then she remembered that recently, she'd taken to arming herself. Randall hadn't searched her for a hideout knife. She had one slipped into a clever little sheath inside her boot that Kevin had helped her make. Apparently, all his family carried knives as a family tradition. And from what she knew of his family back in Kansas, Win could hardly blame them.

She certainly didn't reach for it now. She just kept it in mind. When she got her chance, she'd be fighting with more than just her wits.

She came back to the first and most awful thing that pounded in her head harder than the horse pounded as it galloped along.

Was Kevin dead?

She itched to reach for her knife.

TWENTY-SEVEN

They were a long time reaching the peak the pigeon flew over. They looked all around but no sign of a hideout. No sign of Hawkins. No sign of a pigeon. There were trails, but none of them more worn down than others.

The country was higher, and snow sifted down. The trail they were on crested above the tree line, then led down to sickly, bent trees nearly too high to grow, then thicker trees that towered overhead, even though from where the group stood, they looked down at where the trees grew. If they went down, they'd soon be swallowed up in dense forest.

"Remember how many people have been shot from cover since we've come out here." Molly thought of the evil men pursuing them as she, Kevin, and Andy were sleeping on the ground, still a day out from Bear Claw Pass.

The three of them had crawled into the darkness away from the firelight and watched two men unload their guns into the abandoned blankets. A fine welcome to Wyoming Territory.

Win had been shot, though they assumed the bullet was

aimed at Kevin, then Falcon had gone to track the would-be killers, and he'd been shot. Later on, Win and Kevin were attacked again. Then Wyatt, then Rachel. No one died, but they'd come too close, too many times.

Molly looked down at the steep descent. A likely place for an armed man to hide. They'd better ride easy.

Or uneasy in this case.

"Do we release another pigeon?" Wyatt had one hand resting on top of the pigeon crate to balance it.

John rode over to him. "Yep, no way to know which way to take from here."

He opened the crate while Wyatt steadied it. Slid another bird out of the door and quickly closed it. "Keep a sharp eye."

Everyone nodded. He released the bird. It flew straight east.

The only direction without a trail, and a direction at odds with where the other bird seemed to be heading.

"That one's going to Casper," Cheyenne said.

"Let it get out of sight." Falcon rode up close. "I don't know if a homing pigeon might follow its friend, but in case that could happen, let's wait a spell."

The bird vanished from sight.

"I envy that bird its fast wings," Molly said, mostly to herself. She'd ridden up on Wyatt's left while John was on his right. Falcon and Cheyenne were a few paces ahead of them on the trail, Sheriff Corly at their side.

Wyatt rested one gloved hand on her back, drawing her eyes from the spot where the bird had been lost in the distance.

He smiled.

They really did need to have that talk.

John reached for the crate. He tossed the friendly bird gently into the air. It spread its wings and went flapping east, too.

A third pigeon headed east.

"Two left," the sheriff said. "We're running out of chances."

Molly said a quiet, intense prayer for the Lord to lead them all, including the pigeon. John released the second-to-last bird. It soared like an arrow in flight, heading north. The center trail, into the thickest woods.

They watched to pinpoint where it flew out of sight.

There was a long trail downward and another peak beyond. The bird went on north, straight and steady, beyond the next peak.

They were a long time riding down, then back up. Everyone was wary. Molly found her nerves taut as she tried to look for hidden gunmen. There were too many likely places for an outlaw to stand guard over the trail.

At the top of the next peak, the mountain was white with snow but not above the tree line. The trees held the snow better than that last barren peak. It was growing colder by the moment. The icy wind penetrated Molly's coat, and no one else could be much better. The way was impossible to guess. No obvious tracks. The snow was packed and slippery. Trees seemed to surround them, and snow fell heavily enough they couldn't make out a trail anywhere.

A stream gushed out of a crack in the mountain nearby. Despite the cold, it was a stunning place. The stand of evergreens with their lush needles was broken here and there by the bare branches of an oak or cottonwood or a copse of aspen trees.

Molly looked at the beautiful, forbidding forest. The snow had turned to needles of ice, and her fingers were numb with cold.

They had one bird left.

John looked each of them in the eye. "This is it. We'll follow it as far as we can, and if we don't find it or find some trail that gives us a way to travel, we'll have to go back."

"And probably have to make a deal with Kingston," Sheriff Corly said bitterly.

It burned every one of them to let the man go, but to capture Hawkins, who had committed multiple murders, they might have to agree to his terms.

Molly caught Wyatt's hand, and she prayed silently. She saw Falcon and Cheyenne whispering with an intensity that made Molly think they were sharing a prayer.

Wyatt lifted her hand and kissed her gloved fingertips. Their eyes met.

John quietly said, "Amen."

He reached in the cage for the last pigeon and tossed it in the air.

It took off like a shot straight north. At least it wasn't going to Casper. They all watched, all hoping and praying.

The bird didn't soar onward, over the next peak and out of sight.

Instead, it landed.

A long way down, in a thick stand of trees. But it definitely found its stopping place. It'd gotten home.

Molly's heart sped up. "Did you see it?"

"I did." Cheyenne reined her horse toward the trail, Falcon only a horse length behind.

"I surely did." The sheriff kicked his horse to follow. John went next.

Wyatt, his eyes sharp and ready for trouble, said, "I'll bring up the rear."

Molly looked at him for a long second. There was so much ahead of them. The first thing was going to be hard. If their prayers were answered, they'd be facing a cornered killer. Fighting for their lives. If they weren't answered, an evil man would go free, and he'd attacked them before. Just because he'd been found out didn't mean he might not come at them again.

Nodding, Molly leaned across the distance between their horses and kissed Wyatt soundly on his cold lips.

He kissed her right back. "Get going, woman."

He smiled at her, and she nodded and headed after John.

They were almost there. Almost to what was likely the hideout of a murderer.

A cowardly murderer who hurt defenseless women. But someone had shot Wyatt near Hawkins's place. Molly hadn't considered Hawkins a likely suspect for the crime at the time. Now she knew he was almost for sure guilty. It was a cowardly act, and that sounded just like him.

Though they rode bent low, every one of them kept a sharp eye out, and not a shot was fired. They reached a clearing, and a tumbledown cabin stood there, brush grown up close to it on all four sides. A shanty of a barn behind it.

"Hawkins! Come out." John surprised them all with a powerful voice. Threatening. Furious.

No one stirred. The snow came down heavily, twisting and dancing on the wind.

"It's empty." Cheyenne clucked to her horse and rode it straight toward the cabin.

"Cheyenne, no, wait." Falcon pulled her up, when she wouldn't have stopped for too many people.

"What is it?"

"We'll leave tracks. Look, there's a nice even powder of snow all around that place. The trees block the wind. If we all ride up there, and he's out hunting or finding firewood, he'll see we've been here. Let's hide the horses in the woods and think about how to approach the cabin. Maybe I could walk in from the back, pick spots where the snow is swept away, then hide in the house to wait for him. The rest of you hide in the woods."

At that moment, one of the pigeons fluttered up from the back of the house and flew to them. A second one came soon after. They landed on the crate, and Wyatt tucked them inside. He had a pocket full of seed, and he tossed more grain to them. They happily cooed and fluttered as they pecked it up.

"It looks like a one-room cabin. No one's in there, but it's the right place. The pigeons prove that." John swung off his horse and led it into the woods. "Let's see how this fool likes someone coming at *him* from cover."

"Let's get off the trail quick and hope any tracks we left are covered by snowfall." Cheyenne went toward the opposite side of the trail.

"I watched our back trail. With the wind and the rocky path, there's not much to see." Falcon followed his wife.

"And, Falcon," John said, "I can tell you're a fine tracker, but if one of us goes in that house alone, I want it to be me. I'm a trained investigator, and I might see something in there you'd miss. Clues aren't always obvious."

"I need to get in there, too," the sheriff said. "This is in my territory, and I'm the only recognized lawman here."

Falcon didn't reply.

John vanished from sight into the woods to the east. Falcon went to the west, the sheriff hard after him.

"You go in on the same side as John, Molly," Wyatt said. "I'm going to take a few seconds and fill in some hoofprints and footprints with snow."

The woods weren't easy to walk through. The trees were shouldered against each other. Old oaks and heavily needled pines, their branches weighed down with snow. Young trees growing spindly in the shade of their elders. Ancient tree trunks, broken off, almost impossible to get around. Prickly scrub brush filled in all the empty spaces.

Molly picked her way, following John's footprints. By the time he had his horse tied, she was there, and he took her reins and hitched her horse beside his.

Then Wyatt came. She watched him smooth out the snow with an expert eye. But as he came close, well out of sight of the trail, he quit.

"I'm going to circle around and come in from the back." John slipped away, leaving Molly and Wyatt alone in the cold forest.

Snow came down on their heads, light but steady. The wind had let up enough that their coats kept them warm.

"Let's get closer to the trail so we can see if anyone is coming," Wyatt said.

Molly followed.

He picked a hiding spot wisely, a boulder with bushes around the front of it. They were covered, but the trail was close enough to see easily.

Settling in behind the boulder, Wyatt crouched so he could watch, but for how long? They could be here for hours. All day. Maybe forever.

"This might be our best chance to have that talk, Molly."

And she knew he was right. It was time. It was past time.

She settled in beside him and whispered, "I've had plenty of time to think, and I know it would be wrong to marry you."

"Before you start . . ." Wyatt slid an arm across her shoulders and pulled her close to kiss her. His lips were cold. His nose brushed hers and she shivered, but a nice kind of shiver.

When the kiss ended, Wyatt said, "I expect something awful happened to you. I want you to know it's not going to change a thing."

She wished desperately that she could believe him. But she couldn't. "It will change *everything* when your wife is hanged for murder."

~

"Where are you taking us?" Win had never been out this way before. It was the most rugged country she'd ever seen.

"Shut up."

Uncle Randall was a worthless excuse for a relative, but Win didn't say so because she didn't trust him not to hit her, and she needed to think clearly and be strong enough to fight when her time came.

Information might be useful later though. "What were you in the Jeffers school for? If my father killed your parents, why did you all go?"

"We had no one to watch out for us. We'd all been in trouble. So when Oliver went, they scraped together this and that little crime and just pitched me and Clovis in with him."

"This and that little crime?" Win said it but didn't expect an answer. And she didn't get one.

Instead, Randall went on with his story as if it were a fond memory. "Killing Ma and Pa, Oliver set us up on easy street with that. The school gave us the only education we'd had, fed us, and kept us warm in winter and dry in the rainy season. Ma and Pa's house hadn't done that."

"And only at the price of your parents' lives," Win said. Again she spoke mostly to herself, but this time Randall slid the hand he had around her waist to her opposite arm and twisted it.

"Ouch, stop." She deliberately said it loud enough her father could hear. She was curious what he'd do.

"Leave my girl alone, Randy. She'll be easier to tote along if she's not hurt."

Randall loosened his grip with a cruel laugh. "The girl's never had a switch taken to her. She's got a mean mouth, and I don't like it."

"Might not be too late to teach her some manners." Pa's eyes met Win's, and there was only evil. "I've a mind to take her along with us. She can do the cooking. Be a proper daughter now that she's a widowed lady."

Ignoring those words to keep herself from crying, Win looked at Rachel. Unconscious this whole time. It struck

Win suddenly how unlikely that was. Yes, she was exhausted. Only just up from a week in bed, and during that time, she'd eaten and drank only what sips they could urge down her. It made sense she was weak to the point of collapse. A normal woman would be. But Rachel was tough. The type of woman to carry a knife in her boot and maybe worse.

The type of woman to dig deep and stay conscious, and also perhaps to feign unconsciousness, waiting for her chance to fight.

Win faced forward so no one would see that suspicion—and hope—on her face.

With or without Rachel, Win planned to fight these men who had hurt Kevin.

God, please, please, please let him be alive.

She very much hoped it was *with* Rachel, but Win would fight nonetheless.

The horses were slowing. Win suspected it was because they were tired. But she also noticed the wide trail into the rough country had narrowed and was climbing.

She was watching intently, wondering if a spot in the trail would take all Randall's attention, and she'd have her chance to leap from the horse and vanish into the woods.

She saw a bird fly high overhead. It looked like a pigeon. After a few minutes, she saw another, flying in that same straight-arrow direction. Trying not to draw attention to herself, she quietly waited and saw a third one.

Then no more.

Strange, but she wasn't sure why. Maybe the way the birds flew hard and fast straight east. But it wasn't uncommon for birds to fly in a straight line, was it? But three of them spaced out like that?

And pigeons? She'd seen some roosting in the barn at the RHR, but she couldn't remember seeing one out in the wild. Where did pigeons roost out here? But it stood to reason that they did.

Dismissing it, she hung on and waited for her chance.

TWENTY-EIGHT

*F*alcon slipped through the woods to the back of the house, Sheriff Corly close behind. Just as he came around from the west, McCall came from the east.

Their eyes met, and John's narrowed, but he didn't say a thing. The need to be silent won the day.

The back of the ramshackle cabin was close enough to the woods that there wouldn't be a long line of footprints. Falcon figured he could smooth them out without much trouble.

Falcon found a few bare spots blown clear of snow. Lightly, he covered the distance to the back of the house and heard fluttering and cooing from inside.

John came up behind him. Falcon glanced back and saw that John had stepped in the same spots as Falcon, less of a trail to cover. The sheriff came last and was covering their tracks with decent skill.

"We found more pigeons." Falcon smiled at John, who nodded.

They went into a small back entry, just a little wider than the door. A small slit in the east wall let the pigeons in. There were neatly built coops here, a smaller set of only four coops, but otherwise they were like the coops at Hawkins's house. There were two pigeons inside. And two more coops with their doors open.

Falcon led the way into the main cabin, and it was the work of two seconds in the single room to see it was empty.

"He's been here." The sheriff pointed to a few unwashed dishes sitting on the table. A skillet on a small potbellied stove. The sheriff went to the stove. "The fire has burned down, but there's still some heat. He must've slept here last night."

There were three cots in the room, one on each wall except for the side with the fireplace. The entry door was pushed far to one side of the building so a cot would fit.

"All three of them must've met here." Falcon looked around, but there wasn't much else to see. "Wyatt said Hawkins was known to go off for a few days now and again. I'll bet he and his brothers met here, talked over who all they'd robbed and killed lately. They probably did it when Clovis was still alive, then the two of them kept at it after he died."

"And when they couldn't get away, they'd send a homing pigeon to talk to each other."

"Or arrange a meeting date." The sheriff rubbed his hand over his mouth as he considered it.

"I told Cheyenne I'd be staying inside, waiting for Hawkins to come."

"You left your woman out in the cold while you're inside?" John smirked at him as if he liked taunting.

"Yep, she's a tough woman, and she knows I'm better finding a trail than her, and better hiding one."

"I'm married to a tough woman, too." John's smirk changed to a genuine smile. "She saved my life the first time I met her by knowing her way around in the wilderness. She'd've stayed outside, too, if we decided it was best."

John studied the room. "Not much here, but let's look under the cots, under everything. If I was gonna stash information about my lawbreaking, where better than a secret hideout?"

Falcon headed for a crate on the floor, shoved under the closest cot. It looked to hold a few clothes and not much else, but he had to start somewhere.

~

Wyatt didn't let go of her, and she desperately needed him to.

"I don't know where to start." Molly tugged away and faced the trail.

Wyatt rested his hands on her upper arms and pulled her around to face him. When she met his eyes, she felt a chill rush down her spine.

Somehow, right now, being held was like being taken prisoner. It was like the sheriff and his shackles, the prison door swinging shut.

"Please, let go. I-I can't tell you this if—if we're touching." She swallowed hard. "When I'm done, you may not want to touch me ever again, and it will tear me apart to feel your hands leave me in disgust."

He let go. "What happened, Molly? What could a sweet little woman like you do to—"

"I killed my father." She shoved the words out. Words

she'd never spoken aloud before. Not even to Kevin. She covered her face with both hands, so she couldn't look at Wyatt, couldn't see what was in his eyes. A bone-deep trembling that she couldn't control threatened to break her apart. Her face felt flushed. Her head, her whole body, felt as if a fire burned inside. As if her great, dark secret was consuming her.

"I v-vowed—" Her teeth chattered until she couldn't speak. She'd kept fear inside for years and years, and now she'd said the truth aloud. Now she might hang. She deserved to. "I vowed to never speak those words. I've prayed for God to forgive me for what I've done and protect me from the punishment I deserve. But it's like holding in terror that builds until it has the pressure of a steaming kettle. Now that I said it, I can feel that it's been grinding inside me from the moment that gun blasted and my pa clutched his chest, dropped to his knees, and pitched forward next to my ma's body."

She stopped speaking again and covered her face more tightly with her trembling hands. It was still as vivid as the moment it happened. She could remember the roar of the gun. The way Pa staggered back, looking at her with stunned eyes. She could smell the blood, smell the sulfur, the stench of the smoking gun.

"You killed your father?" Wyatt's voice sounded as if he were far away.

His question helped her go on. "Yes, I shot him dead. I came in to find Ma on the kitchen floor, bleeding, unconscious. Pa turned on me. And it wasn't the first time he'd done it. But he never hurt me like he hurt Ma. This time though, there was such fire in his eyes. Such a love of hurting

Ma, and now those eyes were on me. He swung a fist, and I lurched back. Hit the wall. There was a gun belt hanging from a nail behind the door. I was so afraid and so angry. He'd hurt Ma so many times."

"That's where you learned healing, doctoring your ma?"

She nodded. Glad Wyatt had interrupted her story and taken her out of that room full of death. "After years of cruel beatings, he'd finally gone too far. But I didn't know that yet. I'd seen Ma on the floor, not moving, plenty of times before. I fumbled that gun out of the holster and aimed it. He laughed, taunted me. 'You gonna shoot your lovin' papa, little girl?'"

She thought of those words, that ugliness. "I—I pulled the trigger. If—if I'd done it because I was afraid, only afraid, I would believe it was self-defense. But I hated him. I'd hated him for so long. I know in my heart how badly I wanted to kill him." She started shaking again. She felt like there were tears inside her, but they'd turned to stone in her chest, and she couldn't make them fall. She had to bear the hard pain of them forever.

Wyatt touched her shoulder. She ducked away. His hand followed and rested on her as she shook. The strength of it might hold her together when she seemed about to fall apart.

"He killed her. And you walked in on it?"

Nodding, she didn't think more words could come free.

"And you've never told anyone? Kevin had to know." His hand, steady and strong.

Kevin, her big brother. Her kind brother who'd done everything he could to protect her. "I wanted to tell him. I knew I should go to the sheriff and confess. But Kevin's need to protect me was so strong I was afraid he might insist *he'd* pulled the trigger. He might convince the sheriff to arrest him instead of me. He might've been the one to hang. He might've laid down his life."

"No greater love, that sounds like Kevin." Wyatt hung on to her but not so tight she couldn't talk.

"He came running in from outside only seconds after it happened. He'd heard the shot. I was standing there, holding the gun. Pa dead next to Ma. I didn't know she was dead then, but Kevin checked." Inhaling a jagged breath, she said, "He said, 'I'll bury them. Don't let Andy see this.' And then he dragged them outside. I heard Andy and rushed to him to keep him in bed. Kevin loaded Ma and Pa over two horses and rode away. I never saw them again. Once Andy settled back to sleep, I cleaned up the blood, and that was the end of it."

"Kevin never asked about what happened? And he never told you where they were buried?"

Shaking her head, she said, "He had to guess I'd shot Pa, but it was like those bodies. We buried it. We never spoke of it. No one missed them or asked after either of them. Ma never went to town. Pa was hated and feared because he rode with the night riders. No one even knew they were gone." Molly slid her hands into her hair. "It's too much like the story of Hawkins's parents. And we're talking about hanging him."

Wyatt's arms closed around her, and it brought her back from the ugly past. She couldn't decide if he wanted her still, or if he was comforting her before he said goodbye. If he didn't say it, she would.

TWENTY-NINE

*M*olly, I—" Wyatt started but then shoved her away.

He took one second to see she was devastated, but there was no time to explain. He heard hooves on the trail, but not the one right near them. The sound came from the side of the cabin. "Hush, someone's coming."

He got on his knees behind the boulder and saw Cheyenne across from him down the trail a ways, just before the clearing.

Their eyes met. She nodded and jerked her head toward the cabin to tell him she heard the riders, too. Then they both ducked out of sight.

Molly had a gun. He now knew she was familiar with them. Shuddering, he wondered what it did to a woman to carry that kind of secret for so many years. He wondered if she was capable of loving a husband.

She was on her knees, gun drawn, well below the top of

the boulder. Her eyes open, ears listening, but staying out of sight to any riders.

The clopping of horses, two critters, Wyatt was sure. Two? How did Hawkins find someone to partner up with? One brother, Clovis, dead. The other, Randall, locked up. Wyatt slipped sideways to peer between the thick but leafless bushes, then gasped and jerked his head back. He clapped his hand over Molly's mouth when she looked at him in wild confusion. He shook his head and touched the muzzle of his gun to his lips, then released Molly's mouth. As if she were the one who'd made a noise.

The horses came on. Wyatt stayed down. He'd considering jumping out as they rode into the clearing, getting the drop on them, trusting Cheyenne to do the same. But that was before he'd seen who it was.

Four people.

Two of them Win and Rachel. Though Hawkins and Kingston rode easy, they both had a gun in hand. And no threat of "stop or I'll shoot" would be believed when that put Win and Rachel in the cross fire.

The horses came around to the hitching post at the front of the house. Wyatt peeked out on the side of the boulder toward the clearing. He just didn't know what to do. He should have attacked. He should have shot both of them in the back once they'd turned their horses to hitch them. The bullet probably wouldn't go through them to hit the women who rode in front of them.

Shooting someone in the back was the act of a coward. But he should have done *something*.

He could have charged out of the woods and sprinted

across that clearing while they faced away, jumped up, and pulled one man off his horse, left the other to Cheyenne. Tough as she was, he didn't like the idea of her tangling with an armed killer. But Win might've helped. Rachel appeared to be unconscious.

Where were Falcon, John, and Sheriff Corly? Then it hit him—where was Kevin? He'd been in town. Was he dead? He had to be, or these two would've never gotten the women away from him.

Wyatt had thought Falcon was dead the day Falcon, Kevin, Molly, and Andy had descended on the ranch. Then for a time Kevin and Win had been missing, and they'd feared the worst.

Now Wyatt's stomach twisted with the fear that Kevin might've been shot in what had to be a jailbreak.

Wyatt was sick of all this trouble. He wanted to go back to busting broncs and dodging angry bulls. That's the kind of peaceful, quiet life he loved.

With the men's backs to them, dismounting, dragging their prisoners down, Wyatt stepped out from behind the boulder, his grip unshakeable on Molly's arm, and darted across the trail to Cheyenne's side.

Cheyenne rose from where she'd been concealed, her expression grim. Wyatt closed the distance between them. He noticed Molly wasn't being dragged. In fact, she was coming along fast enough he had to move, or she'd be dragging him.

Wyatt got close enough he dared to whisper. "Rachel looked all in, and Win looked terrified."

Cheyenne shook her head. "Rachel opened her eyes and

saw me. She winked. She's only acting unconscious. Which means she's ready to fight. Win was pale as milk, but determined not terrified."

"Where's Kevin?" Molly broke in.

Cheyenne looked at Molly, her jaw so tight it was likely to crack her teeth.

"He wouldn't have let them take her, not without a fight." Wyatt saw Molly's eyes fill with tears, but she squared her shoulders and swept the wrist of her coat across her eyes. A woman who didn't cry when there was a battle to be fought, maybe later when she had time to spare, but not right now.

"I'll kill both of them for what they've done to Kevin." Molly raised her gun until it pointed to the sky, then turned to march down the trail.

Wyatt grabbed for her and missed.

Cheyenne got a grip on his arm that made his fingers go numb. "I'll help you, Molly. They're headed into the cabin, and Falcon is in there." Cheyenne let go of Wyatt and fell in beside Molly.

After a second of doubting this was the right approach, Wyatt caught up to them and walked between them. They'd left him room, and he knew that was more than good luck. They knew he'd come, expected him to come. Counted on him coming. He felt the need to plan, to talk through what they'd do, but there was no time.

He picked up the pace, and they kept up until they were running.

~

"They've got Rachel and Win." John stepped away from the single window. There was barely room for his broad shoulders between the door and bunk, but he pressed his back against the wall and drew his gun. He did all that in about a second, in time to see Falcon do the same on the other side of the door.

Falcon leaned to risk a look out the window at the men coming up to the hitching post. "Hawkins must've broke Kingston out of jail. What happened to Kevin?"

"And what about Gatlin?" Sheriff Corly asked. "Hawkins may have just killed two men."

The sheriff took quick stock. There was nowhere in here to hide, no more space beside the doors. He opened the back door and stepped through, leaving it open an inch.

"My brother." Falcon felt his head heat up. Rage, killing fury. He drew his gun, pointed it at the floor.

"Watch who you shoot. Mind the women."

Falcon glared at him so he'd know how insulting that warning was.

John jerked his head in a quick nod, best he could do to apologize. "I hope they don't go around back. No footprints out here."

"Hush up. They're coming. Out front." Falcon pressed his back against the wall, his gun pointed down. John's pointed up. Footsteps.

"What is this place? Why are we here?" Win's voice. Falcon was getting to know his little sister-in-law. She was the softest of all of them. But to him, her voice sounded falsely whiny. He suppressed a smile. She had a game of her own going on. Little sister was ready to fight.

Not a sound from Rachel. Falcon remembered how long she'd been in bed. But she was a tough woman.

By gum, she'd shaken off a bullet to the heart.

He wouldn't count on her, neither would he count her out.

The door was shoved open. It hit John in the face, but he was ready for it and made nary a sound. No one seemed to notice it didn't open all the way.

Win got shoved inside. Falcon could have grabbed her, dragged her out of the line of fire, and shot Kingston, and he wanted to so bad he knew it for a sin.

But Kevin. What had happened to his little brother?

Win staggered forward and fell to her knees. Falcon, on high alert, saw her slip one hand under the hem of her skirt and slide a knife from her boot.

Kingston had turned halfway around, away from Falcon, talking to Hawkins behind him. "She still alive?"

"Yep, breathing. Winona said she was ailing."

"Ailing because I shot her." Kingston laughed with crude pleasure.

Win gathered herself, knife hidden in the folds of her skirt. She rose, turned, and saw Falcon. She didn't so much as look at him after that one quick glance. Didn't let pleasure show on her face. She had a cool head in a tough time.

Falcon didn't move. He didn't want a board to creak or a shadow to shift. John was shielded by the door, but as soon as Kingston quit looking at his brother and took one more step into the room, he'd see Falcon. If only Hawkins would come a few steps closer first, so they could grab him an instant after they grabbed Kingston.

Win peeked at Falcon's gun. She got a look on her face

he couldn't understand. All he knew was she looked mad as a rabid skunk. With Kingston's back to her, she raised the knife and sank it hard into the middle of his back.

Kingston roared and spun around.

She let go of her knife and plowed a fist straight into his nose, shouting, "That's for Kevin!"

Hawkins came at a run. He carried Rachel in his arms but shoved her aside just inside the door so she plowed into Falcon.

Falcon steadied her, and her eyes popped open with a quick smile that turned mean.

Hawkins rushed forward.

Blood flowed down Kingston's back. Rachel hit the floor but not from collapsing. She did it deliberately, then kicked hard and high from flat on her back and managed to land a boot straight into Hawkins's backside.

Hawkins hollered with pain.

Kingston turned at the noise his brother made and saw Falcon. He jumped away, ever the coward, to grab Win. Falcon leapt on him, carrying him over backward. They dragged Win off her feet again.

Hawkins turned and ran for his horse. He was on it and galloping around the back of the cabin.

Falcon swung one wild punch after another to stop Kingston, who was clawing at Win to get her in front of him, to protect him from Falcon's assault. They rolled, and Falcon was on the bottom. Win went tumbling backward. A fist plowed into Falcon's face.

He barely noticed John rush outside, then another set of galloping hooves went after Hawkins.

John, alone now against Hawkins.

They came here thinking five against one. All of them against Hawkins. Now it was one-on-one, John against the worst of the lot. The man who'd been killing since childhood.

Then a whirlwind hit Falcon. He thought for a second it was Win, turned into someone nearly as tough as Cheyenne. Then he saw it *was* Cheyenne. His wife had bought into the fight.

A slashing thud ended the fight. Kingston toppled off Falcon. The big galoot landed on poor Win again. Cheyenne shouted something out the door, but Falcon's ears were ringing from so many hard punches to the face that he wasn't sure what she yelled.

Falcon opened his rapidly swelling eye to see his little firebrand wife come to save the day. She twirled her gun with casual skill and tucked it in her holster, her eyes cold on the man lying facedown whose head she'd just bashed.

The sheriff joined the fight after it was over and shackled Kingston's arms behind his back.

Satisfied her outlaw was dealt with, Cheyenne turned to Falcon. "Are you all right?"

He grinned, and she smiled back.

Then her smile shrank. "And how are Rachel and poor Win?" Her eyes scanned around to see who was left standing.

Win jerked her knife out of Kingston's shoulder, wiped it on his shirt, then tucked it back in her boot.

"If Kevin dies"—she more growled than spoke—"I'm going to hang you myself."

Falcon decided maybe not so poor Win after all.

~

Wyatt had let Cheyenne get too far ahead. He heard shouting inside the cabin.

Hawkins charged out, empty-handed. He'd left Rachel behind. John, at a sprint, came out next and slammed shoulders with Cheyenne as she rushed past him to go in. John leapt on the horse standing there—the only one left—and went tearing after Hawkins.

He yelled over his shoulder at Wyatt. "My horse is tied up with Falcon's and the sheriff's right there!" He jabbed his finger at the woods. Wyatt hoped that pointing finger was enough.

Cheyenne yelled, "We're all right. We got Kingston."

"We've got to help John." Wyatt had Molly's hand, and they raced toward the woods as John rode out of sight hard on Hawkins's heels.

The horses were right handy. They mounted up and were close enough to John to hear hoofbeats. Wyatt should have left Molly behind, but when he'd dropped her hand, she'd just kept on coming. There was no time to argue with her now.

They were gaining. Molly leaned as far over her horse's shoulders as Wyatt.

A gunshot split the air ahead, then another.

Molly kicked her horse to get more speed out of it. It was the horse John had ridden in on and a fine animal. Wyatt had Falcon's mount, a long-legged sorrel, as game as any on the ranch.

They rounded a bend in the narrow trail to find John off his horse and running for the woods, his shoulder bleeding.

"Get off the trail," John yelled as he dodged behind a

boulder on the side of the trail away from Hawkins. Bits of rock exploded as he ducked low.

Wyatt grabbed Molly's reins, but she was pulling up already. The aim of the gun shifted so bullets came at them. They threw themselves off their horses, and Wyatt, Molly in hand, charged into the brush. He didn't want to be on the same side of the trail as John. He wanted Hawkins's attention split.

Hawkins quit shooting. The horses were in the way, and John, Molly, and Wyatt were out of sight. All four of the horses milled in the trail, rearing and screaming in panic. One of them kicked out wildly. At last, they gathered themselves and ran back the way they'd come.

Hoping the horses covered any sound, Wyatt moved. Low, as quiet as he could, he closed the distance between him and Hawkins. He wished Falcon was here. Now *there* was a man who knew how to be quiet in the woods.

With the horses gone, Wyatt braced himself for a new round of gunfire. There was none.

Moving faster now, he reached the spot where he knew Hawkins had been. Nothing.

Crouching low, he looked all around, expecting a bullet to come flying, in true dry-gulching style.

Not a sound. Not even the whisper of a footstep or the quiet breath of a man running for his life.

Gritting his teeth, Wyatt called out, "He's gone. I don't see a sign of a trail."

The woods were heaped in leaves. There was snow, but it wasn't deep enough to make a smooth coat on the forest floor. The wind tossed the leaves and sent the snow scudding here and there.

John came fast. Molly caught up. The three of them exchanged a look, then Molly said, "We need the best trackers. We need Falcon and Cheyenne."

All three of them turned and ran for the cabin. They met Cheyenne and Falcon, coming fast. Before they reached the two trackers, they heard a high yell of pain. All five of them whirled to face the forest.

"What was that?" Molly edged closer to Wyatt, and he felt her shudder. He slipped an arm across her waist.

"It sounded like Hawkins to me. It sounded like fear." Cheyenne pulled her gun and checked the load.

Another shout. Hawkins for sure.

Win came running down the trail.

"You were supposed to watch Kingston," Cheyenne growled.

"He's tied up and unconscious, and the sheriff and Rachel have guns on him. He's not going anywhere." Win heard the next shout. Then she smiled as Hawkins emerged from the woods, being shoved along by Kevin.

John strode forward and said, "I'll take him back to the cabin. Let's get the horses caught and head back for the jail."

He nodded at Kevin—they had matching bleeding shoulders. "Glad to see you made it."

John took hold of Hawkins and turned to march him back toward the cabin.

"You're alive." Win rushed to her husband and wrapped her arms around him. Gently, as if she could see he was a man nearing the end of his rope.

Kevin wrapped both arms tight around her and hugged her close. "You're alive."

They held each other, rocking a bit, utterly silent. Then

the silence was broken by the sound of Win's tears. Kevin held her tighter.

Cheyenne went to Kevin and said, "Did you leave your horse around here?"

Kevin told her where, and she headed up the trail away from the cabin. Falcon jogged along until he caught up with her, and they disappeared into the woods together.

Kevin and Win walked the opposite direction Cheyenne went, arms around each other, talking quietly.

John left them behind, shoving Hawkins along at a fast clip. Win and Kevin moved slower because she was fussing at Kevin's bleeding arm.

Molly headed after her brother to help, but Wyatt reeled her back in like a newly roped maverick calf.

John gone on ahead with Hawkins.

Falcon and Cheyenne gone together.

Win and Kevin leaving them behind.

Wyatt found himself alone with Molly.

"How many times would you say we've been alone together, Molly?"

"Are we counting when you were half mad with fever and when you were bound up in that tight sling so your collarbone would heal?"

"No, we are not counting that."

"How about the nights you sneaked into Hawkins's house at night?"

"Nope."

"I think maybe we should count those."

Wyatt smiled. "Maybe. But alone when there was nothing stopping us from really spending time together?"

"About twice. Three times maybe."

"It has to be at least four times because I've kissed you four times."

"Only three, I think."

Nodding, Wyatt said, "That's right. I didn't kiss you when we woke up together that morning."

"I fell asleep from pure exhaustion, and you mostly just regained consciousness, and you were still bound up in that sling. That doesn't really count as waking up together."

Wyatt smiled. "It doesn't count; you're right." He leaned down and kissed her. "But I would dearly like to do it when it does count."

Molly's eyes went wide as if she might be going to cry. Well, it'd been a hard day. He wouldn't fault her for it. But he hoped she didn't make a habit of it like Win.

"Y-you shoved me away when I told you about my pa."

"There were outlaws coming down the trail."

"I told you the law might come after me, and you turned your back on me."

"That is *not* what happened."

"It doesn't *matter* what happened. I can't marry you, have children with you, and maybe someday hang."

"No, you most certainly can't."

She gasped and pulled away from him. He still had her as good as hog-tied and pulled her back.

"Let me go."

"I *mean*, you most certainly can't hang." He dragged her all the way into his arms. "We are not going to let that happen."

She stopped struggling and looked into his eyes. "We aren't?"

"No wife of mine is going to hang." He smiled. "I'm a powerful, connected man in this territory. I think we can clear it all up."

"I-I-I . . . b-but I *did* it. I'm *guilty*."

He kissed her into silence. When she wrapped her arms around his neck, he decided she was sufficiently distracted.

Pulling only inches away, he spoke just above a whisper. "You wanted to talk, before you could say yes to my proposal. Now we have. Will you marry me, Molly?"

She looked into his eyes. Hers wide with hope and unshed tears.

"Just say yes and help me find a horse." Rachel cut into the touching moment. "I need to go back to the RHR or somewhere and collapse."

They both turned to see a very pale Rachel. They'd forgotten about her.

"Are you all right?" Molly let go of Wyatt, rushed to her, and slid an arm across her back. "You were unconscious when they brought you in."

"John sent me to hunt for you. He caught a bunch of horses. He's bleeding, but it doesn't look serious, and the sheriff got both outlaws loaded. Win and Kevin have already headed out with the outlaws, John and Corly riding with them. We need to get back to Bear Claw Pass. I can put off collapsing for a while, but it's already been a long day, and it's not half over."

"Let's go." Molly started walking off with Rachel.

"Wait a minute." Wyatt caught up to them. "Aren't you going to say yes?"

"Kevin, I can't, not with a killing in my past."

279

"Tell me what you did." Rachel, in her typical straight-forward fashion, seemed the perfect person to talk to.

After Molly told her tale, Rachel said, "You didn't break any laws. It was self-defense."

"No, you don't know how I felt. You can't know the anger in my heart when I pulled that trigger."

"I've never killed a person, Molly," Rachel said. "But I've been in a tight spot a few times and thought I might have to. It leaves a wound on your heart, in your mind. You think about being executed for it because it's such a bad feeling that you think you deserve to be punished. That feeling is something you've just got to live with. A nine-year-old shooting her father who'd just killed her mother and was coming at her, that's self-defense.

"If Kevin disposed of the bodies, that's against the law. But it's not a real *serious* crime. If it'd been murder, then he's aiding and abetting. But since it's self-defense, no one will kick up a fuss. We should tell the sheriff, and when he doesn't arrest you, you'll feel better."

Molly flinched when she said *sheriff*.

"Or we could just go on keeping it a secret for the rest of your life. I won't tell." Wyatt slung his arm across her back and said, "Whatever you do about the sheriff, marry me first."

They reached the clearing with the cabin. Four horses remained.

"Let's head on." Rachel seemed determined to interrupt Wyatt's proposal. "We'll leave one more horse for Cheyenne and Falcon, they're supposed to come back with Kevin's. Let's catch up to the others."

Wyatt swung up on horseback just as Molly did. Then

Rachel. He probably should have boosted Rachel up. She looked a little shaky. But she made it. They caught up with the others in a few minutes, then Falcon and Cheyenne came along soon after. All of them with their problems finally solved.

Wyatt could only hope.

THIRTY

$\mathcal{A}$ nd then I shot him." Molly had insisted on talking to the sheriff before she'd agree to a wedding. A hanging right after she said "I do" would be upsetting for everyone, that is . . . even more upsetting than being hanged.

And it was hard for something to be *more* upsetting but just in case.

Her heart pounded like a drum. Her face was so hot she had to believe she was seconds from having flames shoot out of the top of her head.

And not the heat of embarrassment. That was too mild an emotion. The heat of guilt. The heat of knowing what she faced, suspecting what she deserved.

"A clear case of self-defense, Miss Garner. Don't you worry about it." Sheriff Corly patted her on the shoulder. Almost in a fatherly way.

"No, I hated him. I wanted him dead. I wanted to shoot him." Now that she'd started talking, she couldn't seem to shut up. She'd explained her anger. Explained her intent. She didn't think self-defense quite covered it.

"Most folks that shoot someone in self-defense have such feelings, miss. I ain't arresting you for it."

"Are you sure you get to make that decision, shouldn't a jury decide?" She didn't want to walk out of here free and have them change their minds after a stretch of consideration. That would be something else hanging over her.

"Molly"—Wyatt dragged her back a few steps from the lawman—"hush now. No sense begging the man to arrest you."

"Nope, no jury necessary." Sheriff Corly settled into his chair and laced his fingers together across his rather rounded belly. "It don't matter if you were mad as sin and wanted him dead. He'd shown himself to be a dangerous man with evil intent toward you. And by my reckoning there is no doubt he meant you terrible harm. You acted to protect yourself. It's only a shame you didn't get there in time to save your ma. You did the only thing you could do to save your life." The sheriff nodded at her. Then in a kind voice, he said, "I'm right about this, Miss Garner. I understand the law. And I listened well to your confession. It qualifies as self-defense, and a jury would agree with me. A man who puts his hands on a woman, as your pa did your ma and you, well, there's no place for such a man, not in Kansas and not in Wyoming."

Sheriff Gatlin, who was pale and had his arm in a sling, said, "Wish I'd been there to shoot him for you, miss. That's a powerful burden for a youngster to carry with her all these years. I hope it sets just a bit easier in your mind to have confessed to what happened."

Through the trembling, through the heat of guilt and fear, Molly could say honestly, "It does set easier. Thank you both kindly. I wish now I'd talked to a lawman right at the time.

But there were dangerous forces in Kansas then, and even lawmen chose sides. I was too afraid."

Both the lawmen nodded. Sheriff Corly said, "You're free to go. There isn't even the necessity of any of you speaking at the trial for these men we brung in. Sheriff Gatlin is a witness to the jailbreak. To Hawkins shooting two men, including a lawman, to get his brother free. And we've got enough evidence from Hawkins's house to lock him up without any of you needing to stand as witnesses. We don't put up with such as he's done, not here in Wyoming. My only regret is we didn't know about it sooner. We could have saved a few of these young women."

Cheyenne said to Wyatt, "We need to bring Jesse in to be arrested."

Wyatt nodded. "First thing."

"I'd like to attend the trial anyway," Rachel said. "Kingston shot me, and I heard him brag of it to his brother, who said they'd planned it right down to the route I was taking to Casper. That's conspiracy to commit murder. Attempted murder. And gloating about attempted murder."

"Uh, Miss Rachel." Sheriff Corly rubbed his belly as if he was fond of being prosperous enough to have it. "Gloating's not exactly a crime. Probably oughta be, but—"

"I know." Rachel swept his words aside. "But it made me mad enough I'm going to attend the trial and make sure neither of them gets away with anything. Kingston's got a way about him, blaming everything on his brother, acting like he was only involved a little bit. He even acted like that about waylaying me on the trail and shooting me in the heart. I don't want the jury to believe him."

"So be it, Miss Hobart. The trial will be tomorrow afternoon. We want to give Sheriff Gatlin here a chance to rest, or we'd have it right now."

Nodding, Rachel said, "I'll be here." Rachel turned to Cheyenne. "Now I'd like to go back to the ranch. I need a chance to rest, too."

"Not before the wedding."

Every eye in the place turned to Molly when she said it. And she smiled, but it was a private smile of joy. Only for Wyatt.

THIRTY-ONE

*T*his is the third wedding we've had in a very short time," Cheyenne said, leading the way to Hogback's diner, just like she led everywhere.

Wyatt watched his bossy big sister and decided he wasn't going to be heartbroken to have the RHR ranch house to himself . . . well, himself and his wife. That made him smile.

Rachel had gone to the hotel and rented a room. She'd told them congratulations but said she was going to rest until the sheriff needed her to testify at the trial tomorrow.

John stayed with the prisoners. Sheriff Gatlin was ailing and wasn't much help, and Sheriff Corly shouldn't be alone with those two outlaws, who'd proven to be dangerous.

Kevin had stopped at the doctor's office and been bandaged up while the rest of them told their stories, but they waited for him, then went to find the preacher to hold a wedding ceremony.

"I'll fix your shoulder better when we get home," Molly whispered to Kevin.

Parson Brownley was visiting the family of a widow and taking them a meal. Mrs. Brownley said he'd be back within the hour, and she'd send him to the church. In the meantime, the Hunt family would share a meal and make some plans.

Hogback had fried chicken for dinner and nothing else, so that's what they all had. Win told them there were restaurants that had choices, but that seemed like a lot of fuss.

The food was coming to the table by the time they all sat down.

"I came out best in all of this." Wyatt gave Cheyenne, straight across from him, a sassy smile.

"No, you sure enough didn't." Falcon gave him a brotherly swat on the arm.

"Molly's the best cook," Wyatt said.

"We won't starve." Falcon looked at his wife as if he didn't have one worry in the world, though he probably should have.

Kevin, at the foot of the table, slid one hand behind Win's neck. "Do you want to live in your father's house? I'd be fine with a cabin with a couple of rooms and a few acres to farm. I know your pa's house holds no good memories for you."

Kevin didn't seem overly worried about Win's cooking, only her feelings. Still, Wyatt quietly gloated. He had the best cook, and the prettiest wife, too, but he was too smart to say *that* out loud.

"I'm going to think of it as my mother's house. I intend to think of her when we move there."

"If you're sure," Kevin said. "I'll live there only if you agree."

287

"I am sure."

Kevin leaned close and kissed her, softly and not for long. It wasn't at all proper. But he did it anyway.

Wyatt thought of a few more things they needed to clear up. "So it seems our name really is Hunt."

"Yep, for a while, I was worried Win and I were first cousins." Kevin gave her a wide-eyed look.

She smiled back.

"Our pa, Clovis, is a brother to Randall but no blood relation to Oliver. Both men changed their names," Kevin explained.

"They'd've never passed themselves off as rich men with the Tennessee accents," Win said. "Oh, there are Southern folks who move north, but they have fancy family ties that they trot out and boast about. Those boys had nothing. No high-steppin' kin, no wealth, and Pa needed both to weasel his way into high society and marry my ma."

"They probably stole enough money to keep up appearances," Molly said. "That's how they got every penny they ever had."

They finished their meal. As they stood, Cheyenne said, "It's nice to get to have a real wedding."

Falcon came to her side. "Did you want a bigger wedding? A real one?"

"We had a *real* wedding, and don't you forget it." She laughed, her eyes glowing with love. "What I should have said is, it's nice to have the family together for one."

"Ours was for sure a quiet business," Win said. "Quick and quiet and followed soon after with an attack and a fight for our lives."

"Let's think of that ride on the river and the night in the wilderness as a honeymoon." Kevin hugged her close, and she smiled as bright as the noonday sun.

"And ours was after we'd arrested those cow-stealing bums and rescued Amelia Bishop," Cheyenne said.

"The wedding was for sure the bright spot in that mess." Falcon followed along after Kevin and Win, walking on the cold, blustery boardwalk toward the church.

They saw Parson Brownley step out of the parsonage. He spotted them and waved. The man did purely love pronouncing a wedding.

"We'll all be here for this one." Wyatt took Molly's hand, and they walked along, hands swinging. He wondered at how much his life had changed since Pa had died and torn up all their lives.

"You know something?" It must've been his tone of voice, but every one of his family stopped and turned to look at Wyatt. "We talked about honoring our parents. And every one of us, except Cheyenne, had trouble doing that."

"Even I did," Cheyenne admitted. "Because I had Clovis for a father most of my growing-up years, and he wasn't a man I could honor."

"Well, look at us." Wyatt looked around the small circle they'd formed there on that cold street in Bear Claw Pass, Wyoming. "Look at how much our lives have improved because of Pa and that stupid, thieving will. Molly and Kevin and Falcon have added so much to our lives. And we'd've never met them without Pa's will. Look even at how Win found justice for her mother and maybe can discover some of the things hidden about her ma's family. All the cheating and stealing and even murdering our fathers did led us right here." He pointed to the boardwalk beneath their feet.

"It's a good place." Wyatt's grip on Molly's hand tightened. When he spoke of murder, it wasn't just Hawkins who'd brought that evil into his family's life. It was all Molly had endured with her pa's cruelty. And they'd survived it all.

He thought he saw a lighter spirit settle on his family's shoulders.

Molly said quietly, "We honor our fathers by being a light in the world. By believing in what's good. By being better than we might have grown up to be."

Wyatt smiled down at her and suddenly the family was smaller, even with them all standing right there. It was only him and his Molly.

She nodded.

He bent and kissed her and said, "Let's go get married."

A few minutes later, they stood before the parson, a happy family. A family that lived in such a way any decent father would be honored to call them his.

"Dearly beloved, we are gathered here today . . ."

And they were, truly gathered together in a family.

Three beautiful brides.

Three brothers in arms.

All of them had found love on the range.

EPILOGUE

*I*t was summer in Wyoming Territory, and after a year, Molly had definitely decided she liked the place, despite the hard beginning.

Being in love with a fine man made it easy to face any hardship a winter in the Rocky Mountains brought her way.

So much had changed in a year it was like a whole new world.

One big change had Cheyenne chafing. But she'd agreed, no roping, no branding, no throwing nor hog-tying cattle.

It might be hard on the baby that would be coming before winter.

She proclaimed that she didn't believe it, but Falcon had lost his first wife when she was bringing a baby, and he tended to panic.

Today, because it was the Lord's Day, Wyatt had been persuaded to leave off the branding and come along for a visit with Win and Kevin at their home.

They had family dinners often enough, mostly at the

RHR, but they hadn't had one since Win's baby had been born. Now, with Win up and around, Molly had convinced Wyatt to go straight to Kevin and Win's after church. Today Win would get the meal started, but Molly would finish things up.

She was excited to see her new niece, and she wanted to tell everyone she had her own baby on the way. Wyatt knew, but she wanted to tell Kevin and, now that Andy worked at Kevin's ranch, she could tell them both at the same time.

Kevin and Win were still staying close to home. But Falcon and Cheyenne had been at church. Molly had convinced them to come along for the noon meal. It hadn't been hard.

They rode into the yard, and Molly caught herself shaking her head, as she did whenever she looked at the massive house.

Kevin met them at the door, the baby in his arms. Molly's heart warmed until it tingled to see her brother holding his child so gently. She couldn't wait until it was Wyatt's turn.

As they dismounted, Andy came out of the ramrod's house and helped Falcon and Wyatt stable the horses.

Molly beat Cheyenne by a pace and claimed a turn holding the baby.

Kevin laughed but gave little Dorothy up with good grace.

Win was moving around the kitchen. She had a roast on and potatoes stewing. She'd known Molly and Wyatt were coming because they'd finally figured out how to train the pigeons, and they now carried messages between the three families. It was a very convenient system.

Adding Cheyenne and Falcon was no problem. The roast was large, the potatoes were plentiful.

Molly was a while working because she wanted to make a fine dessert and her special garlic biscuits, but at last they were settled in to eat. Baby Dorothy was down for a nap, and they could all eat together, like they had a year ago.

"We're done with the new room on my pa's old place." Cheyenne smiled. "It's been nice being there. It's brought back fond memories of my parents that I'd lost track of."

Cheyenne looked sideways at Falcon. "It's not big, even with the new room. Do you want a nicer house? We could build one. I'd make Wyatt help."

Wyatt snorted. "You wouldn't *make* me. I'd be glad to help." He slid his arm across the back of Molly's chair. Wyatt was next to Falcon on his other side and straight across from his big sister.

Falcon took a break from his slice of tender roast beef and mashed potatoes to take Cheyenne's hand. "It's the biggest house I've ever lived in, not counting the few nights I've slept in the main house at the RHR. Nope, it's plenty for me. If we want more room, I can add another room on."

Cheyenne nodded, and their hands tightened, their eyes held. "I'm happy wherever and however I live as long as you're with me."

"And we get the RHR." Wyatt settled back. He heard the wooden rungs creak and remembered his ma fussing at him not to lean back on his chair. It was a fond memory, too.

When the meal was finished, Win said, "I found something in the attic that I'd like you to see. And Wyatt and Falcon, I'm hoping you'll help Kevin bring a few things down."

"I could've gotten it, Win." Kevin rolled his eyes at her, but he had a grin on his face.

"I've got a few chores to see to," Andy said, rising. "Do you need another strong back or can these old men handle it?"

With good-natured teasing the men told him to get on back to work.

"Before you go, Andy . . ." Molly glanced shyly at Wyatt. She felt a blush pink her cheeks.

Wyatt took her hand and gave her an encouraging nod. They'd discussed it, and she'd asked if she could make the announcement, but now it was a bit hard to speak the words.

"I've got a little one on the way."

Everyone around the table whooped. Kevin rose and pulled her into his arms. Win was next, then Andy. The men shook Wyatt's hand, and everyone gave Molly a hug.

Win whispered to her, "I know you already love your baby, but you won't believe what it feels like to be a ma. It's like a mama grizzly wakes up inside you, ready to fight and die to protect your child. The love is so big, so beautiful." Tears came to her eyes, and Kevin dragged her close with one arm and kissed her dark curls.

Andy gave Molly one last hug, his grin huge, then he headed for the barn.

The rest of them trooped upstairs.

"Leave all the doors open," Kevin said. "Dorothy usually takes a good afternoon nap, but we need to be able to hear her if she wakes up early."

When they reached the attic, Molly saw that everything had been moved around. Dust covers pulled off various crates and chests, including a row of paintings.

"Win, these are beautiful." Molly walked over to the line

of portraits, all of them over three feet high including their ornate gilt frames.

Four pictures in a perfect row.

"The first two are my grandmother and grandfather, next is my mother, and the last is my mother holding me."

"Why isn't there a portrait of your pa?" Wyatt asked quietly. Molly suspected if there had been a picture, Wyatt might've offered to haul it away to burn.

They didn't talk about Win's pa much. She'd wanted no part in attending the hanging of Oliver Hawkins and Randall Kingston. They'd both richly earned their punishment, especially as more and more came out about their criminal dealings.

But that didn't make it easy for Win to talk about.

"I'm not sure why there's no painting of him. My guess is, my grandparents . . . my ma, too, come to that, realized Ma had made a terrible mistake. No one wanted to add him to the family gallery. I'm surprised he didn't burn these. He probably would have if he wasn't such a lazy old beast."

Molly studied the pictures. "You look more like your ma than your grandmother, though you have her eyes."

Win's bright blue eyes were a match for the grandmother and the child little older than a toddler.

"I believe I was four or so when this was painted, it was just before we came west. Once I found this, I remembered a few things about it being painted. Vague memories of being told by my ma to sit still." Win smiled, the memories good ones. Molly was glad she had them.

"We're closing up the attic and may close the second floor before winter. We are living in the rooms you used, Molly.

There are two of them, and little Dorothy is in the second room. We're right by the kitchen"—Kevin shrugged—"the rest of the house is just wasted space that takes a lot of hard work to heat."

Molly knew that, though they lived in a mansion and had enough to eat, times were hard for Kevin and Win. Their cattle had mostly been stolen or neglected. Hawkins had spent Win's ma's money. They had vast land holdings but to build up a herd to make use of that land would take years.

"What is all this up here, Win? Old trunks, chests, furniture." Wyatt flipped the lid up on one. "Have you searched for treasure yet?"

"No, I had no interest in it while I was expecting. I just didn't want to have to spend time thinking about Pa, and I was a little too round to spend much time on the stairs. But now it was finally time, and I came up here and found things I wish I'd had all along."

Wyatt bent and pulled up a handful of papers. "You probably should go through all of this. How can you know if it's valuable? We could help you."

He flipped through a stack of loose paper, yellow with age. A thick oversized packet slipped out and dropped to the floor. It hit with a slap that drew Molly's eyes as it skidded to Falcon's feet.

It was a folder of some kind made of sturdy leather with a button and string tying it shut. Falcon bent to pick it up and read aloud, "'Winona Hawkins Trust.'"

Cheyenne had worked with him for a while, but Falcon took to reading and arithmetic like fire to straw. He now spent part of the family money on books and had a nice shelf full of them.

Molly gasped at the words. And she heard other such noises as Falcon handed the packet to Win.

Win quickly unwound the string and flipped the folder open, then drew out some very official-looking documents. Fine paper, large formal script at the top that read *Last Will and Testament*. Then her grandmother's name.

Below it, in a smaller size, was a page full of the script.

Win read quickly. "My grandparents left me a trust fund. It was very explicitly left to me and was to be turned over after my marriage. It can't be accessed before."

"How big a trust fund?" Cheyenne, always plainspoken, asked.

Win told them, and it earned another gasp all around.

"Remember, Wyatt, when you offered to sell some of your cows to me this fall instead of doing a roundup, and I'd pay for them over time?"

"Yep, the offer is still good."

Kevin grinned and said, "We'll take them all."

The whole group laughed at the load that had just been lifted off Kevin and Win's shoulders.

Kevin slid an arm across Win's back. "Your grandparents, probably with your ma in full agreement, did this to protect you from your pa. They knew you'd need protection, even before all his evil toward your family."

After some deep investigation, it was now believed that Hawkins had killed his in-laws. He'd been sly about it, but there were lawmen back in Chicago who well remembered the unusual circumstances of their deaths. It was assumed that one of the reasons he'd taken his family west was to avoid answering questions. He'd never admitted it, and he was beyond questions now.

Win swung around and looked again at the pictures of her grandparents.

Wyatt said, "When we talk about honoring our parents, Win, you've got grandparents to honor and a ma who was a good woman. And Cheyenne has her first pa, and we've both got our ma, Katherine. Molly, your ma was a decent woman, and, Falcon, so was yours. We need to stop worrying about how to honor men who weren't honorable and remember there were a lot of worthy parents in our lives."

Molly went to his side. "And we'll all do our best to be honorable ourselves, so our children don't have to worry about answering such hard questions."

She slid her hand to her still-flat belly and vowed to God that, with His help, she'd be the best, most faithful mother who ever bore a child.

"Three brothers," Kevin said. "Our pa, Hawkins, and Kingston. Three brothers who never spent a moment trying to be good men. And their parents didn't, either."

He looked to Wyatt and Falcon. "We're going to do better than that for our children."

Wyatt nodded.

Falcon smiled.

"Let's haul these pictures downstairs and hang them in a place of honor," Win said with a firm nod.

"You go on down," Kevin said sternly, but with a twinkle of amusement in his eyes, as he wasn't one to give orders overly. "We'll see to carrying these."

"We'll keep the coffee warm and have cobbler to serve after these pictures are hung," Win said.

It was a happy afternoon. One spent with laughter and a family none of them had known they had and none of them had wanted. An afternoon full of love on the wild ranges of Wyoming.

Together, three brothers in arms, three sisters by marriage, had formed a family of the heart.

ABOUT THE AUTHOR

Mary Connealy writes romantic comedies about cowboys. She's the author of the BRIDES OF HOPE MOUNTAIN, HIGH SIERRA SWEETHEARTS, KINCAID BRIDES, TROUBLE IN TEXAS, WILD AT HEART, and CIMARRON LEGACY series, as well as several other acclaimed series. Mary has been nominated for a Christy Award, was a finalist for a RITA Award, and is a two-time winner of the Carol Award. She lives on a ranch in eastern Nebraska with her very own romantic cowboy hero. They have four grown daughters—Joslyn, married to Matt; Wendy; Shelly, married to Aaron; and Katy, married to Max—and six precious grandchildren. Learn more about Mary and her books at

maryconnealy.com
facebook.com/maryconnealy
seekerville.blogspot.com
petticoatsandpistols.com

Sign Up for Mary's Newsletter

Keep up to date with Mary's latest news on book releases and events by signing up for her email list at maryconnealy.com.

More from Mary Connealy

After his father's death, Kevin Hunt inherits a ranch in Wyoming—the only catch is it also belongs to a half brother he never knew existed. But danger follows Kevin, and he suspects his half brother is behind it. The only one willing to stand between them is Winona Hawkins—putting her in the cross hairs of a perilous plot and a risk at love.

Braced for Love • Brothers in Arms #1

You May Also Like . . .

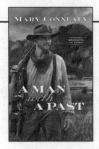

Falcon Hunt awakens without a past—or at least he doesn't recall one. When he makes a new start by claiming an inheritance, it cuts out frontierswoman Cheyenne from her ranch. Soon it's clear someone is gunning for him and his brothers, and as his affection for Cheyenne grows, he must piece together his past if they're to have any chance at a future.

A Man with a Past by Mary Connealy
BROTHERS IN ARMS #2

Growing up in Colorado, Josephine Nordegren has been fascinated by, but has shied away from, the outside world—one she's been raised to believe killed her parents. When Dave Warden, a rancher, shows up at their secret home with his wounded father, will Josephine and her sisters risk stepping into the world to help, or remain separated but safe on Hope Mountain?

Aiming for Love by Mary Connealy
BRIDES OF HOPE MOUNTAIN #1

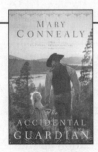

Trace Riley has been the self-appointed guardian of the trail ever since his own wagon was attacked. When he finds the ruins of a wagon train, he offers shelter to survivor Deborah Harkness and the children she saved. Trace and Deborah grow close working to bring justice to the trail, but what will happen when the attackers return to silence the only witness?

The Accidental Guardian by Mary Connealy
HIGH SIERRA SWEETHEARTS #1

⬧BETHANYHOUSE

More from Bethany House

On assignment to help America win the War of 1812, Evan MacManus is taken prisoner by Brielle Durand—the key defender of her people's secret French settlement in the Canadian Rocky Mountains. But when his mission becomes at odds with his growing appreciation of Brielle and the villagers, does he dare take a risk on the path his heart tells him is right?

A Warrior's Heart by Misty M. Beller
BRIDES OF LAURENT #1
mistymbeller.com

Left to rue her mistake of falling in love with the wrong man, Maisie Kentworth keeps busy by exploring the idle mine nearby. While managing his mining company, Boone Bragg stumbles across Maisie and the crystal cavern she's discovered. He makes her a proposal that he hopes will solve all their problems, but instead it throws them into chaos.

Proposing Mischief by Regina Jennings
THE JOPLIN CHRONICLES #2
reginajennings.com

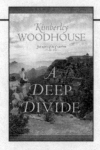

When her father's greedy corruption goes too far, heiress Emma Grace McMurray sneaks away to be a Harvey Girl at the El Tovar Grand Canyon Hotel, planning to stay hidden forever. There she uncovers mysteries, secrets, and a love beyond anything she could imagine—leaving her to question all she thought to be true.

A Deep Divide by Kimberley Woodhouse
SECRETS OF THE CANYON #1
kimberleywoodhouse.com

⬧ BETHANY HOUSE